D0877252

THE
SUPREME
ADVENTURE
OF
INSPECTOR
LESTRADE

THE
SUPREME
ADVENTURE
OF
INSPECTOR
LESTRADE

M.J. Trow

🜸

STEIN AND DAY/*Publishers*/New York

FIRST STEIN AND DAY PAPERBACK EDITION APRIL 1987
The Supreme Adventure of Inspector Lestrade was originally
published in hardcover in the United States of America
by Stein and Day/*Publishers* in 1985.
Published in Britain as *The Adventures of Inspector Lestrade*
Copyright © 1985 by M. J. Trow
Printed in the United States of America
STEIN AND DAY/*Publishers*
Scarborough House
Briarcliff Manor, N.Y. 10510
ISBN 0-8128-8313-6

The Man in the Chine

Melville McNaghten pushed the ledger away from him. He buried his knuckles in his eyes and drew his fingers down his cheeks, taking less care than usual not to disarrange his faintly waxed moustaches. Three years' work, he mused to himself. A lot of good men, a lot of panic and in the end – nothing. What was it Her Majesty had said? 'We must improve our detective force.' Five women had died – or was it more? Over two hundred men arrested, hundreds more questioned. He shuddered as he thought of the fiasco of Barnaby and Burgho, the bloodhounds who had not only not caught the murderer, but had lost their handlers in the fog. And that idiot Charles Warren who had wiped the anti-Jewish slogans off the wall. He'd gone back to the army now – best place for him. And who was the buffoon who thought of photographing the dead eyes of Catherine Eddowes in the hope that a likeness of the murderer would appear on the plate?

He was glad at least, he reflected, that *he* hadn't been involved in that lunacy. He was the first policeman on the case – the first real policeman anyway. Again, the four names caught his eye – *his* suspects, *his* deductions. Nothing provable, of course, nothing absolutely tangible. But enough for him. Enough so that if he whispered just one of these names in the street, the vigilantes of Whitechapel would swarm from their hell-holes with noose and zeal. He could practically hear Mr Lusk, their chairman, wringing his hands in anticipation.

A knock at the door brought him back to the present. He snapped shut the ledger.

'Come.'

Under the lamp's flare he saw the trousers of a constable enter the room.

'Inspector Lestrade, sir.'

McNaghten straightened his cravat. 'Show him in.'

The constable's trousers were replaced under the light by those of the inspector. McNaghten swept the ledger quickly into a side drawer of his capacious desk. Lestrade stood with his back against the door, watching every move with a wry smile.

'The Ripper file, sir?'

'What?' the suddenness and volume of McNaghten's reply indicated that he had heard perfectly well.

'The ledger.' Lestrade walked more fully into the light, gesturing to the drawer as McNaghten locked it.

'Er . . . yes.' McNaghten was more reasonable as he sat squarely again in the chair. He swept his hand across his whiskers and straightened his cravat again. Lestrade remained motionless, hands in the pockets of his voluminous Donegal. McNaghten sighed and resigned himself to the unspoken question –

'Lestrade . . .' Too formal, he needed familiarity. 'Sholto . . .' Lestrade felt the avuncular arm metaphorically creeping across his shoulder. 'You know I cannot divulge a word of these contents . . .'

It wasn't enough. Lestrade had not moved. McNaghten read his mind. 'Yes, I know you were on it, but it was Abberline's case.' It still wasn't enough. McNaghten stood up abruptly and the two men faced each other across the darkening room, their faces lit from below, like the inhabitants of Madam Tussaud's. 'Damn it, Lestrade. It is classified.' McNaghten hated dealing with subordinates, especially those as discerning as Lestrade. He was a thorn in his side, an itch he couldn't scratch. The Head of the Criminal Investigation Department turned to the window. Outside the rain was driving listlessly over the river and the arc lamps below. 'One day,' he talked to the heavy London sky, 'one day they will write about it. One day they will open my files and they will know.'

'I shall be a hundred and thirty-eight,' said Lestrade.

'Damn it, Lestrade,' McNaghten whipped round. He'd already said that and it weakened his argument to repeat himself.

Lestrade smiled. He raised his hands in a gesture of defeat. 'I understand, sir,' he said. He turned up his collar and made for the night. At the door he stopped. 'Goodnight, sir.' The smile was chill.

The door closed and McNaghten slammed a paperweight on his desk. How typical of Lestrade to want to know. But he could not know. Nobody could. In a hundred years, when they officially opened the file he was about to consign to the archives, it wouldn't matter. He, Lestrade, all of them would be dead.

Lestrade's trousers under the light were replaced by the swish of an electric-blue skirt. 'Father?' McNaghten's daughter swept into the room.

'Ah, my dear,' McNaghten's professional face vanished. He was a family man again, in the bosom of his daughter. Miss McNaghten *was* dreadfully large. She was also dreadfully capable.

'Come along, Father. Time for home.'

McNaghten had a brief glimpse of his pocket watch before his daughter threw his Donegal over his shoulders. Three minutes past the half hour. 'Call the cab, Father.' McNaghten dumbly obeyed. He had long since ceased to think it odd that he who gave orders so unthinkingly in the line of duty should take them so unthinkingly in the line of domesticity. The constable wasn't in the corridor. Damn. He set off in search of him in the outer office.

In his absence, Miss McNaghten bustled round the desk, deftly produced a key identical to her father's and unlocked the desk drawer. A further deft movement and the ledger was under her pelisse and the drawer relocked.

McNaghten returned. 'Downstairs,' he said. 'Constable Dew will drive us home. Oh . . .' he remembered the ledger. It must go in to the safe. Miss McNaghten read his mind and blocked his way. Her tone and her logic belied the panic in her heart, thumping beneath pelisse, ledger and matronly bosom. 'The Commissioner, Father.'

'God,' mumbled McNaghten, as though they had axed his pension. 'It's tonight, isn't it?'

'Yes, and Cook has bouillabaisse.'

'Ah, I wondered why she walked like that.'

His daughter's gentle push nearly sent him reeling through the door. They clattered down the darkened corridor, lamps flickering on the institution green and cream. The ornate lift jarred and whirred its way to the ground floor. They stepped into the wet, chilly night. Constable Dew, never the same since he saw the corpse of Marie Kelly, held the door open for the McNaghtens. The police cab rocked as the Assistant Chief Constable's daughter entered. The hack recoiled several paces, bracing its back. While McNaghten Senior fastened the door, his daughter flicked the ledger out of the opposite window. A gloved hand caught it and the cab clashed its way out of the cobbled courtyard and along the Embankment, now green with the river's mist.

From the shadows, a figure emerged: Inspector Lestrade, in his damp Donegal, rain dripping from his Derby hat. He smiled down at the ledger and the little silver key. Moving to the nearest light, away from the drips, he opened the book. He flicked rapidly through the pages and pages of evidence, statements, depositions, theories. The letters met his gaze – *I am down on whores and I shant quit ripping them till I do get buckled*. He knew all that. Nothing new, nothing different. It was the last page he wanted. There it was, the list of four names, stark in McNaghten's copperplate.

Lestrade smiled and his smile broke into a chuckle and his chuckle to a roar. He slammed the ledger shut. So Abberline took my advice, he thought to himself. And McNaghten. They listed all four of them. He was pleased. He knew his name appeared nowhere in the ledger. He knew he would not be remembered when they opened this file a century hence. But it didn't matter. It was enough for Lestrade to know that he had been right. It was that which time and again made his existence seem worthwhile. He did like being right.

'Sergeant,' Lestrade was inside the building again, the ledger under the flap of his Donegal.

The sergeant, who had been dozing, stood up at his desk.

'I'm going to Sir Melville's office – papers he wants me to check.' He made for the lift. 'Oh, at your relief go to Sir Melville's. Give a message to Miss McNaghten – tradesmen's entrance. Tell her . . . tell her thanks and apologise to her. I shall be unable to join her this evening as planned. Pressure of duty.'

Lestrade felt the sergeant's eyebrows lower again behind his back and the smirk develop. 'Oh, and Sergeant,' Lestrade was still walking, still with his back to the man. He paused, turned round and smiled. 'Don't let me catch you asleep again.' The sergeant stiffened and tensed his shoulders. One good discretion, thought Lestrade, deserves another.

'Very good, sir,' mumbled the sergeant. 'Mind how you go.'

Lestrade was in the lift, raising his eyes heavenward at the inevitable cliché of that phrase. 'Goodnight, Dixon.'

When the good doctor alighted from the Southern Railway Company's train he was not in the best of moods. To begin with, his morning eggs had not been to his liking, and his mail had been late – three bills. Then the journey had been draughty and damp; the *Telegraph* full of misprints. But what had really irked him, as he took his hansom in the station forecourt, was the reason for his visit to the metropolis – to see his publisher. There had been no reply to his letters – it did not bode well.

He didn't notice the wet streets or the whipping wind. The jolting annoyed him from time to time, but they were soon there, outside Blackett's the publishers.

He was ready for the revolving doors, having caught his Gladstone in them last time. 'Do you know your bag is going round in the doors?' the doorman had asked him. 'He's a big bag now,' the doctor had answered through clenched teeth, 'he must go his own way.' It was a different doorman this time, for which the doctor was exceedingly grateful.

'Dr Conan Doyle . . . how nice . . . how nice.'

'Mr Blackett, you have not replied to my last four letters.'

'Dr Conan Doyle . . . it's . . .' Blackett was uncomfortable, shifting from leg to leg, wringing his handkerchief from hand to hand.

'You like *The White Company*?' Conan Doyle was relaxed, sure.

'Indeed, sir, indeed. A fine book – rich in historical detail. But . . .'

'But you don't like *The Refugees*?'

'It's not that I don't like it, Doctor . . .'

Conan Doyle sat motionless, cold eyes fixing his publisher.

'It's not . . . finished,' continued Blackett.

'It will be.'

'Of course. Of course. But the public likes new things. Crime – suspense.'

'Like *The Sign of Four*?'

'Yes.' Blackett leaped at the memory, then was less

sure. 'But . . . er . . . Mr Holmes of Baker Street?'

'What of him?'

'Well – ' Mr Blackett was at his most obsequious – 'did he mind? I mean we do have the laws of libel.'

'Oh come, Mr Blackett. My stories of detection bear no relation whatever to the actual work of Mr Holmes. It would be more than my writing career or my medical practice is worth.'

'Well, as long as you're sure. That is the kind of thing the public wants. Plots, international intrigue.'

'Rubbish. Inconsequential bread-and-butter.'

Conan Doyle stood up purposefully.

'I would be grateful if you would return my manuscripts. I shall take my business elsewhere. It is obvious that the firm of Blackett has no concept of good literature. It wants twopenny trash that even the . . . *Strand Magazine* would turn its nose up at.'

Conan Doyle reached the door.

'By the way; that hand.' He pointed imperiously at Blackett. The publisher stared at his arm as though it had been severed. 'Come, come, man – the fingers.'

'Wh . . . what of them?' Blackett was startled.

'Unless I am mistaken – Grockle's disease. We get a lot of it in Southsea. Poor chap – probably a terminal case. Good Morning.'

Across the Solent from Southsea lies Roman Vectis, the Isle of Wight. There was no moaning at the bar when Lestrade put out to sea. Merely a stiff wind straining from the south-west. The steampacket bore him faithfully to Ryde and from the pier he took the train to Shanklin. He was nautically attired, as befitted the occasion, in pea jacket and peaked cap. But it was not a day for a jaunt. McNaghten had received the request. The grudging telegram for help. A body, it said. Found two days ago. Not a pleasant sight.

What bothered the Hampshire constabulary of course

was the season. It was now late March; by the end of April, the tourists would be coming to the Island in vans and flies. Money, the Island's life blood. There must be no leakage, no panic. McNaghten had seen the point. He had seen what panic had done to the East End.

It surprised Lestrade therefore, in view of the need for secrecy, that the whole area of the Chine should be ringed, not only by constables, but by troopers of the Hampshire Yeomanry. He tackled his contact, a Sergeant Bush, about it as soon as he could.

'Ah well, sir,' was the sergeant's reply, 'it's Her Majesty, y'see. She's at Osborne for Easter – and we can't be too careful, can we?'

'Quite so,' replied Lestrade, but for the life of him he couldn't see how the presence of the Hampshire Carbs, complete with helmets and plumes, around the Chine could protect Her Majesty some miles away at Osborne. From what McNaghten had told him, this didn't sound like a Republican terrorist killing. But then McNaghten hadn't told him much. As Lestrade correctly surmised, McNaghten didn't know much.

He followed Bush and the two constables down the winding path that had been hacked in the Chine wall. The breeze from the sea caught them as they turned a corner. The sergeant ducked under a rope cordon and seemed to disappear through a cleft in the rock. The constables took up their sentinel position on the path.

'You'll need to watch your step,' the sergeant's voice echoed. Lestrade emerged in a world of total darkness. The smell was ghastly.

'Can we have a light, Sergeant?' he asked.

He felt a hand grip his arm.

'Inspector, this is not going to be pretty.' The sergeant was grim.

'I've been in the Force fifteen years, Sergeant. You get used to the sights.'

But Lestrade wasn't ready. Not for this one. Bush's

arm swept up to strike the match and higher to show the 'sights'. A foot or so from Lestrade's face was the head. One eye had gone, the mouth gaped open, a gash in the livid skull. The hair stood on end, like a manic shrub blasted by the sea wind. The face flickered in the unreal sulphur glow. Lestrade swept Bush's arm down and the match went out. There was a silence. None of the three men in the chamber breathed. Lestrade turned for the entrance and breathed fresh air again. The helmets of the constables reassured him. Do I look as green as I feel? he asked himself. Come on, man, pull yourself together. You've been fifteen years in the Force. And these country bumpkins need your help.

Recovered, checked, in command, he faced Bush again. Now the sergeant *was* green. 'I'm sorry, sir,' he croaked, 'I can't get used to it. I've seen some "sights". Drownings, you know. Suicides in the Chine. Off of Culver Point. But this . . .' The sergeant's voice tailed away.

'Makes you glad of the sunshine,' commented Lestrade. 'Can we get to the beach down here?' He pointed ahead of him. Bush nodded. 'Be so good as to ask your man to stay here. Let's walk awhile.'

On the beach, drying now under the sun of the late morning and safe for an hour or two from the onslaught of the next tide, both men had a chance to clear their brains. At the back of each was a hideous head. Lestrade had not had time to view the rest.

'Tell me again,' said Lestrade.

'Well, sir. Workmen found it . . . er . . . him. Two days ago, it was. Let's see, Tuesday it would be. The Chine needed repairs. Erosion, you see. The land slips and we do get fierce winds in the winter. Well, the tourists will be here soon. Why, these sands are knee deep in donkey . . .'

'Spare me the holiday brochure, Sergeant.'

'Yes, sir. So, anyway, these blokes were chipping

away at the cliff face in that particular area of the Chine when they found this crack.'

'Fissure.'

'Bless you, sir. Being of an inquisitive nature, these fellers cleared the rubble and went in. Well, at first they couldn't see nothing. Then, when they strikes their lucifers . . . well, there it were. They got hold of old Tom Moseley then and there – he's the local constable. Old Tom ain't very quick but he got the sense to rope off the place and inform me and I sent a telegram right away to Pompey. I don't think I expected them to send to Lunn'un though, sir. I mean, Scotland Yard itself – well!'

Lestrade sat on a breakwater, following the line of sandstone cliffs with his eyes. Above them a solitary gull wheeled and dipped, scanning the sea for movement.

'Pompey got the coroner over, but told him he was to leave . . . it . . . where it was.'

'Cause of death?' asked Lestrade, flicking the guano deftly from his cuff.

'Coroner didn't rightly know, sir. Said he'd been dead for a long time.'

Lestrade stood up. 'Get me a lantern, Sergeant. We must go back.'

This time Lestrade went in alone. He felt safer of his own emotions without Bush. The stench was still nauseating, but the steady light of the lantern gave the corpse a less hideous, less unreal aspect. This time Lestrade gave the task in hand his full concentration, his full professionalism. The body before him was male. Age – uncertain. He would guess about forty. The skin was the colour of old parchment, but here and there the bones of the skull were visible, a muddy, sickly white. One eyeball, or what was left of it, dangled from sinews on to the cheek. The other eye, sightless and pale, stared straight ahead. The clothes, muddied and drab, were those of a seaman perhaps – or a farm labourer. The dust of the sandstone had powdered them with grey and rivulets ran down the chest and arms where rainwater had seeped in. The bones protruded through. The hair caught his attention again – matted and long and grey – but, curiously, standing on end. He dropped to his knees and held the lantern at the floor. Gaiters. The man had been a farm labourer. What he saw next jarred him somewhat. The hands. Coarse, rough, almost devoid of flesh, but the nails were long – three or four inches long each one, curling out black and sharp. No working man grew his nails like that – he hadn't the leisure or time. For a moment, an image of mandarins came to mind. He had seen photographs of the Empress, and even a few of the Chinamen in his own city had nails like that. But the next moment he had dismissed it. What could be the connection? Opium? Secret Societies? He told himself to keep his mind open, not to be parochial. It wasn't every day a hideous corpse turned up in a beautiful valley in an English coastal resort.

Back to the matter in hand. Theories could come later. The body was propped up in a standing position, the legs turned in with the weight of the trunk, but it was clear that ankles, wrists and neck had once been tied. Strangulation? That was possible, but there was not enough of the neck left to tell. There was no more he could do. In the cramped space of the chamber it was too dark and airless for further work. He returned to the sunlight, older, wiser. He gave instructions for the body to be removed, and would supervise it himself. He must talk to the coroner, check the chamber measurements and look for clues. He must talk to the labourers who found it . . . him, to the Shanklin Chine Company.

But first Mrs Bush, rotund, homely, busy, was clattering around her kitchen. Lestrade sat in a with-drawn huddle seeing the dead face before him as Grace was said.

'Shepherd's pie, Inspector Lestrade?'

★

The labourers were unhelpful. They had been working under contract for the Chine Company for seventeen years, man and boy. The Chine had been closed earlier than usual the previous year because of a landslip. By early September, the ropes and chains had been strung up and the gates locked. Was it possible for anyone to enter? Yes, if they had a key. But in daylight, with a body? Unlikely. A night-time job, then? Certainly, but the path was treacherous and steep, with sharp turns and jutting ledges. It would have to be someone who knew the place – and knew it well. One false step, carrying a full-grown man, and it would probably have been two bodies in the Chine.

It took Lestrade a week to interview all those who had regular contact with the area. At the end of it he was satisfied that no one knew anything. The inspector of works commented that there was evidence of rock-cutting and new mortar in the chamber, that the height had been altered and the body in effect bricked in.

'Are you familiar with the works of the late Mr Allan Poe?' he had asked Lestrade.

'Fleetingly, sir.' Lestrade had pondered the similarity already, as he faced the eighth consecutive shepherd's pie presented with glowing pride by Mrs Bush. But the connection didn't help him. Or did it? He had an uneasy feeling as he crossed to Portsmouth to the coroner's office; and it wasn't just the rolling and pitching of the steampacket.

'Dead for several months, I'd say.' The coroner was poring over a severed limb arranged tastefully on a slab. 'Yes,' adjusting his pince-nez, 'several months.'

'Cause of death?'

The coroner stopped his routine examination of the matter in hand and straightened. 'I'm not sure.' He twanged off his surgical gloves and rinsed his hands under a tap. 'Are you familiar with the works of Edgar Allan Poe?' Lestrade experienced an immediate *déjà-vu* –

either that or the coroner was the inspector of works's brother. 'Fleetingly.' He really had had this conversation before.

'The short story called *The Black Cat*?'

'The cat is walled up in the cellar with the deceased?'

'Just so. No cat in the Chine chamber, eh?'

Lestrade shook his head. 'Are you telling me,' he asked, 'that the cause of death was . . .'

'Suffocation, I suppose,' was the coroner's verdict. 'That would have resulted before the other things – starvation, madness.'

'And the nails? The hair?'

The coroner wiped his hands on his waistcoat. He was uncomfortable. 'A ghastly thing. Shocking. Mind you, I can't account for it. Never seen anything like it myself, not in twelve years. Bizarre. That's the word. Bizarre.'

'What do you make of the man's occupation?'

'From his clothes, a labourer, I'd say. Smocking on the chest. Not from round here, though. Not the right pattern. Ah, but this was odd.' The coroner rummaged in a cluttered drawer. 'What do you make of this?' He handed Lestrade a piece of dirty material, metallic and torn.

'Military lace?'

'I am impressed, Inspector. Army, cavalry probably. But officer's certainly. How many officers of cavalry do you know who become farm labourers?'

'I take your point, sir.' Lestrade frowned, the plot deepening so fast as to make his head spin. But it was a clue, a tangible piece of evidence.

'And this is even more interesting.'

Lestrade saw, in the weave of the scarf, fragments that had been tucked under the collar of the corpse, the name 'Peter', embroidered in a coarse, childlike hand. 'What do you make of that?'

'As yet, sir, precisely nothing. But it's early days yet.'

The coroner showed Lestrade to the outer office. 'The

lad will show you out. Spilsbury?'

A short-sighted urchin with acne lurched from an adjacent room. 'Look at him,' the coroner muttered. 'My cousin's boy from Leamington. He wants to be a coroner one day.' Under his breath to Lestrade, 'No hope, no hope at all. I think he's suicidal, you know.'

Not wishing to be a burden to Sergeant Bush any longer and totally unable to face his tenth supper of shepherd's pie, Inspector Lestrade moved in to Daish's Hotel. Daily he walked on the pier, breathed in the salt air. Daily he returned to the Chine, asked himself over and over – who? why? What, after all, did he have? A body. The body of a middle-aged man, walled up in an improvised cave at a popular holiday resort. The man was a labourer, named Peter, who may or may not have had contact with the army. It was thin, very thin.

But there was one last witness to see. A wild-eyed, melancholy old man with a massive barbed-wire beard mingling with the morning egg and pipe tobacco. Lestrade took a passing haywain by way of the worst roads he had ever travelled to the vast, overgrown country house at Farringford. Its owner, the Poet Laureate, was hobbling in the garden on his stick, examining with failing eyes the daffodils on the rolling lawns.

'Who is it?'

'Inspector Lestrade, sir, of Scotland Yard.'

'Lestrade of the Yard?' Tennyson would do anything for a rhyme.

'Very good, sir, very droll.'

'I don't usually see visitors, Inspector.'

'Quite so, My Lord.'

'Tea?'

Lestrade bowed. From nowhere, a butler brought the silver and the porcelain.

'Cream and sugar, sir?' The butler was pompous – he

disliked policemen.

Lestrade felt uncomfortable in the presence of genius. He was not one himself and he was acutely aware that the Laureate did not tolerate visitors gladly. It was even rumoured that he leapt from rear windows and fled through orchards rather than face his butler's announcement of imminent guests. He had better get this over with. It would probably be of little value anyway.

'Forgive me for disturbing you, My Lord. I am told you are a frequent visitor to Shanklin Chine – out of season.'

'When I am at Farringford, I often wander there, yes.'

'You have a key?'

'No. My man calls on the gatekeeper when I wish to enter.'

'Have you been there recently?'

Tennyson's concentration began to wander. Lestrade busied himself searching in the delicate porcelain for a vestige of the tea. How he loathed the habit of filling only half the cup. He declined the butler's cream puff – for one thing the man had his thumb in it.

> 'Men may come and men may go,
>   But I go on for ever.'

Lestrade flickered a glance at the butler, who remained immobile, pompous.

'Er . . . quite.' Try a different tack, he thought. Eccentricity will out. 'On recent visits did you notice anything unusual?' He cursed himself for that vagueness. It opened the floodgates for senility.

> 'Break, break, break,
>   On thy cold grey stones, O Sea!
> And I would that my tongue could utter
> The thoughts that arise in me.'

Amen to that, rejoined Lestrade silently.

'Did you notice any evidence of digging, My Lord?'
He found himself talking loudly, as though to a deaf
mute or a foreigner. 'Some new work on the Chine wall?
A new cleft in the sandstone?' It was very hard work.

'But O for the touch of a vanish'd hand,
    And the sound of a voice that is still!'

That was more to the point. So Tennyson knew
something. He was aware that there had been a murder.
The papers had not yet released the story. The Noble
Poet was hiding something.

'What makes you say that, My Lord.'

Tennyson stared unblinkingly under the over-shad-
owing brim of his Wide-awake. 'Forgive me, Inspector.'
His tone was different. 'Sometimes I forget myself. Vain
of me, isn't it, to quote my own work?'

Lestrade tried not to show he had not been following
the drift of the last few minutes. 'Do you know anyone
called Peter?' he asked.

Tennyson rose with the aid of stick and butler.
Lestrade followed him towards the great house.

'Why are you asking me these things?'

'We have found evidence of foul play in the Chine, My
Lord. The body of a man whose name may have been
Peter.'

Tennyson stopped and faced the inspector. He
motioned the butler to go ahead.

'Inspector, I am not long for this world now. I have
seen a great deal in my lifetime. Much sorrow . . . much
sorrow. My mind is not so clear. If a body fell at my feet I
doubt if I would notice it. The shadows are closing in.
There are some days when I cannot tell if I am talking to
men or ghosts.'

Lestrade, not usually a man of sympathy, patted the
Laureate's arm. 'Thank you for the tea, My Lord,'
seemed warm enough.

Tennyson was quoting again –

> 'If thou shouldst never see my face again,
>   Pray for my soul. More things are wrought by
>   prayer
> Than this world dreams of.'

He motioned the butler to him and hobbled on up the lawn. Lestrade waved his hat in token that he would find his own way out.

> 'Twilight and evening bell –' he heard the Poet
>   declaim,
> 'And after that the dark!
> And may there be no sadness of farewell
> When I embark.'

Lestrade embarked on the steampacket later that afternoon. He had assured the authorities that there were further lines of inquiry to follow up and that the case was far from hopeless, but he was not very far forward. The local papers had been leaked the story – inevitably. And the name 'Peter', the labourer's smock and the notoriety for the Chine were all there. The editor had had the good taste to suppress the grisly details – or the coroner had been unusually tight-lipped.

No time for Lestrade to return to London. Instead he took the train, by easy stages, via Swindon and the wide gauge of the Great Western, to Haverfordwest. He was annoyed at having missed his connecting boat and had to spend a wet, cold night in the town with what appeared to be a single street. If there were further delays tomorrow, he ran the risk dreaded by all full-blooded Englishmen in a Welsh town – a dry Sunday. Methodist revivals and Mr Gladstone's Licensing laws had combined to kill Haverfordwest.

As it turned out, Lestrade would have preferred a dry

Sunday to the wet Saturday he got. The ship lurched and rolled in the inhospitable Irish Sea. Lestrade, never a good sailor, found his stomach and his mind whirling together in speculation and nausea. Irish soil felt solid and safe. The cab clattered along Sackville Street and on into the suburbs. Dublin was still a lovely city, elegant, wealthy, English. And if there was an air of hostility, if the men and women did not look you squarely in the face, it wasn't to be wondered at. After all, wasn't that unprincipled maniac Gladstone playing with Home Rule? Playing right into the hands of the Fenians? And Salisbury couldn't last long – the Irish MPs at Westminster would see to that. At least, so *The Times* said and Lestrade had a great respect for that newspaper. Not that he was a political policeman, but he believed in keeping abreast of affairs.

Lestrade alighted at the barracks of the 13th Hussars to have his feet run over by their new maxim-gun detachment. Not wishing to appear unmanly before these fine fellows on manoeuvres, he buried his teeth into the rim of his bowler and drove his head a few times against the nearest wall.

'Did ya have a nice trip, sor?' chuckled the cabbie on his perch.

Lestrade flashed him a livid scowl and no tip and limped painfully into the regimental offices. The surgeon duly saw him, bandaged both feet and left him in the orderly room. It was some hours before the object of the inspector's visit arrived. Two burly privates appeared and lifted Lestrade between them down the corridor, across the courtyard and into the office of the colonel. The walls were hung with regimental trophies and photographs and the whole room had an aura of cigar-smoke and horse linament.

'Boys,' a sharp voice barked behind him. Lestrade leapt an inch or two and instantly regretted it, landing full on his bruised toes. Colonel Templeton-Smyth strode past him to his desk. He was a man of average height, brisk and straight-backed, with the inevitable military moustache, clipped somewhat thinner than Lestrade's own. He had the face of a hawk, clear blue eyes, firm chin and tanned, parchment skin – rather an odd hawk, really. He threw his forage cap on to the desk and unhooked the short, astrakhan trimmed patrol jacket before flinging himself into his chair.

'Boys,' he repeated, sliding a cigar box across to Lestrade. 'What do you think of 'em, Sergeant-Major?'

'Inspector, sir, Inspector of Police.'

'Ah, yes, of course. Sorry. Find these rank things confusin', what?'

'I think that boys have their place in the scheme of things, sir. They will at very least be boys.'

'Ah, yes, but you are a policeman. Right?'

Lestrade nodded.

'You must know some of these youngsters. You know, the ones old Barnardo doesn't get. I've got an idea . . .'

'Forgive me, sir' – Lestrade was trying to be formal, despite the throbbing in his toes – 'but I'm on important police business.'

'Ah, yes, 'course. Light?'

Somehow Lestrade leaned forward and puffed gratefully on the cheroot. The grandmother tolled the hour of four.

'Ah, tiffin.' The colonel rang a silent bell near his desk. 'But the prevention of crime, man. That Ripper chappie – he was a boy once. We can't wait until they grow up twisted and bitter. We've got to train them, make them into useful citizens. Now, my idea . . .'

'With respect, sir,' Lestrade cut in.

'Ah, yes, 'course. Fire away. Ha! Good that, what? Military joke, don't you know, fire away!' Templeton-Smyth saw that Lestrade was not amused. 'Well, to business.' His face straightened.

'I am making inquiries into a suspected murder which took place recently at Shanklin on the Isle of Wight, sir.'

'Ah, yes? How can I help?'

Lestrade fumbled in his wallet and threw the scrap of material on to the colonel's desk. 'What do you make of that, sir?'

Templeton-Smyth scrutinised it closely. He took it to the light of the window. Something in the square caught his eye and he threw open the sash.

'Not like that, Corporal,' he shouted. 'It'll never get better if you picquet!'

Back in the room, the colonel answered the inspector's question. 'Officer's lace. Thirteenth Hussars. Shoulder belt.' A pause, then – 'Could be Fourteenth Hussars, of course.'

'Thirteenth.' Lestrade was emphatic. 'This object was found in the lining of the clothes of the deceased, sir. I took the trouble of cleaning it. I also borrowed a copy of Her Majesty's Dress Regulations for Officers from Messrs Gieves & Company, Portsmouth branch. A brief consultation of that told me that the lace belongs, as you say, to a shoulder belt of either the Thirteenth or Fourteenth Hussars. If however you look again at the object' – the colonel did – 'you will notice that one edge of it is brighter, less tarnished than the rest.'

'I don't follow you, Inspector.'

'Your batman would, sir. Any man who has the job of cleaning regimental lace would know that where it is covered by a metal ornament, the lace is clean. The clean area on the scrap you have there corresponds in size and shape with a metal scroll on which a battle honour is blazoned. I need hardly tell you, sir, that the Thirteenth is the only cavalry regiment that wears its battle honours on its pouch belt.'

Templeton-Smyth's jaw fell slack. 'I admire you police chappies. First-class piece of deduction, Lieutenant.'

'That's Inspector, sir.'

'Ah, yes, 'course.' Templeton-Smyth returned the lace. The significance began to dawn on him. 'So this chappie, your . . . er . . . deceased. An officer of the Thirteenth?' His moustaches began to bristle with distaste.

'That is what I am here to find out, sir.'

'Now look here, Lestrade. This isn't on, you know. I mean, officers and gentlemen and all that. Bit unseemly, what? Chappie from one's own mess endin' up done to death.' But curiosity overcame the scandal. 'Tell me, how'd it happen? Sabre? Carbine? Maxim?'

Lestrade ignored these fanciful lunges into mid-air. The man had clearly no notion of the mechanics of murder. 'Have – or had you – among your officers, Colonel, one called Peter? The Christian name, I would surmise.'

Templeton-Smyth strode round the room. 'Peter, Peter,' he mused to himself, stroking the long lean chin. 'Well, I've been with the Thirteenth for fifteen years now since Cornet. There's only one Peter I've known among the officers.'

Lestrade straightened. Was this it? Had his gamble, his expensive, unrequisitioned trip to Dublin, paid off? Did he have a link with this fashionable cavalry regiment? What was Templeton-Smyth covering up?

'Peter Endercott. He's out there.' He pointed to the window.

Lestrade hauled himself upright, grimacing with pain. Those damned gun-limber wheels must have broken his toes. He reached the window. Below, a squadron of the 13th Hussars were going through their sword drill exercises, even though the afternoon was drawing in under a threatening sky. The clash of steel punctuated the harsh commands of the drill sergeants. Lestrade remembered his own days of such practice as a constable with the Mounted Division. He could see four officers standing casually around watching the men go through their paces.

'Which one is he, sir?'

Templeton-Smyth looked oddly at him and realisation dawned. 'Oh, no, my dear chap. Over there.' He pointed beneath a clump of elms, some distance from the parade ground. 'Third grave from the left. T.B., poor chap. Family insisted he be buried here. Full military honours, of course.'

'When?' Lestrade's optimism had already reached his bandages.

'Ooh, three – no, four years ago. June it was. Shame. He made up a good foursome.'

'Foursome?'

'Whist, Captain. Do you play?'

'Er . . . no, sir.'

'Pity. Now there's a good game for boys.'

The door opened and a tall angular woman in a frothy white dress appeared. 'My dear, I'm sorry tiffin is late today. Shall we take it in the . . . oh, I'm sorry, I didn't know you had company.'

Lestrade staggered to his feet. 'Oh, no, please don't get up. Gout can be a frightful business, can't it?'

'This is Major Lestrade, my dear, of the Metropolitan Police,' offered Templeton-Smyth. 'Major, my sister.'

'Inspector, ma'am,' groaned Lestrade, as Miss Templeton-Smyth shook his hand heartily.

'We are discussing a delicate matter, my dear . . .' said the colonel.

'Oh, Robert, my dear, can't it wait? This poor man deserves some tea.' She helped Lestrade to his bandages and steadied him on a wiry arm. 'Girls,' she said as they limped from the colonel's office. 'As a policeman, you must meet some of the wayward ones.'

Lestrade had been here before.

'Well, we have to train them, Inspector, to make something of them. I was talking it over with one of my brother's officers, Captain Baden-Powell, before he left for Malta. He rather ridiculed the whole thing.' The colonel fell into step behind his sister, 'We'll have some tea and I'll tell you of my idea . . .'

So Lestrade had drawn another blank with the 13th Hussars, as he had with Tennyson. He had bruised his toes, been violently sick on the crossing back from Dublin and had been subjected to Templeton-Smyth's interminable ramblings about organising the youth of Britain into some ghastly regiment of paragons, helping old ladies across roads and hiking pointlessly around the countryside. What a fatuous idea – that Baden-Powell fellow had got it right. And how silly Colonel Templeton-Smyth would look in short trousers.

For the next eighteen days, a team of constables working from the War Office tracked down and interviewed the twenty-four Peters who were serving or had served in the ranks with the 13th Hussars. Lestrade was desk-bound while his toes subsided, but he was rather surprised that there were so many of them – Peters, that is, not toes. It was not after all so common a name. He was disappointed not to find anything tangible in the follow-ups. Eight of the Peters were dead, three of them were in jail. Two were abroad and likely to remain so and of the remaining eleven, no links could be established with Shanklin, the Isle of Wight or the disappearance of a middle-aged man in a labourer's smock. At least Lestrade now knew that the smock denoted Norfolk, but inquiries by telegram and telephone to the chief constable of that county achieved nothing – partly because the chief constable did not have a telephone. But there were no reports of a missing person answering to the description of what was once the man in the Chine. Several cats of course were listed and one rather nasty salamander, but no farm labourers, indeed no people at all.

Lestrade was about to conclude that an unidentified
man, whose name may or may not have been Peter, who
may or may not have had association with the 13th
Hussars, had met his end by foul play by person or
persons unknown, when a letter arrived by second
delivery. It was a mourning letter, black-edged and the
message was typed. Lestrade read it just once to realise its
import –

> Just look at him! There he stands,
> With his nasty hair and hands.
> See! his nails are never cut;
> They are grim'd and black as soot;
> And the sloven, I declare,
> Never once has combed his hair.

The postmark was London and it was addressed to
'Inspector Lestrade, Scotland Yard.' The inspector
looked again at the doggerel. Home-made? Yes, he
surmised so. He wished he knew rather more about
poetry but the crammer he had been to had not thought it
necessary and most of his colleagues at the Yard –
Gregson, Athelney Jones, even McNaghten – found
poetry and poets faintly limp and unmanly. The
typescript was odd – slightly uneven with a decided kick
on the letter 'n' so that it stood a little below the line. He
had always thought there must be a way of detecting a
faulty typewriter, but he was damned if he could see
how.

He remembered again the Ripper letters. Two of them
he knew were genuine. Nearly two hundred were from
cranks, oddities who crawled from the woodwork
whenever murder walked abroad. But these two had
carried inside information. And so did this verse – the
hair alone had been mentioned in the local papers and the
case – for such it had become – did not reach all the
dailies. Only the coroner's report, that of Sergeant Bush

of the Hampshire Constabulary and Lestrade's own carried full information. There was the possibility of a leak, mused Lestrade, as he painfully took the lift to the ground floor. Perhaps someone in the coroner's office – that spotty lad Spilsbury, for instance – perhaps one of Bush's constables. But he didn't think so. In his heart of hearts he knew that this letter had been written, and the verse composed, by the murderer.

Well, so be it. This was 1891 and this was Scotland Yard – the foremost police headquarters in the world. This was Britain, the workshop of the world. Forensic science was at his disposal. Here, in the gloomy basement festooned with pipes of gas and water, here were the most brilliant men of science that Europe could boast. If they could not find clues in the letter no one could.

'Fingerprints?' repeated the boffin as he stared at the outstretched letter in Lestrade's carefully poised finger-tips. 'What are they?'

A Death in the Morning

Lord Frederick Hurstmonceux lay on the billiard table in
the gaming room. His normally immaculate hunting
coat was thrown back in tatters, his shirt lacerated and
congealed with blood, as were his hands and face. He had
been dead for some six hours when Lestrade arrived, at
McNaghten's personal request. The house, an extrava-
gant Palladian monstrosity nestling in a curve of the
downs, was still and silent. After the shaking and rattling
of the Daimler Wagonette horseless carriage, that silence
was bliss. A grim butler met him at the door and showed
him into the tiled entrance hall. His policeman's eye took
in the aspidistrae, the elegant sweep of the staircase, the
portraits of the Hurstmonceux, fathers and sons in their
hunting pinks. A row of hushed frightened servants, stiff
in their starched white aprons lined the passageway.
They were unsure how to behave to Lestrade. They
knew he was a police officer and why he was there, but
many of them had never seen an officer from Scotland
Yard, a man in plain clothes. Some of them curtsied,
others followed him with their eyes.

The butler threw back the double doors. Lestrade
blinked in the bright electric light which flooded the
table. He looked down at the body. 'Ruined the baize,' he
murmured.

'Will that be all, sir?'

'Yes. Would you ask Sir Henry to join me here?'

The butler vanished. Lestrade gave the body a cursory

examination. Cause of death he assumed to be severe lacerations and shock. Or blood loss, he mused, as he turned the matted head to find the jugular ripped. Of his clothes only the mud-caked hunting boots remained unscathed. This was messy, a sticky end, even for a country squire of Hurstmonceux's reputation.

'McNaghten?'

The voice made him turn sharply.

'Oh, I expected Assistant Chief Constable McNaghten,' said the voice.

'Inspector Lestrade, sir.' 'At your service' sounded too deferential. 'Sir Henry Cattermole?'

The voice brushed past Lestrade and looked down at the corpse on the billiard table. 'Yes, I'm Cattermole.'

'Assistant Chief Constable McNaghten was unavoidably detained, sir. He asked me to give you his regards. I shall have to ask you a few questions, sir.'

Cattermole had not taken his eyes off the body. 'Come into the library,' he said, 'I can't look at him any more.' Lestrade followed him across the hall. Servants and butler had gone. The library was typical of these country houses, wall to wall with leather-covered books, which no one had read.

'Cognac?'

Lestrade accepted the proffered glass. 'In your own time, sir.'

Cattermole quaffed the brandy and refilled.

'Freddie Hurstmonceux was a bastard, Inspector. A professional bastard. Oh, not in the sense of lineage, you understand. They don't come with bluer blood.'

'I found it rather red, sir.' Lestrade could have kicked himself for the tastelessness of that remark.

'No, Freddie deserved this. Or at least, I'm not surprised by it.'

'Could you tell me what happened, sir?'

'He was out hunting. We all were. Freddie loved having open house and riding to hounds with his cronies.

They all hated him, but he exuded a certain raffish charm. Anyway, we'd got a view and the hounds were off. This was in the Lower Meadow and Freddie, as ever, was off in hot pursuit. Whipping his hunter unmercifully.'

'He didn't treat horses well?'

'Horses, dogs, people. He didn't treat anything well. I've seen him whip a horse to death.'

'You didn't stop him?'

'Damn it, Lestrade. What business is it of yours?' Cattermole paused. Then, more calmly, 'You don't cross a man like Freddie.' A long pause. 'Well, he came through the thicket ahead of me, away to the left. Bertie Cairns and Rosebery were with him, but as he topped the rise he must have left them behind. Ploughed fields there of course, tough going. Freddie was a better rider than any of them. By the time I got to the rise, all hell had broken loose. The hounds set up the devil of a row beyond the wall, I thought they'd got the fox. They were tearing, limb from limb, howling and yelping. But Bertie and Rosebery were galloping down there, taking the wall and laying about them with their crops. It was obvious something was wrong. When I got there it was all over. The dogs were being hauled off and I could see it wasn't a fox. It was Freddie.'

Cattermole buried his face briefly in his hands. Lestrade returned to the subject of the body.

'Foxhounds did that?' he said incredulously.

Cattermole sat back in his chair. 'Impossible to believe? I saw it, Lestrade. They went for his throat. He had no chance at all.'

'Forgive me, sir, I don't mean to be in any way awkward. But this is accidental death. A quirk of nature in the breasts of vicious beasts.' He congratulated himself on having got that out in one breath. And then, perhaps a little pompously, 'I am from the C.I.D., sir, the Detective Branch.'

Cattermole stood up sharply. 'Inspector –' his face was

dark – 'I could have called in the village bobby, but I didn't want huge feet trampling over the last vestiges of what was once a great family. That is why I contacted McNaghten. God knows I had no time for Freddie. He's dead and damned to all eternity. But there,' he pointed dramatically to the massive portrait over the empty fireplace, 'is the fourth Baron Hurstmonceux – and a better man never drew breath.' Henry Cattermole was of the old school, honest and loyal. 'Friendships forged at Eton and Quetta don't die, Inspector.' The inspector took his word for it. 'It's for his sake I sent for the Yard. No fuss, no scandal, you understand?'

'Perfectly, sir.'

'Poor Georgie. Freddie was his only son. The bastard killed him.'

'Would that be on our files, sir?'

'Oh, not literally, Lestrade. He didn't actually put a revolver to his head. But with his . . . ways . . . he might just as well have done.' Cattermole gazed long at the portrait. Then, 'Come with me, Inspector.'

The two men left the house by the vine-covered south wing and crossed the velvet lawns to the stables. Beyond the main buildings here, where the hunters and thoroughbreds steamed after their exercise, they came to the kennels. Lestrade was not taken with dogs. One or two of his superiors were keen on the use of bloodhounds, but they always seemed to urinate on him whenever he had been involved with them. He often wondered whether it was anything personal or whether it was somewhere he had been. In a yard, thirty or forty foxhounds, smart in black, tan and white, licked and snuffled. Lestrade was glad there was no growl, no howl. Not wishing to let Sir Henry believe he was afraid of these curs he extended a sure hand, praying that it didn't shake. A heavy jowled dog, perhaps older, certainly darker than the rest, buried its nose in his palm. Lestrade ruffled its ears. 'Good boy, good boy.'

'Do you notice anything about these dogs?' Cattermole asked him.

Lestrade hated being put on the spot in this way. Give him a burgled tenement, a done bank or even a forged fiver and he was on home ground. But hunting and shooting weekends and country houses were somebody else's patch. He checked the obvious – leg at each corner. None of the dogs had tried to pee on him yet.

'You mean . . .' Long years in the force had given him the slow amble, developed to the point which would give his questioner time to chip in.

'Apart from the blood.'

Lestrade whipped back his hand and hoped that the gesture hadn't been too sudden. He hadn't in fact seen the blood – until now. But there it was, dark and caked around many mouths. Human blood. Hurstmonceux blood.

'They're so docile,' Cattermole went on, 'you wouldn't think that six hours or so ago they tore a man apart, would you?'

Lestrade shuffled backwards as far as protocol would allow.

'That one by you,' Cattermole pointed at the dog which Lestrade had been patting, 'that's Tray, the lead hound. He would have gone for Freddie first. Rosebery said it had him by the throat.'

Lestrade was grateful for the fresh air. Across the courtyard, still in his hunting pinks strode Archibald Philip Primrose, 5th Earl of Rosebery. He was an anxious-looking forty-four.

'Ah, Rosebery. This is Inspector Lestrade – of Scotland Yard.'

'Oh, God.' Rosebery caught the proffered hand.

'My Lord,' Lestrade bowed stiffly. 'Can you shed any light on this unfortunate affair?'

Rosebery looked around him like a stag at bay, his large watery eyes flashing to every corner of the yard. He took Lestrade's arm and led him away down the lawns. Cattermole sensed his air of secrecy and suspicion and walked back towards the house. 'I'll see to your room, Lestrade,' he called.

'Thank you, Sir Henry.'

'Look, Balustrade, there's a Garter in the offing for me.'

'My Lord?' Lestrade would believe anything of the aristocracy, but Rosebery did not strike him as one of those.

'No scandal, y'see. I can't afford any scandal. Not now, I mean, Home Rule is one thing. And the gee gees, but this . . . God, poor Freddie.'

'What sort of man was he, sir?'

'Who?'

'Lord Hurstmonceux.'

'Oh, a bastard. An absolute bastard. He had his moments, mind.' Rosebery chuckled a brittle, distant laugh. 'No, I suppose Freddie wasn't what you would call a decent sort. Look here, er – Balcony – this won't become common knowledge, will it?'

Lestrade had met this kind of pressure before, but from a man like Rosebery, Gladstone's right-hand man, a foremost politician and Peer of the Realm, it was disconcerting. He wouldn't budge Lestrade himself, but an inspector's hands could easily be tied and he wasn't at all sure about McNaghten. Influence and the old school tie were all they once had been, despite the extension of the franchise.

'You can't conceal the death of a member of the House of Lords, My Lord.'

'Death?' Rosebery's tone suggested that he had been misjudging Lestrade. Then, more calmly, 'Oh, quite so, quite so.'

But Lestrade had been quicker. He had read the signs. Rosebery was hiding something.

'Do you think it was something more, My Lord?'

'More?' Rosebery's effort to effect unconcern was pathetic.

'Murder, My Lord.' Lestrade turned to face the man so that their perambulations came to an abrupt end. Rosebery stared at him, his mouth sagging open.

'How?' was all that he could manage.

'That's exactly what's bothering me,' confessed Lestrade. 'I don't know. Yet.'

Rosebery blinked and walked on, following Lestrade's lead. The tone of the conversation had changed. The policeman was now in charge, leading the noble lord around with an invisible ring through his aristocratic nose.

'I take it Lord Hurstmonceux was an experienced huntsman?'

'Oh, yes, ridden with the Quorn, the Cattistock, the best of them.'

'Knew horses and dogs?'

'Like a native. That's what's so damned peculiar.' Rosebery was beginning to open up. 'I mean, he treated his animals badly, God knows. But dogs are faithful curs. They'll stand for a lot, y'know.'

'When foxhounds are on the scent, what do they go for?'

'Well, the fox, of course.'

'Because of the scent?'

'Yes. It's bred into them.'

'And what could make them turn on a man, especially when they are in full cry after the fox?'

Rosebery shook his head. 'I don't know,' he said. 'It's the damnedest thing.'

Dinner was surprisingly convivial. True, Rosebery was still nervous, but the wine flowed and the aristocracy found the presence of a Yard officer more novel than irritating. Lestrade deflected probes about the Ripper case as deftly as he could, but it was obviously still the talk of clubland. He coped remarkably well, for a man of his class, with the vast range of cutlery and silver which would have made Mrs Beeton's head spin. It was a curiously masculine evening. A 'stag weekend' was how Lord Hurstmonceux had termed these functions — by family tradition the last hunt of the season was a 'gentlemen only' affair. Over cigars and port, the third member of the house party, Sir Bertram Cairns, took Lestrade aside.

'They'll be talking Home Rule all night,' he motioned to Rosebery and Cattermole, heads together in earnest conversation by the roaring log fire. 'Bring your glass. There's something I want to show you.'

Lestrade followed Cairns through the house, past his own room and on through endless passages, twisting to right and left, until they came to a locked door, studded with brass. Cairns produced a key and unlocked it. It took a while for Lestrade to take in the contents. The room was obviously some sort of laboratory. Hanging from the ceiling were gruesome birds in the attitude of flight, casting large shadows on the walls. Pigeons disintegrating on the impact of hawks, and shrikes impaling insects on thorns. On the tables and benches was a vast array of glassware, bottles and flasks and tubing. In the centre of the room, the floor was bare, scarred with cuts and stained darkish brown. In jars on the shelves was every assortment of animal, floating in greenish liquid.

'Lord Hurstmonceux was a scientist?' said Lestrade.

'Not quite,' came the answer. Cairns pointed to an oblong box in one corner of the room. At one end of it was a series of black and white keys and the box was divided into compartments with piano wire strung across the base to the keys themselves. Lestrade felt it was legitimate to admit that he did not know what this was.

'The Cats' Piano,' said Cairns grimly.

'Er . . . the cats' . . . er . . .'

'The cats are placed into the compartments and locked in. Then the . . . scientist . . . plays a tune on the keyboard, with the result that the wires spring up and lash the cats from below and the hammers hit their heads.'

'So this is not a laboratory,' said Lestrade, the light beginning to dawn.

'No, Inspector. This is a torture chamber.'

Lestrade noticed for the first time that the walls and door were heavily padded. Cairns caught his eye. 'Noise-proof,' he said. 'These animals around you in the jars. I'll wager any price you like that they were operated on while very much alive.'

Cairns crossed to a desk-drawer and produced a ledger. 'Here – a record of his "experiments".'

'Vivisection,' mused Lestrade.

'Oh, no, Inspector. The public might not like the idea, but true vivisection is at least for scientific purposes. But this – this is sheer sadism – torture for pleasure's sake. And Unnatural Acts,' he added cryptically.

Lestrade flicked through the ledger. Boiling hedgehogs, skewering thrushes on needles, snapping the front legs of foxes, castrating horses with dress-making scissors, blinding goats with hatpins. Hardly the usual pastime of a scholar and a gentleman. And what Lord Hurstmonceux attempted to do with the sheep on his estate was very definitely best left to the imagination.

'How does this help us, Sir Bertram?' asked Lestrade.

'I'm not sure,' answered Cairns. 'But we all know why you're here, Lestrade. This is not a simple death in the morning. It's murder.'

'By dog or dogs unknown?' added Lestrade.

'What do you mean?'

'Let me explain something about murder, Sir Bertram. When I am called in to investigate foul play, I usually have a victim and no murderer. The average killer does not stand over the corpse obligingly with a gun or knife in his hand until I arrive. I piece together the evidence – like the parts of a jigsaw puzzle – and I arrive at conclusions. Now, in this case, I have my murderer – or murderers should I say. Forty of them. But they are foxhounds, sir, and a foxhound cannot stand trial before one of Her Majesty's Justices. There is no precedent for it.'

'Good God, man, I'm not an idiot. Freddie Hurstmonceux was one of the most unpopular men in the country. There must be scores of people who would not have been sorry to see him dead.'

'Very possibly, sir. But unless you can tell me how they did it, I cannot proceed further.'

Lestrade slept little that night. In his room tucked away in the west wing he paced the floor. The oil-lamp cast a lurid glow on the heavy Chinese wallpaper. His bed was appallingly uncomfortable and the room cold. He had not come with the intention of staying but in view of the deceased's no longer wanting them, Sir Henry Cattermole had lent him a nightshirt and dressing gown of Lord Hurstmonceux's. They were a trifle large perhaps and decidedly ornate by Lestrade's rather drab standards, but they would do. He looked out from time to time across the lawns and caught the scurrying moon flickering on the waters of the lake. Occasionally the baying of a hound bore in on him the extent of his exasperation. But as dawn began to creep over the low trees below the house, a theory began to emerge. Well, after breakfast, Lestrade would see whether or not it paid off.

Cairns was all for it. Cattermole had his doubts, but would do a great deal for the good of the family name. Rosebery wished he wasn't there. Within an hour after breakfast, the pack was out with their handlers and the house guests, including Lestrade, mounted and ready to go. Standard police procedure, he had assured them – the reconstruction of a crime. He kept as far as he could from the hounds and each man carried a loaded revolver in case they ran amok again. Lestrade was a fair rider, but he wasn't used to rough country and five-barred gates. He hoped they would encounter neither.

It was a misty morning, raw-cold for early April and totally unlike the clear night. The ground was heavy with dew like tears as Cattermole sounded the horn and the pack moved off. A suicidal groom was riding far ahead with a dead fox over the cantle of his saddle, to draw the hounds the right way. It was an odd sight. A hunt, now rather out of season, if only by a day, with too few men, too few horses, no real quarry and an odd, gloomy silence. There was no jollity, no bantering and even Cattermole's horn sounded chilly and alone. They crossed the ploughed fields of the South Meadow, the horses sliding in the morning mud. Lestrade felt faintly ridiculous in Lord Hurstmonceux's spare pink and the ghastly uncomfortable hat bouncing around on his head. But the fields were a joy compared to the woods. Branches lashed at him as he doubled up to stay in the saddle. Splashed with mud and the dew from leaves he swung away from the path in an effort to find solid ground. His horse plunged and reared, snorting with annoyance at the increasingly less competent man on its back. Fleetingly, Lestrade saw Bertie Cairns across to his right, at the head of a scattered field. Fleetingly, because he saw him at a curious angle while somersaulting over the horse's head.

Lestrade landed squarely on his back, badly jarring his spine as he did so. He had the sense and training to cling to the reins as he fell, so was able to haul himself upright using the horse. There was no sign of the others. He hoped no one else had seen him. Two or three of the straggler hounds rushed past him, leaving him firmly alone. He remounted with difficulty and made for the light at the edge of the woods. Below him, he saw that the hounds had reached the spot where he presumed Lord

Hurstmonceux had been killed. Beyond a low, dry-stone wall, unusual for the area, the dogs milled around, sniffing, yelping, obviously having lost the scent. The groom with the dead fox had done his job well and had effectively lost his pursuers. Cattermole, Cairns and Rosebery sat on their horses, looking around them for Lestrade.

The inspector urged his mount down the furrowed slope. The view in front of him bobbed and leaped. He dug his knees in hard and clung on as majestically as he could. The horizon dropped before him and he was down, wheeling his horse sharply in a circle to join the others.

'Bravo, Parapet,' called Rosebery. The name had lost all semblance of reality so that for a while Lestrade assumed he must be talking to somebody else. 'A yard or so to the left, however, and you would have caught that harrow.'

Lestrade just had time to catch sight of the implement, when it started. The hounds howled and snarled, springing up at Rosebery, jaws snapping as they turned in the air. Cairns and Cattermole drew their revolvers, firing wildly to left and right. Rosebery clung to the saddle for dear life, trying to extricate his plunging horse from the mêlée of dogs. Three or four grooms were hurrying down the slope towards the wall shouting harshly at the dogs. Lestrade drove his horse through the bedlam, caught Rosebery's rein with a deftness which surprised him and led him away over the furrows. By this time Rosebery had taken stock of himself and was controlling his horse. Lestrade swung back with his revolver cocked, but Cairns and Cattermole had done their business well and the hounds were recoiling, calmer now and stunned by the gunfire and the corpses by the wall.

The horsemen rode to higher ground as the grooms and handlers took charge of the pack. Rosebery, gashed and bleeding, slumped in his saddle in shock. 'It's the damnedest thing,' he said, staring blankly ahead.

'You're lucky to be alive,' said Cairns, handing Rosebery his hat.

'At least that lead-hound won't attack anybody else,' said Cattermole. 'I just shot him.'

'It wasn't the lead hound,' mused Lestrade, almost to himself.

'I saw it,' said Cattermole, 'exactly like poor Freddie.'

'Tell me, sir,' Lestrade turned in the saddle to face him, 'when you shot the dog, Tray, who killed him – you or the gun?'

'Eh?'

'I mean – the hounds killed Freddie Hurstmonceux. But who trained them to?'

'Trained?' snapped Rosebery. 'You can't train dogs to go for a man.'

'Yes, you can,' said Cairns, 'but they must have been trained to go for Rosebery, too.'

'No, sir, I don't think so. If my assumption is correct, then this morning's incident was merely an accidental repetition of the original. Lord Hurstmonceux must have been unhorsed. You were lucky, My Lord.'

'We've got to get you back to the house, Rosebery,' Cattermole urged. 'I don't know what you've achieved, Lestrade, except for nearly killing someone else.'

'Sir Henry, please bear with me. I believe I have the answer, but I must see the tenants first. Can that be arranged?'

'Good God, man, there are nearly two hundred of them. Can you spare that time from the Yard?'

It took Lestrade just over a week to interview all the Hurstmonceux tenants. With two or three sergeants to help him he might have halved this time, but Cattermole was insistent for the sake of the family honour that the incident must be hushed up. Lestrade knew all too well that whatever he uncovered here would never become public. Freddie Hurstmonceux had been notorious enough in his lifetime, but no one would be able to make matters worse after his death. The 'laboratory' would never see the light of day. Lestrade wasn't even sure if Cattermole knew about it.

Of the one hundred and eighty-three adults on the Hurstmonceux estate, one hundred and eighty-three had the motive and opportunity to kill their former master. Even some of the children looked murderous. But Lestrade only asked one question – at least he was only interested in the answer to one question: who placed the harrow against the wall in the Lower Meadow?

It transpired that none of them had. Lestrade prided himself on his judgement of men – and women. There were many tenants who would have split Lord Hurstmonceux's head with a hoe, blown it off with a shotgun or sliced it apart with a sickle, but who among them had the ability to kill him in this way? Trained policeman that he was, he noticed the tenants' reactions to the harrow question. They told him the truth. No one had moved it.

He then interrogated, with all the subtlety at his disposal, the handlers of the pack. It was a new pack to the hunt, they told him. Lestrade toyed with the question of whether the seal had been broken, but the gravity of the situation prevented it. Another gem, he mused, lost forever. Where had they been bought? At auction, of course. Lestrade broke the silence he had promised by sending a telegram to the Yard to check. As Lestrade guessed, the former owner could not be traced.

The inspector had one last card to play. Rosebery had gone, nursing his wounds, back to London to wait for his Garter. The funeral for Lord Hurstmonceux was due on the following day, in the family chapel a mile or so from Hurstmonceux Hall. Lestrade would not be there. His presence would not be welcome. The night before he left them, Lestrade crept from his room after dark. He crossed the moonless courtyard to the kennels. Once inside, his heart raced. Once or twice his nerve left him, but each time, he turned back. The dogs slept more or less soundly despite his entrance. But he knew, even in the dark, that one or two of them were awake, watching him. He levelled the revolver, a heavy Smith and Wesson, and prayed. His heart pounded in his ears. Flashing before his eyes he saw again the lacerated corpse of Freddie Hurstmonceux, the congealed blood on his throat and clothing, the dried trickle on the baize of the billiard table. He cocked the pistol – once, twice and somewhere from the depths of his throat came the whispered word – 'harrow'.

The kennels roared into life, hounds snarling and snapping. Lestrade threw himself back through the door, sliding the bolt and collapsing against the wall. He was right. He had proved it. But the house was coming to life, lights appearing in the servants' quarters. Voices and shouts in the yard. Lestrade saw no point in advertising himself. He put the gun away and crept via the shrubbery to the relevant wing. Up the stairway and into his room, before the house returned to an uneasy slumber. On the night before the funeral of the master, everyone was uneasy.

Lestrade travelled back to London by train. The newspapers had carried the headlines – 'terrible hunting accident'. Everything was neat, vague and unexceptional. Lord Hurstmonceux might simply have fallen from his horse. Only Lestrade knew *how*. Someone had placed the harrow by the wall in the Lower Meadow. They had then led the hunt that way, probably as Lestrade had done, getting a beater to carry a scent over his saddle. Hurstmonceux had leapt the wall, hit the harrow or narrowly missed it. What would have been his reaction? 'What's that bloody harrow doing there?' or something similar. Whoever had arranged this had already sold the pack to Freddie, and had taught them to react, viciously and blindly, to anyone who spoke the word 'harrow'.

Well, there it was. All the same, it was fantastic. It was astonishingly risky, uncertain. The murderer ran a risk in drawing on the hunt. He could easily have been seen. How did he arrange the sale? How could he be sure that Freddie would reach that wall first? And that he would use the essential word 'harrow'? That he was alone at the time was the good luck of others who rode in the hunt. Lestrade realised he should have talked to them. But by the time he had arrived, most of them had gone and they could probably have added nothing to the facts of the case. Still, there it was. Risky, uncertain, fantastic, yes. But it had worked.

So Lestrade knew how. What he did not know was who. He would put the evidence before McNaghten, who would brush his moustaches and straighten his cravat and consign the information to the bowels of his incomprehensible filing system. He could then compile a list as long as his arm of those who knew Freddie Hurstmonceux for the cad and bounder that he was. It didn't help him a great deal.

The letter was waiting for him when he got back. A mourning letter, lying square in the centre of his desk. Lestrade inquired why it was separate from the week's mail pile which stood to one side. The desk sergeant explained it had come this morning and looked personal, addressed to Lestrade himself. The inspector opened it. And then he placed it alongside the first. There was no doubt about it. They were written on different typewriters. But the doggerel sounded similar, if this time more informed:

> *Here is cruel Frederick, see!*
> *A horrid, wicked boy was he;*
> *He caught the flies, poor little things,*
> *And then tore off their tiny wings,*

He kill'd the birds, and broke the chairs,
And threw the kitten down the stairs;
The trough was full and faithful Tray
Came out to drink one sultry day;
He wagg'd his tail and wet his lip,
When cruel Fred snatch'd up a whip,
And whipp'd poor Tray till he was sore,
And kick'd and whipp'd him more and more:
At this, good Tray grew very red,
And growl'd and bit him till he bled;
Then you should only have been by,
To see how Fred did scream and cry!

The realisation was borne in on Lestrade. The mourning letters addressed to him at the Yard. No traceable clues in postmark or typeface. Two pieces of verse, each with definite knowledge of the murder under investigation. And, from the style of the verse, written by the same hand. Even Lestrade's unpoetical eye could see that. He placed the disturbing evidence before McNaghten.

The Head of the Criminal Investigation Department brushed his cravat and straightened his moustaches.

The Vicar's Daughter

It took Constable Dew nearly ten minutes to find it in the atlas.

'Here it is, sir,' he told Lestrade, 'Wildboarclough.'

'Ridiculous name,' grunted Lestrade.

'About six miles from Macclesfield, sir, as the crow flies.'

Lestrade did not fly. He caught a series of trains as far as Macclesfield and hired a pony and trap to get him on to the Pennines towards Wildboarclough. It was early May, but there was no sign of Spring up here. He was within a crow's flight of the Cat and Fiddle Inn, one of the highest in England. It was a hiker's paradise, but Lestrade saw no hikers today. As his pony climbed the narrow twisting roads, the snow lay crisp in the hollows. On the higher slopes above him, he saw the sheep, huddling together for shelter against the biting wind. He passed a lamb, dead by the roadside on the open moors. Its eyes had been pecked out by crows – one of those Dew was thinking of, no doubt, that flew from Macclesfield.

As Lestrade rattled into Wildboarclough, the moors were less visible. There were deep chasms here, haunting and dark, sheer cliffs of northern granite rearing up above the bare, still, winter trees. He passed the new post office, specially built for Her Majesty's visit to Lord Derby's estate, and the school. The vicarage was away to the left, above the small, grey church. All the houses were grey, tall and silent, stark against the evergreen clumps of rhododendron bushes.

A housekeeper-shaped woman answered the door as the gardener took charge of the pony and trap. Lestrade explained who he was and was shown into a drawing room. He peeled off his doeskin gloves and cupped his hands over a minimal fire. As he watched it, it went out, leaving a single spiral of smoke. Lestrade contented himself with blowing on to his fingers, trying to bury their tips into the thawing fronds of his moustaches. He stamped up and down trying to remember when he had last felt his feet. The books on the ceiling-high shelves were what he would have expected – theological tomes, discursive works on ecclesiastical history.

'Inspector Lestrade?'

The inspector turned to face a bull-necked, purple-faced man about twice his own width. 'Swallow.'

Was this an old Cheshire custom, wondered Lestrade. Or perhaps a cure for frostbite? He was in the act of complying with the command when realisation dawned – 'Inspector Swallow, Cheshire Constabulary.' Lestrade hoped his Adam's apple had not been too visible as he shook the inspector's hand.

'Bad business,' Swallow grunted.

'What happened?'

'I may as well be blunt,' Swallow announced grumpily. Looking at him, Lestrade wondered how he could be anything else. Swallow crossed to the window and looked out across the sweep of the lawn to the church. 'I advised 'em against it. I said we could handle it. I said we didn't need t'Yard.' Fearing he had been *too* blunt, he turned to Lestrade. 'Nothing personal, of course.'

Lestrade waved the insult aside. 'We all follow orders, Inspector,' he said. 'I'm afraid this thing may be bigger than both of us.'

'Meaning?' Swallow had missed the cliché.

'I can't be sure yet.'

Swallow thumped a framed photograph of a teenaged

girl down on the mantelpiece near Lestrade's head. 'Harriet Elizabeth Wemyss. Aged seventeen. Burned to death.'

'So I gather.' Lestrade perused the photograph. A singularly plain girl, hair parted in the centre. Very old-fashioned. Probably the living spit of her mother. Dead spit now, he supposed. Better not pursue that. Rather unpleasant.

'I saw no damage as I came in,' chanced Lestrade.

'Nay, you wouldn't. This were no ordinary house fire. If it were, d'you think we'd send for t'Yard?'

'Your theory, then?'

Swallow was less sure of himself. 'Look, y'd better come and see for yoursen. The Reverend ain't home yet awhile. He won't mind.'

Lestrade was surprised to see Swallow apparently showing signs of sentiment or at least respect. He followed the burly policeman up the broad staircase, past the stained glass and *The Light of the World*. The body, what was left of it, lay on a bed in a room at the end of a passage. It was barely recognisable as a human form, much less the girl in the photograph.

'I 'ope you've a strong stomach, Lestrade,' grunted Swallow – 'they'll be taking her away t'Congleton later today. If y'want to examine the body y'd best do it now.'

'Who certified the death?'

'T'local doctor. Chap called Marsden.'

'Cause of death?'

Swallow looked askance at Lestrade. Is this t'Yard? he thought to himself. The man's some kind of cretin.

'Burning,' he answered.

Lestrade looked at the neck, or where the neck should have been. Strangulation would be impossible to detect. He looked at the rest of the body, charred and shrivelled. Perhaps a coroner could find something on that wreck, though he'd have to be a damned good one. But Lestrade couldn't. He must assume that burning it was.

'Tell me what happened,' he said.

'Can we go back t'drawing room?' Swallow looked surprisingly green. Lestrade followed him down the stairs. At the bottom the Reverend Wemyss met them on his way in through the front door. Within seconds he was knee deep in cats. Introductions were brief and to the point. The Vicar carried two of his favourite animals through into the drawing room. A third cat had twined itself round Lestrade's neck. Wemyss stopped in his tracks.

'Mrs Drum!' he barked.

The housekeeper bustled in amid the rustling of skirts. The Vicar rounded on her as cats flew in all directions. 'You've had a fire in here!'

Mrs Drum dissolved into instant tears. 'I'm sorry, sir, I didn't think. We had guests . . .'

'Guests!' The Vicar was purple. Mrs Drum indicated Lestrade. 'I have forbidden any fires in this house, Mrs Drum. You will take your notice.'

The housekeeper exited among floods of tears. Wemyss visibly calmed himself down and instructed the officers of the law to sit.

'Please forgive me, gentlemen. As you can imagine, this is something of a trying time for us all.'

'Of course, Mr Wemyss,' said Lestrade. 'It is my painful duty, however, to ask you some questions.'

'Quite so, Inspector. But first, would you like some tea?'

'Thank you, sir.'

The Vicar pulled a bell cord, then settled back to fondle his cats. A maidservant swept in, curtsied and stood motionless. 'Tea, Hannah' – and then as an afterthought – 'no, wait. Of course, I have said no fires. We will have lemonade.'

Lemonade on top of a long cold journey was not Lestrade's idea of a good time. But, then, he was hardly here to enjoy himself.

'I have, of course, already made a statement to Inspector Swallow and his constable,' began Wemyss, 'but I understand it is police procedure to repeat oneself several times.'

'Occasionally, new points come to light, sir,' observed Lestrade. 'Pray continue.' And he could have kicked himself for that remark.

'I was attending a Temperance meeting in Macclesfield. This was, let me see, Thursday. The day before yesterday. I arrived home by trap, early evening. It was already dark. As I alighted and Beddoes was taking the pony, I heard the screams from within the house. I went in and found . . .' He paused, but seemed remarkably in control of himself. 'My wife and my daughter's governess, Miss Spink, were there ahead of me, both hysterical. The charred thing that was once my daughter was lying on the landing floor . . .' Another pause. 'Unrecognisable.'

Swallow slurped his lemonade at an unfortunate, poignant moment.

'I should explain,' Wemyss went on, 'that my wife and Miss Spink had themselves been absent, visiting the local elderly. They had arrived home moments before me.'

'And the servants?' asked Lestrade.

'Only Mrs Drum was in the house. The maid Hannah does not live in and it was her day off. Beddoes we share with the schoolmaster. He had been on the premises an hour or two only, before I arrived. I never allow him in the house.'

Charity, mused Lestrade to himself, did not begin at home in this establishment.

'Have you anything to add?' he asked.

Wemyss stood up, disarranging the cats as he did so.

'God moves in mysterious ways, Inspector. I long ago joined Brutus in his acceptance of death among his dear ones. It must happen one day and, knowing that, I can accept it.'

Lestrade and Swallow found themselves nodding in

unison, like things on sticks at a fairground. They noticed each other and broke the rhythm.

'I'd like to show you something.' Wemyss selected a faded book from the shelf. 'The Annual Register for the year of Our Lord 1767. I have taken the trouble to mark the pages.' He read an extraordinary account. 'A lady was found burned to death in her bedroom in her London house. An old lady, certainly, but there was no source of fire. No candles, no grate, no tallow. Nothing particularly inflammable. She simply burned to death,' concluded Wemyss. 'A sort of . . . spontaneous combustion, I suppose you would call it.'

'You mean, like a 'orseless carriage, Vicar?' asked Swallow, quite perplexed. Wemyss and Lestrade both looked at him, and he sank back in his chair.

'Can that happen, Mr Wemyss?' asked Lestrade.

'According to the Annual Register, it did in 1767, Inspector Lestrade. But no, I think not. You see, I think my daughter was murdered.'

Lestrade looked at the older man. What sort of a murderer would kill a seventeen-year-old girl – the daughter of a vicar? It could have been a sexual crime, of course, but the state of the body made that hypothesis unprovable. It seemed a trifle inappropriate to ask the age-old question, but he did anyway.

'Did your daughter have any enemies, Mr Wemyss?'

'Inspector, my daughter was a shy little girl of seventeen. She had very few friends, poor lamb. We are rather remote up here, you know. But enemies . . . no, Inspector. She hadn't an enemy in the world.'

'Then why do you say she was murdered, sir? And why call in the Yard?'

'To answer your second question first. I have always insisted on the best for my family – the best food, the best clothes, the best education – which is not, mark you, your North London Collegiate School – and, without wishing to offend Swallow here, the best police.'

Lestrade bowed in acknowledgement of the compliment.

'To answer your first question. Because I don't believe in this' – pointing at the Register – 'I do not believe that a person can burn to death by themselves. There has to be a rational explanation. My daughter's body was found upstairs on the landing. There were no fires in the upstairs rooms. It was rather warm for May.'

Lestrade winced as he wondered what a cold May must be like.

'I shall examine the scene of death again a little later, sir,' he said, 'but first I would like to talk to your wife, Mr Wemyss.'

'I'm afraid that won't be possible, Inspector. You see, my wife is distraught. She is staying with her sister in Congleton. I must insist that she is not disturbed. Our doctor has warned that it would be unwise in her mental state.'

Lestrade glanced at Swallow for confirmation. The bluff Cheshire policeman nodded gravely. He had presumably seen Mrs Wemyss, Lestrade conjectured. Her testimony would be unhelpful.

'Then I must speak to Miss Spink.'

'Of course. I shall send her to you at once.'

But Wemyss had not reached the door when a silently weeping Mrs Drum appeared. 'I'm on my way, sir,' she managed between sobs, indicating a valise in her hand. 'Beddoes will send my trunk on. In the meantime . . .' At this point, coherent words failed her completely, and she merely indicated the entrance of visitors by a wave of her hand, clutching a copious white handkerchief.

'Very well.' Wemyss remained unaffected by the woman's distraught state. 'Do not look to me for a reference, Mrs Drum. Your action today obliterates your former unblemished record. My dear Watts.'

Wemyss shook the hand of the new arrival, a handsome man in his mid-fifties, Lestrade guessed, sharply dressed and distinguished. Behind him minced a small auburn-haired man with the narrowest, most sloping shoulders and largest head Lestrade had ever seen. With him, Wemyss was more reserved. 'Swinburne,' and a stiff nod of the head was all he received. The little man nodded in turn.

'My dear Hector, how positively dreadful. We came as soon as we heard. Swinburne hasn't been well. How is poor Dorothea taking it?'

'Badly, I'm afraid. You can imagine what a shock it must have been – finding poor Harriet like that. She's with her sister in Congleton.'

'Harriet?' asked the newcomer.

Everyone looked at him rather oddly.

'No, Dorothea.'

'Ah, of course.'

Introductions were perfunctory. 'Inspector Lestrade of Scotland Yard, Inspector Swallow of the Cheshire Constabulary, my dear friend, Watts-Dunton, the poet. And Mr Swinburne.'

Wemyss led his friend, the poet, to the door, the latter commiserating with him as he went. The door slammed shut and Mr Swinburne stood before it, rather spare and out of place. Lestrade took Swallow aside and asked him to find Miss Spink. He then tackled the little man.

'Algernon Charles Swinburne?'

The little man spun round as if he had been slapped. 'It's a lie, I wasn't there.' And then, more calmly, 'Oh, forgive me, Inspector. I forgot myself.'

'Algernon Charles Swinburne, the poet?'

'I have that honour, sir.'

'Do you recognise the style of this, sir?' Lestrade pulled from his pocket copies of the doggerel connected with the last two murders on his mind. He suspected that this one, bizarre and tragic, may be a third, but couldn't be sure yet.

'They're not mine,' said Swinburne. 'They're probably Browning's.'

Lestrade's professional ears pricked up. Swinburne knew something. 'Indeed?'

Swinburne relaxed a little now and sat on the settee. He reached in his pocket for a hip flask and uncorked it. 'Oh,' he paused, eyes pleading pathetically, 'you won't tell Watts–Dunton, will you? He thinks I've given it up.'

Lestrade waved aside the possibility.

'This Mr Browning. Would you happen to know where he is?'

'Westminster Abbey.'

'Poet's Corner?'

Swinburne nodded.

'You would assume that these verses were written recently?'

'Beats me!' said Swinburne, and chuckled to himself. 'Browning's been dead these two years.'

Another brick wall reared up at Lestrade, but Swinburne was already off on another tack.

'Tell me about police brutality,' he said.

'Sir?'

'Oh, come now, Inspector. When you have a man in custody – what is that quaint euphemism you chaps use – "helping the police with their inquiries" – isn't that it? What do you use? Truncheons? Whips? Thumbscrews?' His voice rose imperceptibly by degrees as he spoke, savouring each word. His knuckles were white as he gripped the arm of the settee. Lestrade narrowed his eyes as he began to see Mr Swinburne's problem.

'Rubber tubing,' he said.

Swinburne's mouth sagged open with pleasure and astonishment. Lestrade became confidential. 'It doesn't show, you see.'

Swinburne's voice was a rasping whisper. 'Where do you do it?'

'Cell Block A.'

'No, no, I mean where on the body? Buttocks, thighs?'

'No, thank you,' said Lestrade, 'I am trying to give

them up.'

He left the room as Swinburne took refuge in his hip flask, and slowly began to tighten the knot of his tie so that his eyes bulged and his colour rose. 'Chastise me!' were the last words Lestrade heard as he made for the stairs.

In the study sat Miss Spink, a prim demure lady in her mid-thirties, hair strained back in the characteristic bun of the professional spinster. Swallow stood behind her like something out of a studio photograph.

'I would like to see you alone, Inspector,' she said to Lestrade. Swallow was about to object but Lestrade's gesture of the head sent him shambling to the door, grunting under his breath the while. 'Mr Swinburne is in the drawing room, Inspector,' Lestrade called after. 'See that he doesn't come to any harm, there's a good chap. And don't let him put your handcuffs on!'

'Inspector?'

'Ma'am.' Lestrade sat down in front of the governess. She was not conventionally attractive, perhaps, but there was a certain something about her. She gazed deeply into Lestrade's eyes. 'I could not bear to tell that oaf,' she motioned to the retreated figure of Swallow, 'but I feel there is something you should know.'

'I am all ears, ma'am.'

Miss Spink swept upright with a rustle of petticoats. She turned her back on Lestrade. 'This is very difficult for me, Inspector. You can't imagine what a shock all this has been.'

Lestrade sensed when a particular approach was needed with witnesses. He laid a reassuring hand on the governess's arm. She gasped and pulled back, but the expression on her face indicated that it had been precisely the right thing to do. She blushed and glanced at the ground. 'Harriet was seeing . . . a man,' she said.

'A man, ma'am?'

'All men are beasts, Inspector,' she suddenly shouted,

then realised the stupidity of the remark. 'Forgive me. Present company is of course excepted.'

'This man – who is he?'

'I don't know. Inspector, I have been guilty of neglect. I beg of you, don't tell the Reverend or Mrs Wemyss. I could not bear them to know the truth.'

'And what is the truth, ma'am?'

Miss Spink began to cry, decorously, of course, into a tiny lace handkerchief. Lestrade was the soul of consolation as she gradually pulled herself together.

'I regularly accompanied Harriet to Macclesfield. Beddoes drove us in the trap. We would visit the library, and the tea-rooms and on fine days walk in the park. Occasionally we would go further afield – to Buxton to the pump-rooms, for example, or Congleton.'

'Go on.'

'Well, about a month ago, Harriet went into Macclesfield alone – with Beddoes, of course, but the disgusting man finds a tavern and stays there until an agreed hour.'

'You were not present, ma'am?'

'No, I was . . . indisposed. When Harriet returned that day, she was excited, agitated. She danced and sang and chattered incessantly, to me, to her mama, to her papa. She would give no reason for this new elation – she was usually so quiet a child – except that her life had changed and that she would never be the same again.'

'From which you concluded . . . ?'

'I could not believe it at first. A young lady of Harriet's refinement, the daughter of a clergyman, but I suspected – no more than that – that she had an admirer.'

Lestrade's headshaking and clicking of the tongue were taken at face value by the strait-laced Miss Spink.

'Pray continue, m'am.'

'Harriet became a different girl. She went into Macclesfield two or three times a week and each time she returned she was ruder, more unbridled. She refused to attend to her studies and took to the vilest habits.'

'Habits, ma'am? Are you suggesting she was embracing the Catholic faith?'

'Why no, Inspector. She . . . smoked.'

'*Smoked*?'

'Here.' Miss Spink produced a tin of tobacco papers from a pocket in her voluminous skirt. 'Shameful, isn't it? A young lady of her refinement. The servants knew, of course, but we were at pains to keep it from her poor parents.'

'And how do you account for the acquisition of this habit, ma'am?'

'That man, that filthy beast whom she met in Macclesfield and whom she went on seeing in that clandestine way. It was he, I am sure, who introduced her to the habit . . . and the Lord knows what besides.'

'I repeat, ma'am. Who is the man?'

'I only saw him once. On one occasion I ignored Harriet's insistence that she go alone to Macclesfield. I went with her. As we neared the park, I saw her signal to a figure in the bushes. It was only a split second, of course, because the figure vanished. I asked Harriet who it was and she laughed and said a friend. I could extract nothing more from her.'

'Could you give me a description of the man?'

'That's very difficult, Mr Lestrade. He was large, big-built, wearing a long coat and a dark hat. I could not see his face. But I knew instinctively that he was a beast.'

'Of course,' Lestrade concurred, his tongue planted firmly in his cheek.

'And you never saw the man again?'

Miss Spink shook her head.

Swallow burst in. 'That Swinburne's a right . . .'

'Thank you, Mr Swallow.' Lestrade stood up sharply, gesturing to Miss Spink. Swallow coughed awkwardly.

'I am to join Mrs Wemyss in Congleton, Inspector. Please treat all that I have told you in the strictest confidence.'

'Of course, ma'am. Would you be so good as to ask Mr Beddoes to see me presently.'

Miss Spink floated out in a profusion of dignity. She tossed her head disdainfully at Swallow and glided across the hall beyond him.

'That one needs a bloody good . . .'

'Quite so, Inspector,' Lestrade interrupted him again.

'Ee, that Swinburne.' Swallow returned to his former topic. ''E's sittin' there, gettin' cats to sink their claws into his legs. Bloody weird, I call it.'

'Bloody weird most of us call it, Inspector. But it is hardly a police matter.'

Swallow shrugged.

Beddoes began by being far from helpful. Trouble at t'Vicarage was something he rather revelled in. A man of his class, he was no deferential tenant and it was clear that he had no time for the carriage folk whom he served. Yes, he had taken Miss Harriet on several occasions into Macclesfield. Yes, he had noticed a change in her mood, but it didn't surprise him. All carriage folk behaved badly to him. They upbraided him, looked down on him, ignored him. So the girl was going off the straight and narrow. Typical. Nothing about the gentry surprised him. A man? No, he knew nothing about a man. But then he had spent his time in Macclesfield at t'Rose and Crown, so he wouldn' a seen nowt, would 'e? But then, nothing about the gentry surprised Beddoes.

It took Lestrade some little time to elicit this slim information, as Beddoes was broad Cheshire and Lestrade wished at more than one point for an interpreter. But as Beddoes rose to go, he threw out a remark which he considered unimportant. To Lestrade it was vital.

'A pedlar?'

'Aye. On't morning of Miss Harriet's death, it were. Soom bloke comes round to sell brushes.'

'What did this man look like?'

'Oh, I didn't see him very close. I'd just come from t'school. Big bloke 'e were. 'Ad an 'at.'

'An 'at.'

'Aye.'

'Beddoes, where is Mrs Drum?'

'Vicar give 'er notice. She's off t'Macclesfield this hour since.'

'On foot?'

'Nay, I took her t'station at Rainow, seein' as 'ow I couldn't go mysen''

'Get your trap, man. We're going after her.'

'It's t'Vicar's trap.' Beddoes was suddenly astonishingly solicitous for his employer. 'Besides, y've got your own.'

'Inspector Swallow has borrowed my trap to pursue his own inquiries. I am commandeering the Vicar's in the name of the law.' Then, more forcibly, 'You wouldn't want to be accused of obstructing the police in the course of their investigations, would you, Beddoes?'

The odd-job man grumbled and muttered as he scuttled to the stables behind the house.

'Y'll not catch 'er now,' he shouted as the trap swung down the gravelled drive out on to the open road. 'T'train from Rainow leaves in ten minutes.'

'Use your whip, man. You're wasting time.'

They did catch Mrs Drum. So desolate had she been while waiting in the cold drizzle at Rainow station that the stationmaster had taken her into the shelter of his office and given her the proverbial cup of tea that did not really cheer. Consequently, while the garrulous Mrs Drum poured her heart out to him and he poured tea into her, she had missed her train. Lestrade had found her, still sipping tea, still in the stationmaster's office. She was not, however, terribly helpful. Lestrade's forthright questions brought her out of her mood of self-pity, but her description of the travelling salesman was vague. He was a big man, she said, but his face was partly hidden by a muffler and his voice distorted accordingly. She thought he had piercing blue eyes, but under the rim of the hat, it was difficult to tell. As to the death of Miss Harriet, Mrs Drum had been in the kitchen, it being the maid's day off, preparing dinner. It was about half past three. She remembered that because she heard the hall clock strike, but the hall clock was notoriously inaccurate. Safer to say it was between three and four. Mrs Drum had heard a roaring noise, and then the screaming started. By the time she reached the top of the stairs, it was too late. What was left of Harriet Wemyss lay blazing on the carpet. Shocked and sickened, Mrs Drum had thrown water on her and all the blankets she could drag from the beds. The smell, she said, was awful and the memory of it would remain with her always.

Lestrade gave the ex-housekeeper time to recover. It had been perhaps half an hour later that Mrs Wemyss and Miss Spink arrived, followed almost immediately by the vicar. Mrs Drum had sent Beddoes for the police, but they arrived later still.

'I can't understand how it happened, sir,' sobbed Mrs Drum, 'it's unbelievable.'

'The travelling salesman,' said Lestrade. 'What time did he arrive?'

'I suppose about half past twelve sir. I told 'im we didn't need brushes but 'e insisted on seeing the lady of the 'ouse. I told 'im Mrs Wemyss wasn't in, but Miss 'arriet came downstairs and took 'im into the drawing room.'

'What did you do?'

'I got on with my work, sir.'

'Did you not think it odd that Miss Harriet should deal with this pedlar herself? Was it not usually your duty?'

Mrs Drum had clearly not thought along those lines before, but she acknowledged that that was in fact the case.

'And what time did this pedlar leave?'

'I don't know, sir. I was in the kitchen most of the day

and you can't see the front door from there. I suppose Miss 'arriet saw 'im out.'

'The pedlar used the front door. Was that not unusual?'

Again Mrs Drum had not thought of that. Again, she concluded that it was.

Lestrade thought now that he knew how the murder was accomplished. And he knew who – or at least he had a description of the man. But he needed to prove it, and to that end he took the protesting Mrs Drum along with the complaining Beddoes back to Wildboarclough Vicarage.

He was in time to see a cab leaving with Watts-Dunton and Swinburne and he thought he heard a superfluity of whip-cracking, but he couldn't be sure. The Reverend Wemyss was somewhat peeved to see the return of Mrs Drum, but Lestrade assured him it was necessary and she would not be there long.

It was nearly dark now and the housekeeper and the policeman ascended the stairs by the light of an oil-lamp, Lestrade once again insisting on overriding the Vicar's newfound aversion to naked flames. Harriet Wemyss's body had been removed to Congleton mortuary, accompanied by Swallow and one or two curious cats. Lestrade viewed the landing area where Mrs Drum had found the blazing girl. There were bad scorch marks on the carpet, through to the floorboards underneath. They formed a visible trail from a door down the corridor towards the dead girl's bedroom.

'What is that room?' asked Lestrade.

'The Chapel of Ease, sir,' replied Mrs Drum, showing signs of being overcome once again at standing on The Very Spot Where Poor Miss Harriet Died. Lestrade opened the door – a conventional middle-class lavatory, complete with blue-flowered porcelain bowl. Much to the distaste of Mrs Drum, he peered into the pan. There was a coloured film floating on the water, he noticed as he lowered his lamp towards it, and burn marks on the wooden seat.

'Has this lavatory been used since the accident?'

'Why, no, sir. Inspector Swallow told us not to touch or move anything. There is another on the other side of the house – as well as the privy in the yard.'

Lestrade was grateful that Swallow was enough of a policeman for that.

'Stand back, Mrs Drum, you are in for another shock.'

Lestrade poised himself, then flipped a lighted match into the pan. It exploded with a roar as a column of livid flame ripped upwards, illuminating the room, the landing and the terrified Mrs Drum.

Lestrade threw towels over the fire and it died, slowly, reluctantly.

'Is that the noise you heard, Mrs Drum, before the screaming started?'

Mrs Drum was standing back against the wall, visibly quivering, nodding silently the while.

'In the kitchen you would not have heard the cigarette – the furtive, clandestine cigarette that Miss Harriet was smoking – hit the water. But it wasn't water, Mrs Drum. Or at least the surface of it was not. It was petroleum spirit, instantly inflammable to a match or a lit cigarette. The poor creature must have gone up like a torch, and in her shock and agony, must have rushed headlong towards the sanctuary of her bedroom. But such was the power of the flames that she never got there. Not in this world.'

By now, the Reverend Wemyss, startled by the noise of the flames and the cry of terror from Mrs Drum, had joined the couple in the almost total darkness on the stairs.

'Come, sir,' Lestrade said to him. 'You and I must have a little talk.'

It did not unduly bother Lestrade that in telling Wemyss all he knew he was betraying an implied confidence to Miss Spink. His priorities were right, he felt sure. What was domestic tension compared with murder? The Vicar of

Wildboarclough listened with an evertightening lip to the whole sorry bizarre story. He could shed no light. He knew of no man. He assumed that Harriet's increased visits to Macclesfield were due to an increasing interest in the newly extended lending library. It had never occurred to him that his daughter had become a libertine and that she had been seduced into the ways of the devil by an anonymous 'seducteur'. He would not tell his wife – the further shock would kill her. When she had overcome her immediate need for Miss Spink, he would dispense with the woman's services – Miss Spink's that was, not his wife's. Dorothea had after all been 'in his service', so to speak, for too long. Miss Spink had not been vigilant. She had known Harriet's secret and had said nothing. It was tantamount to murder. Even Lestrade fleetingly contemplated issuing a warrant as accessory, but he guessed that the governess's conscience was sentence enough.

The night at the Vicarage was cold and gloomy. A morbid stillness lay over the whole house. At one point Lestrade fumbled with a lucifer to light a cigar, but he had to admit that the sudden flare of flame in the house of death seemed unfitting, blasphemous almost. He blew it out and huddled beneath the blankets, chewing the tobacco instead. The cold water in the morning and the iced coffee and cold ham did nothing to cheer or warm him. He ate alone. Even the maid came nowhere near him. He could not find his grief-stricken host to say his farewells. He trod finally on one of the cats and left.

Dr Marsden was in mid-surgery when Lestrade found him.

'Breathe in.' The instruction was issued to an elderly gentleman stretched out corpse-like on a bed in his consulting room.

'I can't be of much help, Inspector.' The doctor blinked at his visitor through a screen of cigar smoke. Ash dropped sporadically on to the patient's stomach, causing him to wince somewhat. 'Shock or first-degree burns or both were the cause of death. Oh, it's all right,' he coughed through the fumes, noting Lestrade's concerned glance at the patient, 'he's deaf as a post. We're quite alone.'

'I was trying to draw your attention to his colour, Doctor. I believe he may have died.'

'Good God.' Marsden brought his hand down sharply on the chest of the recumbent form. 'Breathe out, man!'

Lestrade was relieved to hear the patient gasp and cough.

'Could I ask you a delicate question, Doctor? We are, after all, men of the world. In our professions we both see humanity in all its most naked forms.' He was rather proud of that line.

'Do.' Marsden forced the old man over so that his nose buried itself in his trousers. The look on the doctor's face evinced surprise that the patient could do this.

'Where would you say the worst burns were? Where was the point of impact of the flame?'

'Bum,' snapped the doctor.

'Doctor?' said the policeman in surprise.

'No, no. I've lost my cigar.' Both men peered into the hair of the old man and their eyes met above his head. 'Ah.' Marsden recovered it from the collar of his patient's shirt.

'It was the rectum that received the full force, I'd say. The burns on the upper torso, upper limbs and head were less severe. It must have been the inflammable material of her dress that proved her undoing.'

'The rectum then,' repeated Lestrade, making for the door.

'Bum!' roared Marsden.

'Thank you, Doctor, I am aware.'

'No, no, I've lost my cigar again.'

Lestrade was sitting in his office when the letter arrived. He had his feet in a bowl of hot water and a towel over his

head. For three days he had lost all sense of taste and smell.
For three nights he had not slept. Sir Melville McNaghten
had told him to go home, but he was too busy. The
ever-solicitous Miss McNaghten had sent him hot
toddies and cordials. Lestrade responded with alternate
shivers and fevers. In his bed at night he felt himself
consumed by the flames which in seconds had engulfed
Harriet Wemyss. In the day, he felt as dead and cold as the
man in the Chine.

It was unquestionably another letter in the series, he
realised as he laid the towel aside. A click of his fingers
brought Constable Dew with the goose-grease. He
looked at the grey slime in the cup, and sent Dew away. A
mourning letter – the third such he had received. The same
untraceable postmark, the same untraceable typewriter.
The same untraceable verse.

> It almost makes me cry to tell
> What foolish Harriet befell.
> Mama and nurse went out one day
> And left her all alone at play . . .
> And see! Oh! what a dreadful thing!
> The fire has caught her apron-string;
> Her apron burns, her arms, her hair;
> She burns all over, everywhere . . .

Lestrade slammed his fist on the desk. He was being
played with. This was a game of cat and mouse and he
didn't care for it. He didn't care for it at all. Three murders
– scattered over the country. Bizarre, vicious. What were
the links? The common factors? Poetry of a sort – sent to
the Yard. Sent to him. Lestrade had come to regard
whoever was out there doing these things as a personal
enemy. This was a duel of wits and so far Lestrade had
come off second-best.

Three of Spades

'I do think Dew will do, sir,' Lestrade was saying.

'That's easy for you to say, Lestrade,' McNaghten was answering, 'but this new chap is damned clever. His references are excellent. Dew is all right, but he'll never amount to anything. No finesse. No style.'

'But Eton, sir? A copper from Eton?'

'Oh, I know it's not the usual recruiting source, but you mustn't be an inverted snob, Lestrade. He may not have had the advantages of the Blackheath crammer, but you mustn't hold that against him.'

'I'll try not to hold anything against him,' said Lestrade reaching the door.

'Bandicoot?' repeated Lestrade.

'Yes, sir.'

'You can't be serious.'

'Sir?'

Lestrade paced the floor. He looked again at the young man before him. He stood, Lestrade guessed, at six-feet-four, broad, handsome even. His suit was crisp in grey check and his bowler perched neatly in the crook of his arm. Lestrade was temporarily lost for words. 'Your name is Bandicoot?'

Bandicoot began to take just a pinch of umbrage.

'Bandicoot is a well-established name in some parts of Somerset, Inspector. I, for example, have never met a Lestrade before.'

'Well, you have now.' Lestrade's morning was not going well. Twice on his way in he had collided with the scaffolding still around New Scotland Yard which was in the final stages of being built. His tea resembled something one of the Reverend Wemyss's cats might have done. And now this – a novice constable from a public school. Lestrade sat at his desk and crossed his ankles on the polished, uncluttered top.

'How long have you been in the Force?'

'A little under one year, sir.'

Lestrade looked wide-eyed in the direction of McNaghten's glass-fronted door away down the corridor.

'Have you ever seen a body?'

'I'm not exactly a virgin, Inspector.' Bandicoot found himself smirking, a little surprised by Lestrade's question.

'A *dead* body, idiot!' Lestrade shot upright, bringing his hand down on the desk.

'No, sir.' Bandicoot's smirk vanished and his eyes faced front.

'What made you join H Division, Bandicoot?' Lestrade's tone was now patience itself. 'No, don't answer that. Why did you join the police?'

'Well, sir, it's rather silly really.'

Lestrade somehow knew it would be.

'I joined the Officer Training Corps at Eton. A few chaps ragged me into believing it was the Police Officer Training Corps. It was three years before I found out otherwise and by then I'd rather set my heart on it. In the process I became something of a crack shot, a first-rate swordsman – and my military fortifications defy belief.'

'I'm sure they do, Bandicoot, but, you see, we don't have much call for a *beau sabreur* at Scotland Yard. Tell me, I always thought gentlemen wore top hats, especially Old Etonian gentlemen.'

'Oh, we do, sir, but never before luncheon.'

Lestrade stood corrected.

'Can you make tea?' he asked.

'Er . . . I think so. You use one of those kettle things, don't you?'

Lestrade applauded with a slow, staccato handclap. 'I've always found it helps. In my outer office you will find a constable. Ask him to show you how. And then, when you've made me a cup, I'll show you what a filing cabinet looks like and we'll start some *real* policework.'

Bandicoot was about to go, when Lestrade grabbed his arm. His stare down the corridor caused the younger man to freeze as well. An ample young woman in electric blue was bustling towards them. Lestrade flattened himself against the wall, then raced for the window and the fire escape.

'Bandicoot,' he hissed as he was departing, 'convince Miss McNaghten with that Etonian charm of yours that I am away on a case for a few days, and I'll make you the most famous detective in London.'

It was the beginning of the season and London was already full of weasel-eyed Mamas and blushing daughters; gauche, flat-footed youths and lecherous old men. After the severe winter that had passed, the fashionable areas of Belgravia and Mayfair came alive again in the endless round of balls and soirées. But this season was even more colourful than the last, for a new celebrity had arrived – the ex-slave Atlanta Washington. The press reported his every move. He had been made an honorary member of White's and Crockford's, had stayed at Sandringham with the Prince and Princess of Wales and was rumoured to be having an affair with all three of the Duchess of Blessington's daughters as well as the Duchess herself. He was not without his critics, however, for there were many who shared their white American contemporaries' views that an 'uppity nigger' had no place in polite white folks' company. Washington revelled in the limelight. He wrote equally offensive replies to the offensive letters in *The Times*, and when spat upon in the street, proceeded to horsewhip the culprits in full view of lookers-on and at least four Metropolitan policemen, apparently cowed by the prospect of a wealthy, educated coon. When they at last moved in, Washington accompanied them willingly enough – in fact led the way – to Cannon Row Police Station where he was bound over to keep the peace. Three men in particular hounded him – the three men whom Lestrade was called in to see in Battersea Park on a Wednesday morning early in June. The three men had two things in common – they were all dead and they were all covered from head to foot in black paint.

Their identity did not become apparent until the paint had been removed, and long before their cold corpses had been laid out for final examination by the Scotland Yard surgeon, their families were screaming out for revenge, or if that could not be arranged, justice. McNaghten was being pressurised from above. All three men came from eminently respectable families. Every effort must be made, no stone must be left unturned, etc. etc. Lestrade had heard it all before, but he needed no exhortations. He had received no letter as yet but he didn't need to wait. This was precisely the sort of bizarre behaviour he had come to expect. It was another in the series, all right, and the body count had now reached six.

'Asphyxiation was certainly the cause of death, Lestrade,' the surgeon told him. 'These men had the pores of their skin filled with paint and it was that which killed them. Lungs alone won't do it. The skin must breathe too.'

'How long would that take?'

'Hours, days possibly. You can see the marks on their ankles and wrists where they were tied. Ghastly way to go.'

'They weren't killed in Battersea Park, then?'

'Oh, no. They were placed there, but they died somewhere else.'

Once again Lestrade had his means. He lacked any notion of those other essentials of the detective's art – opportunity and motive. He looked at the names of his victims on his desk. Their families and friends would run into hundreds. It was time to despatch constables, but constables had notoriously flat feet and lacked finesse. He could give Dew and Bandicoot the basics, but the serious questioning must once again come from him.

Bandicoot peered over Lestrade's shoulder. 'Edward Coke-Hythe!' he shouted. Lestrade hurled the contents of his tea cup over his hand, and rushed to the rest-room, screaming as decorously as he could so as not to alert the whole of Scotland Yard to his accident. Bandicoot pursued him.

'A *little* more care,' hissed Lestrade, wincing as he ran his hand under the cold tap. The water suddenly stopped with a harsh, gurgling thump.

'Damn this new plumbing,' the inspector snapped. 'Bandicoot, get me some bicarbonate of soda and hurry, man. I'm about to lose the skin off my hand.'

When the excitement was over, Lestrade placed his bandaged hand carefully on the desk. Dew brought them tea this time and Lestrade made sure Bandicoot was in front of him as he drank it. 'Why,' he began, much calmer now, 'when reading over my shoulder, did you cry out the name of one of these victims.'

'I know him, sir. Or, rather, knew him. Edward Coke-Hythe. I was his fag at Eton. Capital sort of chap. Captain of Fives – and a Double First at Cambridge.'

'Popular?'

'Oh, rather, sir. Poor old Teddy. Dear, this will be a blow to his uncle.'

'Uncle?'

'Doctor John Watson.'

'Watson? As in Watson of Baker Street?'

'Yes. Do you know him?'

'I know him. I have been an acquaintance of his associate, Sherlock Holmes, for some years.'

'Ah, the Great Detective.' Bandicoot beamed.

'If you say so,' replied Lestrade. 'What about these others? William Spender and Arthur Fitz.'

'Fitz what?' asked Bandicoot jovially.

'I'll do the jokes, Constable,' murmured Lestrade.

'No, sir. Sorry. They're not Etonians, or at least, they must have been years my senior if they were.'

Lestrade shook his head. 'They were all in their twenties, healthy, strong, young men. All right, Bandicoot. Time you won your spurs. If you knew Coke-Hythe, get round to his family – they have a town house in Portman Square. Be circumspect, but find out the deceased's movements on or about last Tuesday. Contacts, friends, enemies. It'll probably mean some shoe-leather before this case is over. Oh, and Bandicoot – ' the constable turned in the doorway – 'it's nearly luncheon. Don't forget your topper!'

Lestrade took the Underground to Baker Street Station and a brisk walk to 221B. Outside he saw a wizened old flower-seller, toothless, haggard, with iron-grey hair matted over an iron-grey face. 'Pretty posies, sir?' she squawked at him.

'Really, Mr Holmes, what would I be doing with posies?'

The flower-seller stood up to his full six feet and threw the matted hair savagely on to the pavement. 'Damn you, Lestrade, it took me nearly two hours to get that lot on.'

'Sorry, Mr Holmes. Is the good doctor in?'

'Who?'

'Watson.'

'I suppose so. Tell Mrs Hudson to put the kettle on, will you? I've sleuthed enough for one day.' He set to, sorting out his merchandise, while Lestrade went in search of his quarry. Mrs Hudson, the housekeeper, dutifully scuttled away to do her master's bidding. Watson was asleep over the newspaper in front of a roaring fire.

'Doctor Watson.' Lestrade cleared his throat. The doctor did not move. Again, 'Doctor Watson.' Louder still, 'Watson.' Then in a stage whisper, 'Your publishers are here.' Watson leapt to his feet, newspapers flying over the carpet.

'Damn you, Lestrade.' It began to sound like the refrain from a phonograph. 'That blighter Conan Doyle keeps publishing articles under my name and all you can do is make jokes at my expense. Can't the law touch him?'

'Whichever of you refers to me as "imbecile" and "ferret-faced" will discover what the law can do soon enough,' Lestrade felt it his duty to remind him. 'In the meantime I fear there is more pressing business.'

Watson replaced himself on the armchair and the papers on his lap. 'Ah, yes, my nephew. Dreadful, dreadful.'

'My condolences, of course. What do you have for me?'

'Not a great deal, Lestrade. We are not a close family. To tell you the truth, I hadn't seen Edward for some years – not since his fifteenth birthday in fact. Recently, of course, one has read various unfortunate things in the papers. This business with that black fellow, that slave johnnie. But I could have seen it coming.'

'Oh?'

'At Eton he was something of a hellion, I believe. His father threatened to cut him off, stop his allowance and so on, but incidents still occurred. There was some business with the tweenie and talk of a missing hundred pounds. I didn't pry too deeply.'

'Did your nephew have enemies, Doctor?'

'Dozens, I should think. My family have a knack of annoying people, Inspector.'

'You never spoke a truer word, Watson.' Holmes entered with armfuls of flowers, wigs, etc.

'Good God, Holmes, you look damn silly in that frock,' Watson chortled.

Mrs Hudson brought the tea. 'Here, Holmes,' Watson went on, 'you'd better be mother. Ha ha.' His laugh fell a little hollow in the face of Holmes's cheerless scowl.

'Look at this fire, Lestrade,' he said. 'Flaming June and Watson has a roaring fire.'

'I've been in India, Holmes. I feel the cold more than somewhat.'

'Who's that, Doctor?' asked Mrs Hudson, pausing at the door.

'Get out, woman!' shouted Holmes. 'To what do we owe the honour, Lestrade?'

'There's no such phrase, Holmes,' muttered Watson.

'You've clearly been in India too long, Watson,' snapped Holmes. 'You're beginning to confuse the Queen's English with pure Hindoostani.'

'Which brings me to my visit,' interrupted Lestrade, to calm the tension of the atmosphere more than anything else. 'The death of Doctor Watson's nephew, Edward Coke-Hythe.'

'Ah.' Holmes sat down, stuffing the voluminous skirts between his knees and reaching, without taking his eyes off Lestrade, for his meerschaum. 'I have a theory about that.'

Lestrade gritted his teeth. This wasn't why he had come, but Holmes had been useful in the past and for all his irritability and elitism and short temper, Lestrade had a grudging soft spot for him. Holmes lit the pipe and the flame lit his lean haunted features momentarily before they disappeared in a cloud of smoke.

'Revenge,' Holmes savoured the word. 'It's elementary, my dear Watson,' he said to the good doctor's quizzical look.

'I thought you never said that, Mr Holmes,' said Lestrade.

Holmes scowled. 'We all have our off-days, Lestrade. This black fellow – what's his name? Philadelphia?'

'Washington.'

'Bless you, Lestrade,' Watson chipped in.

'Yes. Well, Watson's nephew publicly humiliated Washington – or tried to. Washington resented it and retaliated brilliantly. He killed him and his two cronies in a perfect poetic murder. He not only turned them black – thereby forcing his deformity on them – but he killed them with blackness. His blackness.'

'Isn't that a bit obvious, Holmes?' Watson was speaking Lestrade's thoughts.

'No, no, Watson. You medical men, you're so black and white.'

'Oh, droll, Holmes, very droll,' chortled Watson.

Holmes ignored him.

'It's a double bluff, Lestrade. Precisely because it *would* be so obvious, Washington knew he would be safe. It's elementary, in fiction and life. Take my word for it, Inspector, Washington's your man.'

Lestrade looked at Watson. 'In the absence of another motive, gentlemen, I may as well start there.'

Holmes opened Watson's bag and pulled out a syringe. 'Join me, Lestrade?'

'No thanks, I don't,' the inspector answered.

Holmes disappeared into an adjoining room from which, shortly afterwards, emanated the most appalling noise of a bow on the strings of a violin.

'I'll see you out, Lestrade,' said Watson. 'Sorry I couldn't be of much help.'

'Not at all,' Lestrade said. 'Holmes has proved one thing to me.'

'What's that?'

'Atlanta Washington is an innocent man.'

'Oh, quite. He's not well, you know.'

'Washington?'

'No, Holmes. One day, that habit of his will kill him.'

'One day it will be against the law as well,' mused Lestrade as Mrs Hudson gave him his hat. 'It would be a sad thing, Doctor, if the Great Detective were to die in prison, an incurable addict.'

Lestrade reached the street. Above him a sash window flew up.

'Lestrade,' hissed a voice. Holmes peered out, violin gripped in his fist. 'I must apologise for Watson. He hasn't been well. He caught something in India. Never been the same since. You saw the symptoms. Giggling, sniping at me. He's supposed to be a professional man, for God's sake. Anyway, there it is. Sad, eh?'

'Very,' said Lestrade, tipped his hat and walked away.

He couldn't leave Coke-Hythe's family entirely to Bandicoot. Having given the young constable time to interview them, he took a cab to Portman Square, and in his most enigmatic, Scotland-Yard manner, pursued his inquiries. Bandicoot had been surprisingly thorough. No doubt the Old School Tie had helped, but Lestrade went doggedly over the same ground, priding himself on his superior reading of facial expressions, casual gestures, but at the same time feeling that the metaphorical Blackheath Crammer Tie around his neck was decidedly inferior. Yes, Ned had been something of a lad. Never in trouble, Lestrade understood. No, he didn't care for black people, but that surely was understandable. After all, his cousin Rudolph had succumbed to a native assegai during the Zulu War when Ned was at a very impressionable age. And this slave chappie was flaunting himself somewhat. But really, Ned had grown a little apart from his family of recent years. He seemed to spend most of his time in Cambridge. And so pausing only to throw together a few necessaries in a Gladstone bag,

Lestrade caught the evening train.

Most of the students had in fact gone down for the summer vac. The air was clear and cool as the inspector wandered through the town, down Silver Street and Sidney Street in his search for lodgings. He found a modest hotel near the college of his destination, Magdalene, and collapsed gratefully into bed.

He was up with the lark to hear cheery laughter in the punts below and the watery wobble of timber in rowlocks. 'Care for a dip?' a red-faced man in a boater and blazer called to him as Lestrade stuck his head out of the window in an attempt to focus.

'It's a little early for me,' he managed as cheerily as he could. As he washed and shaved, he heard the champagne corks pop and the sound of female laughter trickle over his window ledge. The town came to life with the ringing of bicycle bells and the clatter and jingle of dray horses.

Lestrade downed his hearty breakfast of bacon, eggs, toast and coffee and emerged into the morning sunlight. He felt out of place in his black serge and bowler amidst the stripes and straw and on a whim he entered Fosdick's, the University outfitters and bought himself a blazer and a pair of flannels. He resisted the spats as being a little risqué for a man of his position and was not entitled, of course, to a college badge.

The Master of Magdalene greeted him on the steps of his college. He was a vast man, with flowing dundrearies which had gone out of fashion twenty years before and a mortar board which hid, Lestrade suspected, a totally bald head. He was helpful after his fashion and between showing Lestrade the river walk, the chapel and the three Van Dykes so generously benefacted to the college, explained that he had never really known Edward Coke-Hythe or his friends and he had liked them even less. He might perhaps try the Albino Club in Jesus Lane.

'I am sorry, sir,' said the man on the door of that august institution, 'you are wearing a black tie. I cannot possibly allow entry to a man in a black tie.'

Lestrade flashed his identification. The doorman hesitated, then stepped aside. He showed Lestrade into a perfectly white interior – the walls, ceiling, even the furniture gleaming in ivory. Against the far wall was a piano, without ebony keys. One or two young men lounged about in white suits. Lestrade explained who he was and asked if any of them had known Edward Coke-Hythe. After a few in-suckings of breath, murmurings of 'Jolly bad form' and 'Chuck him out', the inspector was finally introduced to Hartington-White, the club's president, Fellow of Peterhouse and all stations west.

'Look here, Inspector, I mean arriving in a black tie is one thing, but asking personal questions about a member.'

Lestrade's mind turned for a moment on the exact meaning of the word 'member', but this was merely a club for eccentrics. He need look no further into an innocent and unconscious double-entendre, unless, of course, Hartington-White knew that Coke-Hythe's member was now lying black as the ace of spades along with the rest of him on a slab in Cannon Row Morgue.

'Edward Coke-Hythe is dead, Mr White. A police officer in the course of his inquiries is entitled to ask any questions, personal or otherwise. The fact that the deceased was a member of your club does not interest me one jot . . . Alternatively, it could be very illuminating.'

'Meaning? – and that's Hartington-White, by the way.'

Lestrade noticed the other man nodding in the direction of a few other club members.

'What is the aim of your club, Mr Hartington-White?'

'Aim? Why, recreation of course. Any member of the University is eligible.'

'And no one is black-balled?'

'That's not a term we care to use.'

'Don't you like the colour black, Mr Hartington-White?'

'I beg your pardon?'

'The decor, the black tie, even the piano keys. Isn't the purpose of this club to remove what you consider to be the black peril from white society?'

'Really, Inspector. Isn't this a little preposterous?' But Hartington-White was uneasy, his grin very fixed.

'Wasn't Edward Coke-Hythe running an errand for you? Isn't that why he was in London, in fact, since he kept his rooms in the north of town here? Wasn't he furthering the cause of white supremacy by attempting to humiliate the ex-slave Atlanta Washington?'

'That's insane, Inspector.' Hartington-White was on his feet, shouting. 'Now, I really must ask you to leave. Y . . . you do not have a white tie.'

'Neither do I have my answers,' Lestrade shouted in return. Then quieter, 'Nor blood on my conscience.'

Instinctively he heard the whirr as the billiard cue hissed through the air. He ducked and drove his shoulder into his opponent's groin. Grabbing the corner of the rug as he went down, Lestrade overturned a second attacker and kicked Hartington-White in the pit of his stomach. When he finally got up, Lestrade realised that his speed and his boot had eliminated only one permanently. The man with the billiard cue lay gripping his crotch with a distant look on his face. In front of Lestrade were four members and a footman, two of them armed with billiard cues. It had been some time since Lestrade had had to defend himself from such an attack – not since he was a sergeant at Wapping New Stairs in fact. The device he had used then, though hardly regulation police issue, was still in his pocket now. He was never without it. He deflected the sideways swipe of Hartington-White's cue, gripped the man's arm and jerked him forwards, twisting him round so that his arm locked under his jaw.

Lestrade's left hand produced the Apache dagger, a needle-sharp stiletto with brass rings that went over his knuckles. The tip of the blade rested an inch away from Hartington-White's left eardrum.

'A step closer, gentlemen, and your revered President will be bleeding all over the carpet.'

They stopped, hesitated, looked at each other.

'For God's sake, do something,' screamed the President. 'The maniac will kill me.'

'The door, gentlemen,' hissed Lestrade, tilting his adversary's head further back. 'I want it shut with you on the other side of it.'

'Do as he says.' Hartington-White's voice was strained almost to inaudibility.

One by one, they dropped their guard and backed towards the door. One by one they left the room. Hartington-White was a big man and Lestrade knew now, if he had not known before, of his somewhat murderous tendencies. He was taking no chances. He spun round and drove knee and knuckleduster simultaneously into the pit of his stomach. The Club President went down, vomiting as he did so.

Lestrade knelt to one side of him to avoid the mess and flicked his switch blade under his chin. 'Now, Mr Hartington-White, where were we? Ah, yes, you sent Coke-Hythe to London, yes?'

Hartington-White nodded, gulping for air.

'To bait Atlanta Washington?'

Another nod.

'To kill him?'

Hartington-White's head remained still. Lestrade's knife edged closer.

'If necessary,' the Club President whispered.

Lestrade put the weapon away, found his boater and looked around the littered room. Furniture lay in disarray. The member with the damaged member lay moaning in the corner. The President knelt, furious and shaking and in pain in the middle of the floor.

'Expect a visit from your local constabulary, Mr Hartington-White. The charge will be incitement to riot and attempted murder. By the time the police, the Church, the do-gooders and the press have done with you, there won't be much left of the Albino Club.' He glanced at the door. By now there would be reinforcements outside – a little army of racialists bent on preserving their anonymity behind the gleaming white walls of an eccentric gentlemen's club. Even an Apache knife wouldn't serve well against all of them.

'Don't bother to get up, I'll see myself out. 'And the inspector threw himself bodily through a plate-glass window.

When Lestrade came out of hospital three days later, events had moved apace. McNaghten was far from pleased at the ruckus at the Albino Club and one of the members had demanded a full apology. Lestrade refused and countered his principal's intervention by ordering the arrest of those present the day he had been attacked. All in all, it was unfortunate and had not got Lestrade much further. He assured McNaghten that he was on top of the case but could not promise him an imminent arrest.

There were still stitches in the inspector's face when he called in expert advice by visiting the studio at St John's Wood. Studio it may have been, but to Lestrade it resembled a palace, vast and sprawling, each room hung with paintings, expensive tapestries and filled with lavish furniture. As luck would have it, Lestrade arrived in time to feel very out of place at a garden party in the grounds. A shifty-looking, rather neurotic man with furtive eyes and thinning hair pinched his sherry. Lestrade recognised him as Mr Burne-Jones, the Pre-Raphaelite. He and the name were all Lestrade remembered from a crash course in modern art five years ago when he was involved in the

Frederick Leighton Fake Swindle. His quarry that day in St John's Wood he had never heard of, but a footman pointed him out.

'Mr Adma-Talema?' said the inspector.

The host of the party turned to the inquirer. He adjusted his pince-nez and responded, 'Something like that. No, don't tell me. You are a reporter from the *Daily Graphic*, an art critic and your last piece so provoked an artist that he smashed a canvas over your head?'

'Something like that,' replied Lestrade. 'Actually I am from Scotland Yard.'

'Really?' said Alma-Tadema 'I have never met a real detective before. Apart from . . . oh, but he doesn't count.'

'May we talk in private, sir?'

The artist took leave of the admiring circle around him, took two drinks from a passing tray and thrust one at Lestrade. They walked through a cloud of white peacocks on to a broad terrace and into the vast sunlit studio itself. An enormous canvas rested on three easels in the centre of the room. Partially draped, it was an ancient scene, classical and grand.

'Do you like it?' The artist asked, and grinned.

'Indeed,' said Lestrade, hoping he would not be lured into a conversation on the merits of gouache or the traps of chiaroscuro.

'So do I.' Alma-Tadema replenished his own and Lestrade's glasses with the finest claret cup Lestrade had ever tasted. 'Tell me something, I thought you police-chappies never drank on duty.'

'Most of us don't, sir. But if I may say so, most of us don't get offered claret of this vintage.'

'My dear . . . er . . . Inspector, is it? Not only have you a discerning eye for art, but you are also a connoisseur of the vine. A lucky day for me indeed.'

'I hope so, sir.' Lestrade produced a tin from his pocket. 'Be so good as to have a look at the contents of this.'

Alma-Tadema opened, sniffed, peered closely through the pince-nez, placed an exquisitely manicured finger in and licked it. 'Enamel,' he said. 'Black enamel. Aspinall's probably.'

'Is enamel paint unusual, Mr Ala-Tameda?'

'Indeed it is. It's not readily available yet and of course quite unsuitable for canvas. But the French are using it a lot on their blasted bits and pieces.'

'Don't you like the New Art, Mr Mala-Teda?'

'Oh, in its way, it's all right, but you can't build an Underground station that looks like a peacock. There isn't enough of the classical in art nowadays. Not like the Romans,' he said, waving in the direction of his canvas. 'You know where you are with Romans.'

'You said Aspinall's enamel?'

'Yes, that is the firm that produces it.' Alma-Tadema buried himself in a bureau. 'It's deuced expensive; even I only have . . .' He stopped. Lestrade crossed the room to him.

'Something the matter, sir?'

'They've gone. Six pots of Aspinall's black enamel. Gone.'

'When did you last see your enamel?'

Alma-Tadema chewed his thumb. 'Well, let's see, it must have been – Tuesday last, or Monday.'

'It may be crucial, sir.'

'Yes, yes of course, Inspector. Monday, week before last. I'm certain it was Monday because I had one of my sitters cancel at short notice. I was not too displeased. I hate painting portraits. Give me Romans every time.'

There was a pause.

'Inspector, may I ask why you came to me with this paint?'

'My chief recommended you, sir, as a prominent man in paint-consistency.'

The artist laughed. 'Well, I'm flattered. But what is

this in connection with?'

'You don't read the newspapers, Mr Alma-Mater?'

'Only the art reviews, I'm afraid. Shockingly narrow of me, isn't it?'

'Had you read the headlines, sir, over the past ten days, you would know that three young men were found dead in Battersea Park. Each one had been painted black from head to foot. It was that very act of painting which killed them.'

'Good God!' Alma-Tadema sat down with astonishment. 'But that's incredible.'

'What is more incredible, sir, is that the paint seems to have come from your studio.'

Realisation began to dawn on the artist.

'I see,' he said, the smile leaving his face for the first time that day. 'So you came to me for expert technical advice and I end up as a suspect.'

'Not such a lucky day for you after all, then, Mr Alda-Tamer?'

'Indeed, no,' replied the artist.

'Who has access to this studio?'

'Oh, almost anyone. It's locked at night, of course and only the butler and I have keys, but during the day it's always open. Unless I have a finished canvas. The place is always full of people. You saw for yourself. It's open house. My hospitality is renowned, I blush to admit.'

Lestrade walked to the glass doors. 'I am sure you have no plans to leave Town, sir, but please contact the Yard if you do.'

'Yes, of course, Inspector. I am only too anxious to clear this matter up.'

'May I suggest you take better precautions, sir? This little piece, now – ' indicating the Roman canvas 'what might that be worth?'

'I have been offered eight thousand for that one.'

It was Lestrade's turn to be astonished. It was more money than he would make in a lifetime, if he continued straight.

'Pounds?'

Alma-Tadema guffawed heartily. 'Don't be unrealistic, Inspector . . . guineas.'

The family of Spender had aristocratic connections, but they themselves lived in a tawdry house in a tawdry suburb in Notting Hill. They were more anxious for blood than the Coke-Hythes had been and infinitely less polite. With his customary ease, Lestrade was able to defend himself and the Yard against the oft-heard cry from the deceased's grandfather in the corner: 'What are you fellows doing about it?' A combination of wheedling and bluff on Lestrade's part provided all he was ever likely to know about the late William Alphonse Spender. He was twenty-four, single, without a post ('job' was far too common a word for the Spenders), and kept unfortunate company. No one in the family seemed really upset to see him go; no one in the family seemed very surprised that he had met so 'sticky' an end. If only they hadn't sent him to Harrow in the first place, this would never have happened. Still, it was probably for the best. No, William had no real aversion to blacks, it was just that he enjoyed tormenting people. Coke-Hythe was obviously the instigator of the recent notoriety. But it was such a minor incident. Only the radical press would be so common as to blow it up out of all proportion. Enemies? Well, even the family conceded that William was an unlovely lad, but they could think of no one, no real individual, who stood out. Except of course for that ghastly black person. He had a motive. Why hadn't he been arrested?

Arthur Fitz had no immediate family. His parents had died in an avalanche some years before while visiting Switzerland and the boy had been bounced around various distant aunts who ended up cursing themselves for not being distant enough. It was this very distance which gave them an air of guilt. They had failed the boy. The least they could do now was to ensure that his murderer was brought to book. But Arthur spent most of his time in clubland, in disreputable company and his various aunts suspected that he was very horribly in debt.

Clubland proved chilly and unhelpful. Lestrade tackled some – Arts, Army and Navy, Crockford's. Bandicoot tackled others – White's, Boodle's, Naval and Military. Dew held the horses. Their collective inquiries yielded almost nothing. A lot of shoe-leather worn, a lot of frosty silence, a lot of angry letters about police intrusion to McNaghten and the Commissioner. Lestrade's reputation began to sink in the mire of accusation and inefficiency. It was turning, slowly but surely, into a nightmare.

Lestrade was shown into the expensive suite of rooms occupied for the past four months by Atlanta Washington, the ex-slave. The inspector had not really known what to expect. Before him stood a handsome, dapper man about his own age, immaculately groomed with a rose in his button-hole. On each arm he wore an incredibly beautiful white girl, one of whom Lestrade thought he recognised as a former courtesan belonging to Lord Panmure.

'You sure took your time.' The Negro grinned, displaying a row of pearly white teeth. 'Honies, run along now, Atlanta wants to talk to de man.' He swung his body across the floor, as though to an imaginary tune, shooing the protesting girls out of the door in a flurry of feathers and furs.

'Well, now, Inspector honey, to what do I owe de pleasure?'

'I am pursuing a murder inquiry.'

'Right on. Why don't you siddown dere an' I'll have

some mint julep sent right up, y'hear.'

Lestrade sat.

'I hope you won't take long. I's expectin' ma hominey grits in a liddle while an' I sure hates tuh be kept waitin'.'

'Atlanta Washington,' Lestrade stood up again, 'I arrest you in the name of the law. You are not obliged to say anything, but anything you do say will be taken down . . .'

'Now, hold it, man,' the Negro interrupted. He looked squarely at Lestrade for a moment. 'Aw, shit.' He pulled off his elaborate thick, curly hair to reveal a much less impressive balding pate underneath. Next, he unhooked his immaculate false teeth to reveal a few scattered brownish ones beneath.

'All right, Mr Lestrade, the show's over.' Even the phoney plantation accent had gone. 'What am I charged with?'

Lestrade sat down, triumphant. 'You're not,' he said. 'But I had to get through that barrier somehow.'

Washington grinned. 'You're smart and no mistake.'

'Why do you do it?' asked Lestrade.

'What – the lingo? The teeth? The rug?'

Lestrade nodded.

'It's a long story, Inspector.'

'Take your time, sir.'

'My father was Booker T. Washington, a slave. Maybe you read his book, *Up from Slavery*?'

Lestrade had not.

'Well, I was born a slave, like he was. Momma used to wash the Massa's clothes on the plantation – Georgia. Poppa was what they call in the States an "uppity nigger", but like all Negroes, he knew how to hide it. The lingo I was just using – and not fooling you with – is plantation jive. You see, the way to stay out of trouble and to stay alive is to act dumb, to play Sambo. Jig around a lot, roll your eyes and talk' – and he broke into it again – 'like de whities expec' a Sambo tuh talk. That way' – lapsing back – 'you don't get noticed. When the Lincoln soldiers came in '65 we were all told we were free. I was lucky. I went North with Poppa and learnt what freedom really meant. It meant the brothers living like pigs in Harlem while the white folks get the jobs and the handouts. You know how many black police there are in the great United States? How many black doctors, lawyers, judges, teachers? None, Inspector, none. Even the nigger minstrels on the stage are whities blacked up with burnt cork. That's the freedom Lincoln gave us. And they killed him for it. So I decided to hit back. Poppa wrote his book and got famous – and rich. So I became a celebrity – an educated nigger. Popular? No, I'm not. Whities hate me 'cos I'm black. But they're fascinated, too. They can't keep away because they're afraid of me. They're afraid that one day all my kind are going to be smart and sassie, and it scares the shit out of them. So, it's all a front, Inspector. The hair, the pearly teeth, the jive, it's what people expect. And who am I to let them down?' A pause: 'Tell me, do you think my secret is safe with you?'

'Did you kill those men?'

'Hell, no. I may be a coon, Inspector. I may be an ornery bastard. But I've never killed a man and I couldn't start now. Yes, I horse-whipped a couple a couple of weeks ago when the insults and the spittle came on a little too strong. But that's it, that's as far as it goes.'

'Do you know the studio of Lawrence Alma-Tadema?' Lestrade surprised himself in getting it right.

'If he's the photographer fella in Piccadilly, yeah.'

'What can you tell me about Aspinall's enamel?'

Washington looked blank. 'Nothing.'

Lestrade got up. He was impressed by the man's sincerity.

'Mr Washington, when are you leaving the country?'

The ex-slave put back his teeth and refitted his wig.

'Why, any day now, suh, fo' sure.'

Lestrade nodded his approval of that.

'What's gettin' you, man? Jus' 'cos some Massas in de cole, cole groun'.'

'I am wondering,' said Lestrade, 'how many more there are going to be.'

This time, the by now inevitable letter was a long time coming. Lestrade mechanically traced, as far as he was able, the last day in the lives of the three dead men. They knew a lot of people, were usually, though not always, in the public gaze and the contacts all drew blanks. The common factors in their lives, their tenuous friendship based on a love of limelight and of devilry, produced nothing that was concrete. No leads, no suspects. But, then, the letter came.

> As he had often done before
> The Woolly-headed black-a-moor
> One nice fine summer's day went out
> To see the shops and walk about.
> Then Edward, little noisy wag,
> Ran out and laugh'd and wav'd his flag;
> And William came with jacket trim
> And brought his wooden hoop with him;
> And Arthur, too, snatch'd up his toys
> And join'd the other naughty boys;
> So one and all set up a roar
> And laughed and hooted more and more
> And kept on singing – only think –
> 'Oh, Blacky, you're as black as ink.'
> He seizes Arthur, seizes Ned,
> Takes William by his little head;
> And they may scream and kick and call
> Into the ink he dips them all;
> Into the inkstand, one, two, three,
> Till they are black as black can be.
> They have been made as black as crows,

> *Quite black all over, eyes and nose,*
> *And legs, and arms, and heads and toes,*
> *And trousers, pinafores and toys –*
> *The silly little inky boys!*
> *Because they set up such a roar*
> *And teased the harmless black-a-moor.*

A longer verse than usual, mused Lestrade, and more of a story perhaps. No extra clues in letter-head or paper type or print, but there was something else – a signature.

'What do you know about Agrippa?' he threw at Bandicoot, who had just come in with an armful of written statements.

'Which one?'

'All of them,' answered the inspector, annoyed to find that his lieutenant seemed to have such knowledge at his fingertips.

'Well, there was Marcus Vipsanius Agrippa, the Roman General. If my Classics serve me correctly, he commanded Octavian's fleet at the Battle of Actium in 31 BC.'

'Did he like Negroes?'

Bandicoot thought hard. 'I think you must be confusing him with Scipio Africanus, sir. He was one.'

'Who are the other Agrippas?'

'Herods I and II – as in the New Testament. Puppet Kings of Judaea allowed to rule in name only by Roman order.'

Lestrade rubbed his eyes and lolled back in his chair. He was getting nowhere.

'Why do you ask, sir?'

Lestrade looked at him. No harm, he thought, in showing the letter to Bandicoot. Perhaps his literate brain, naïve and fumbling policeman though he was, might shed some light on the poetry.

'Oh, *that* Agrippa!' Bandicoot chuckled.

Lestrade sat bolt upright. 'What do you mean, "*that*

Agrippa"?'

'Well, I didn't realise it was a joke, Inspector.'

'It's no joke, Bandicoot, I can assure you. Are you telling me you know this poem?'

'Yes, of course. Don't you?'

Lestrade looked like a man whose prayers had been answered. 'Dew!' he roared, 'fetch us a pot of tea. And toast. Bandicoot, have a cigar. You've earned that at least. We could be here for some time.'

'It comes from a series of, well, I suppose you'd call them cautionary tales for children, sir. As a boy Nanny was always reading them to me. I grew up with them. I thought everybody did.'

'We didn't all have your advantages, Bandicoot.' Lestrade felt himself sounding more like Mr Keir Hardie every time he opened his mouth.

'It's called *Struwwelpeter*, written by a doctor-chappie to amuse his little patients, I believe.'

'Strew what?' asked Lestrade.

'*Struwwelpeter*. I suppose . . . er . . . German wasn't really my strong point, but I seem to remember it was written as *Shock-headed Peter* in the English version.'

Lestrade's jaw dropped. 'The man in the Chine,' he murmured.

'Sir?'

Lestrade unlocked the confidential file in his bureau drawer. He threw the letters down on the table. 'I have received one of these after each murder. Do they all come from *Shock-headed Peter*?'

Bandicoot perused them. After a while – 'Yes, *Shock-headed Peter* all right, but they seem shorter. Bits must have been omitted.'

'Examples?'

'Oh, Inspector, I haven't read these for years, but, look, in this first one for example, the last line or so has gone. You've got –

> *And the sloven, I declare,*
> *Never once has combed his hair;*

'Then it goes something like this –

> *Anything to me is sweeter*
> *Than to see Shock-headed Peter.'*

Lestrade remembered the awful spectacle of the corpse in the Chine and wholeheartedly agreed with that sentiment.

'Anything else?'

Bandicoot thought again. He was getting into his stride now.

'Yes, this second one refers to a verse called "Cruel Frederick". He whips a Mary, sister, nurse, whatever she is and of course he doesn't actually die in the poem. I assume all these letters refer to murders.'

'Correct – to date six of them.'

'Well, I can see the picture now – the dog Tray ends up sitting at a table with a napkin on, eating Frederick's pies and puddings.'

Lestrade wandered around the room, swigging from the inelegant cup.

'With the Harriet story,' Bandicoot went on, 'I seem to remember great play about the girl's pet cats and nothing being left in her pile of ashes but her scarlet shoes. Presumably the murderer couldn't arrange it quite as neatly as that – to fit the rhymes exactly.'

'Well, he hasn't done a bad job so far. The Wemyss family were crawling with cats.'

'This last one is called "The story of the Inky Boys" – black-baiting. Agrippa is some sort of magician who champions the coons' cause and dips the baiters in a huge pot of ink.'

'Or Aspinall's black enamel,' chimed in Lestrade.

'It isn't clear from the poem whether they die or not of course. But the picture with it, I believe, indicates that they don't.'

Lestrade stopped pacing. He put his cup down and lowered himself on to his elbows on the desk next to Bandicoot.

'How many more cautionary tales are there?' he asked.

'Lord, I don't know, sir. A few. I don't know.'

Lestrade snapped into action, 'All right, Bandicoot, get to a booksellers, to the British Museum, wherever you have to, but get a copy of that book. It's a perfect text for the murders so far. Our friend isn't likely to deviate now. That's why he didn't include the lines about *Shock-headed Peter* after his first murder. It would have tipped me off too early. Chances are he doesn't think we've got him yet, but we have. I'm giving this to McNaghten, it might take the pressure off us all . . . Oh, and Bandicoot, before you go.'

'Sir?'

'Well done. We'll make a policeman of you yet.'

While Lestrade was briefing McNaghten about the advances he had made, making as little as possible of Bandicoot's role in it all and while Bandicoot himself was hunting purposefully through the Westminster book-shops, Albert Mauleverer lay dead in the well below Guy's Cliffe. A labourer found the body by chance and alerted the Warwickshire police. They had no clues, no evidence, no motive and no suspect. And it was only by chance some days later that Lestrade happened to see a tiny piece in the *Police Gazette*. 'Body found in well. Gunshot wounds.' By now he had the book in his possession, *Struwwelpeter by Dr Heinrich Hoffmann, Pretty Stories and Funny Pictures*, published 1845. Immediately he recognised the hallmarks of the 'Story of the Man that went out Shooting'. He read it again as he sped north on the morning train. In the poem, a hare did it. Having stolen the Man's spectacles and gun, while he is asleep, the hare shoots him when he has fallen into a well. Once again, the result in the poem is not murder, and there was various nonsense about the Man's wife drinking coffee nearby and the hare's child being splashed by it. But Lestrade knew only too well by now that none of this was nonsense. Some maniac was grimly acting out these cautionary tales, as meticulously as possible. But who? And why? There were just not enough answers. One thing and one thing only could be formulated about the murderer – he was damnably clever – and another thing – he was still, despite Lestrade's possession of the book, one step ahead.

Lestrade booked in first at the Clarendon Hotel at the top of the Parade. He had walked from the station, but felt the time well spent in that he had the opportunity to study the spa town of Leamington for the first time. Very like Cheltenham, he thought to himself, but when you've seen one spa, presumably you've seen them all. The wide streets, the leafy avenues, the opulent extravagance of shop fronts and offices, all bore testimony to the wealth and stability of the middle classes of the provinces. Lestrade was glad to change into his lightweight suit and he fancied the sun was strong enough for his Cambridge boater, a little battered around the brim though it was.

At the police station however, they were less than helpful. A portly sergeant eyed Lestrade from head to toe before offering him the use of a station cab. Lestrade took a constable with him and they drove to the morgue. This corpse was less bizarre than the last few, but no less grisly. The right side of the head was that of a man of middle age, greying hair and heavy features. The left side of the head was not there at all – merely a mass of dark congealed blood with pieces of whitish bone visible. Lestrade had seen such wounds before, but unfortunately, the young constable had not and he gracefully

floated to the floor as the attendant lifted the blanket.
Lestrade went on checking the body and asking the
attendant mechanical questions, while the constable was
carried out, his helmet resting on his chest.

'Three days ago, you say?'

'Yes, sir. He were brought in 'ere dead as mutton. I
cleaned him up a bit but apart from that 'e 'aven't been
touched, 'ere are his glasses.'

The attendant held up a shattered pair of spectacles.
Lestrade noted the green Norfolk jacket, the crumpled
bloodstained deerstalker and then he examined the
shotgun. Standard twelve-bore, handsome piece. One
barrel discharged.

'Is this the gun that killed him?'

'I don't know.' The attendant shrugged. 'That's your
job.'

Impervious to Lestrade's scowl, he shuffled off,
blowing hard on a pipe of vicious tobacco, his head
wreathed in smoke. Lestrade looked at the wound again;
point blank range, both barrels he'd say. He went out
into the sunshine and found the pale constable leaning on
the station cab. He attempted to stand to attention at the
inspector's approach.

'All right, lad. Cigar?'

The constable declined with a pathetic faraway look on
his face. Lestrade lit up, savouring the moment.

'Who found the body?'

The constable rummaged in his pockets for his
notebook.

'Half a dozen eggs, two . . . Oh, sorry sir. The wife's
shopping.'

Lestrade paused in mid-puff. 'Wife? How old are you,
Constable?'

'I shall be twenty in the autumn, sir.'

Lestrade began to feel his age. It was the beginning of
the end, of course, when policemen began to look
younger than you did.

'Joseph Glover, sir. A labourer from Bubbenhall.'

'Where?'

'Bubbenhall, sir. It's a village' – the constable rummaged again and produced a map, which he laboriously unfolded on the rump of the horse – '. . . five miles from here.'

'Near Guy's Cliffe?'

'Oh no, sir.' The constable's concentration followed his finger again over the map. 'Eight miles from there, sir.'

Lestrade thought aloud. 'Now, what was a labourer doing eight miles from his village? What time of day was the body found?'

The constable referred to his notebook, 'Approximately half past seven in the evening, sir. Saturday, July the twenty-fourth.'

'This Glover – anything known? Try it without the notebook, Constable,' as the young man's head bent to the book again.

'Well, sir,' the mental effort was obviously crippling the constable, 'ploughing champion for the county three years running. One of the best hedgers I've seen. And he seems to eat a lot of other people's pheasants.'

'Right, Constable. That doesn't exactly constitute "form", but never mind. Give me the reins. I'm getting out of practice. And you keep your wits about you; I want to get home by tomorrow.'

They found Joseph Glover lashed to a ploughing team, two massive Clydesdales, huge and gentle, plodding through the furrows. Behind their tossing heads and the dust flying as they walked, could be seen a pair of gaitered legs and the odd flash of a switch.

'Ay up, Jewel, ay up, Dinkie.'

Lestrade crossed the furrows, the constable scrambling behind him.

'Joseph Glover?'

The little man growled under his breath and pulled the

horses up short. He unhooked the reins from his neck.

'Who wants to know?' The truculent little labourer came up to Lestrade's tie-knot.

'Inspector Lestrade, Scotland Yard.'

'Scotland? You're a bit far from home.'

Lestrade bent over so that their noses were touching. 'Obstructing the police can get you five years, Glover. What would happen to your horses then?'

Glover flung himself back against the huge, glossy flank of one of them.

'Don't worry, Dinkie, I won't let him take you.'

'I'm from Scotland Yard, Glover, not the knacker's yard.'

Another gem wasted. Only one of the Clydesdales snorted in appreciation.

Glover hitched himself to the team again and switched them into action. 'I gotta get on,' he growled. 'Ploughin' contest next week at the Abbey.'

Lestrade looked to the constable for explanation.

'It's nearly harvest, sir. You don't plough at harvest time. You plough in the Spring.'

'Is he . . . er . . . all right?' Lestrade mouthed the words silently, nodding sideways at Glover, who chewed his grass with still more determination and annoyance, staring fixedly ahead.

'Oh, yes, sir.' The constable giggled. 'Each summer there's an agricultural fair at Stoneleigh Abbey, Lord Leigh's estate. It was his land the body was found on.'

'Why were you at Guy's Cliffe on Saturday last?' Lestrade asked Glover.

'Sparking.'

Lestrade turned to the constable for translation.

'Courting, sir.'

'What was the young lady's name?'

'Now look . . .' Glover broke off as he caught the look in Lestrade's eyes.

'Do you know what a treadmill is, Glover? Do you

know what it feels like treading down on those rungs, fifteen minutes on, two minutes off, six hours a day?'

'Louisa Ellcock. Works for the folks in the big house at Guy's Cliffe.'

'The Mauleverers, sir.'

'Tell me,' said Lestrade.

'I was on me way to visit Louise. Promised we are. Well, I cuts across the fields from Old Milverton Church and there he was. I seen his gun first, sort of gleaming in the evening sun.'

'Never mind the poetry, go on.'

'I went over and saw him. Stuffed down the well 'e were. Dead.'

'Did you hear any shots?'

'On and off. But I'd walked near ten miles, there was lots of sportsmen about that weekend.'

'Did you see anyone about? Acting suspiciously?'

'That's a bloody daft question' – and then, softening the tone – 'beggin' your pardon, of course. But I had me mind on other things. I was 'oping to do some suspicious actin' meself in a minute. Know what I mean?' The jab from the elbow and the wry grin fell a little sourly on Lestrade. He wanted evidence, not rural erotica.

'This Louisa Ellcock. Where can we find her?'

'Now then, I don't want 'er bothered. Not in 'er condition.'

Lestrade stopped walking and raised a disapproving eyebrow.

'Chances are, Glover, that when your "suspicious actions" and 'er interesting condition produce something, the little bastard will have a dad rotting inside.' He dug Glover in the ribs with his elbow: 'Know what I mean?'

Guy's Cliffe House was tall and oddly foreboding. It was set back from the water, swirling and spraying over the weir. In the strong afternoon sun Lestrade and the

constable crossed the rickety wooden bridge. Their
occasional bursts of conversation were drowned by the
noise of the rushing water and the rank, stagnant smell
near the mill. The inspector inspected the well. If there
had been blood, it had been washed off by rain or water
from the well. The area around it was hopelessly
trampled with countless footprints – Mauleverer's,
Glover's, a dozen or so policemen's, newspapermen's
and doubtless sightseers'. And somewhere, Lestrade
pondered, somewhere in the Warwickshire dust, the
footprints of the murderer. Lestrade's murderer. Lestrade's man.

Louise Ellcock was of little help. She was terrified that
Lestrade would tell Mrs Mauleverer of her 'secret'.
Lestrade told her her secret was safe with him, that he had
other fish to fry. She showed him gratefully into the
drawing room. Mrs Mauleverer joined the officers of the
law there.

'Inspector Lestrade, ma'am, of Scotland Yard. This is
Constable . . . er . . .'

The constable consulted his notebook.

'Prothero, ma'am.'

'Of the Warwickshire Constabulary,' Lestrade com-
pleted the sentence for him.

Mrs Mauleverer urged them to be seated.

'A distressing time, ma'am,' commented Lestrade.

'We can dispense with the solemn looks, Inspector
Lestrade. I am naturally distressed at the sudden and
ghastly death of a fellow human being. But the fact that
that human being happened to be my husband is purely
coincidental. Sherry?'

Lestrade glanced at Prothero. 'You needn't take this
down, Constable. Wait with the horses.' The constable
left.

'Mrs Mauleverer.'

'Inspector.' Mrs Mauleverer swept to her feet and
poured some pale sherry for Lestrade. 'You must think

me very unfeeling.'

'Not at all, ma'am. You have had a very trying time. May I ask you a few questions?'

'I cannot tell you more than I have told the local police, Inspector.'

'I have not yet consulted the local police, ma'am. The young constable is merely my guide around the neighbourhood.'

'You don't know Warwickshire then, Inspector?'

'No, ma'am.' Lestrade followed his hostess with his eyes. She walked away from him across the room. The sunlight fell on the dark green and gold of her velvet gown. It caught the lustrous black curls too, falling, no, cascading was the romantic word, over one shoulder. Mrs Mauleverer was a very beautiful woman, fine-boned, with dark, smouldering eyes that flashed in the pale, melancholy face.

'My husband and I were married for three years, Inspector. He was twenty years my senior and had spent most of his life in Africa. He was an engineer of sorts. I first met him in London five years ago. He was suave, debonair, travelled. I had just been presented at Court and Mama was anxious for me to make the perfect match. I was a fool, Inspector. I didn't have the courage to call a halt, to say no, this is not what I want. Women are slaves still. I felt it was my duty and I accepted when he proposed. It had not been easy for Mama. Papa had died some years before, and at least Albert offered us financial security. Oh dear, this all sounds so mercenary.'

'Not at all, ma'am.'

'It didn't last.' Mrs Mauleverer began to pace the room, wringing her hands. Occasionally her dark eyes fell on Lestrade and hurriedly looked away. 'Albert was attentive for a month, perhaps two and then he began spending more and more time away. Shooting weekends, card parties, always without me. Oh, I busied myself in the area. The poor are always with us,

Inspector. I helped with charities and joined committees. I redecorated this house, this cheerless mausoleum Albert brought me to. It didn't help. It didn't fill the place of a husband.'

Lestrade sensed her sadness in the very shadows of the room.

'You were no doubt surprised, Inspector, when I did not appear to weep for my husband. You are no doubt surprised that I am not in mourning. But, you see, my husband died three years ago. I barely recognised the man they found in the well.'

There was a profound stillness between them. Lestrade mentally shook himself. He was thirty-eight years old, had been twenty years in the Force, fifteen of those with Scotland Yard. He'd known dozens, scores, possibly hundreds of bereft widows, yet none had affected him like this one. There was an honesty and a dignity about this woman that strangely touched him. In the silence his hard-bitten heart went out to her.

'The day of the murder.' He cleared his throat and blustered on. 'Tell me about that.'

'It was a day like any other.' A pause, 'No, not quite like any other.' She began again, 'It was the day someone murdered my husband. Tell me, Inspector. Is it wrong for me to want revenge – even revenge for the death of a man I did not love?'

'I am not a judge and jury, ma'am.'

'But you could be an executioner?'

'If I had to kill a man in the course of my duty, ma'am. On occasions we are issued with firearms.'

'I rose at half past eight. My husband had already gone out for the day. He had taken luncheon, in a knapsack, and his gun. He had apparently told Louisa, my maid, that he would not return before nightfall. I suppose it crossed my mind briefly that he had gone to Coventry to see . . . well, another woman. In the morning I busied myself with my correspondence. I heard distant shooting; it may have been Albert . . .' Mrs Mauleverer suddenly started: 'It may have been the shot that killed him. God. The well is only a few hundred yards away, Inspector, though we cannot see it from the house. In the afternoon I drove with Louisa into Leamington. I called at Warwick first and had tea with the Countess. It would have been about nine o'clock when the police called with the news. There had been an accident. Albert was dead.'

'You identified the body?'

'Yes, at Leamington that night.'

Their eyes met in the evening sunshine. The look spoke of all the emptiness in the heart of Mrs Mauleverer. And perhaps too in the heart of Inspector Lestrade.

'I can't tell you any more,' she said. 'My husband was a hard man, remote, silent. I have thought of who would wish him dead. I can think of no one who cared enough to pull the trigger. Isn't that a tragic thought?'

Lestrade rose and put the empty glass on the table.

'Thank you, ma'am. It cannot have been easy. I will take my leave of you.'

'My name is Constance, Inspector. It has not been easy. But you have been kind.'

'If I should need to contact you again . . .'

'I had planned to spend a while with my mother in Camberwell after the funeral.'

'If you would be so kind as to inform Scotland Yard of your London address . . .'

'Of course.'

'And Mrs Mauleverer . . . Constance . . . if I can one day be of help to you . . .' Lestrade took Mrs Mauleverer's hand and kissed it. She smiled.

As he crossed to the station cab and motioned to Prothero to move the horse on, the lines from *Struwwelpeter* came again into his mind –

> *The poor man's wife was drinking up*
> *Her coffee in her coffee-cup;*

The gun shot cup and saucer through;
'Oh dear!' she cried, 'what shall I do?'

'Watch what you're doing with those infernal pins.'

Lestrade entered the trophy room of Stoneleigh Abbey to the sight of Lord Leigh being fitted for a new uniform. He stood with left arm raised while a pair of tailors buzzed around him, putting the finishing touches to his tunic.

'This busby is ridiculous!' he roared. 'It's too tight and too high. If I break into a canter it'll fall off. Who the hell are you?'

'Inspector Lestrade, My Lord. Scotland Yard.'

'Oh.' Lord Leigh recovered quickly. 'Hamburger and Rogers, military tailors. Presumably you know who I am.'

'May I speak to you in private, sir?'

'Oh very well. Gentlemen, call again in a week – and make sure this tunic sits better, will you? I shall be a laughing stock at the Review.'

The tailors dismantled the elaborate silver and blue uniform until His Lordship stood in his scarlet combinations. Lestrade thought how uncomfortable they must be in this hot weather.

'What is it, Lestrade?' A valet appeared from nowhere and helped His Lordship into a silk smoking jacket. 'I am a busy man.'

'Quite so, My Lord. A body was found on your property at Guy's Cliffe on Saturday last. Can you help me?'

'No.'

'Let me put it another way. I have come a long way at the taxpayers' expense to find out who killed a man. And perhaps to prevent that person from killing again.'

'Hmmm.' Lord Leigh poured himself a huge brandy. He did not offer one to Lestrade. 'I knew Mauleverer, of course. Even offered him a commission in the Yeomanry once. He couldn't have had a troop, of course. I mean he was an outsider. But a Lieutenancy. I could have got him that. Anyway,' Leigh swung onto a wooden frame on which a saddle rested, 'he refused. I never cared for him after that.'

'Did you kill him?'

Leigh sat bolt upright in the saddle. 'Damn you, Lestrade. I shall talk to your superiors. Anyway, if I had killed him, I should have used a sabre.' Leigh made a dramatic flourish with his right arm and returned gratefully to his brandy. 'I didn't dislike him enough to keep him off my land. The truth is he was a damned good shot – and a sportsman.' Leigh suddenly changed his tack. 'Anyway, what are you fellows doing about it? A murder takes place on a chap's land and you have the nerve to come round here accusing me. If this is the best old Jack Lamp can do . . .'

'Jack Lamp, My Lord?'

'County's Chief Constable. Blue Lamp they call him.'

'Original,' grunted Lestrade. 'No, My Lord, Chief Constable Lamp did not call me in. I have reason to believe that the murder of Albert Mauleverer is one of a series. It's not him, it's not your land. It's not even Warwickshire. It's just that it fits a pattern. That's all.'

'Do you Yard-wallahs always talk in riddles?'

'Forget it, My Lord. You saw nothing suspicious yourself?'

Leigh shook his head.

'And none of your people – servants or tenants – reported anything to you?'

'Not a thing. Look, Lestrade, I don't want to sound callous. Can I make a suggestion?'

Lestrade was grateful for the meagrest of straws.

'Mauleverer's wife. They didn't get on, you know. Common knowledge. I think she did it.'

Lestrade felt himself going white. Constance Mauleverer had flashed into his mind throughout a restless night.

He could not forget the pale, haunted face. For a moment he thought of forcing the brandy, glass and all, down Leigh's throat. Then perhaps a quick backward flip over his saddle and frame. In the end he settled for a professional opinion.

'A shotgun is not, in my experience, a woman's weapon, My Lord. Poison, yes; dagger, perhaps; pocket pistol, at a pinch. But shotgun, never. I'll see myself out.'

Lestrade stopped momentarily on his way to the door, which was miraculously opened by the vanishing valet. Leigh was prancing across the floor, posturing with a drawn sword.

'Mark my words, Lestrade, cherchez la femme.'

Lestrade hated the quarterly inspectors' meeting on the third floor. True, the new buildings had a polish and grandeur that Whitehall Place had lacked, but it was still the same in-fighting, the endless bitching about whose Division had managed the most arrests and endless exhortations from the Commissioner and McNaghten about greater care, more vigilance, good hard police procedure, with less money to do it with.

The first point on the agenda that dreary, drizzly August day was police pay.

'A strike?' McNaghten was gradually turning crimson from his cravat upwards.

'That's what they say,' Athelney Jones sat back in the leather armchair. Lestrade looked at him across the room. Jones was a round man, florid and moustachioed, his black-braided inspector's tunic straining across his paunch. He played with his thumbs, smug that he had efficiently landed the problem in McNaghten's lap. The Head of the Criminal Investigation Department threw it back. 'It's your problem, Jones. When I was constable we were glad of two guineas a week. Your men have pensions, free uniforms, sickness benefit, even jars of macassar. Tell them from me that I won't have the

Metropolitan Police a laughing stock. Look at this – he slapped a copy of *Judy* down on the desk. It showed a policeman staring blankly at huge fingerprints on a wall. 'This kind of public scorn we can do without. Jones, if you hear the word "strike" again you have my permission to flog the bounder who uttered it.'

Jones growled under his whiskers something about McNaghten not being human. McNaghten heard it, but chose to ignore it. 'Well, Lestrade. Your case.'

Lestrade shifted the papers on his lap. He hated this. Especially now. Of course the others had unsolved or unsolvable cases. But this one he had already begun to take personally. It was an affront to his expertise, perhaps his whole career.

'Seven murders,' he said, leaping in at the deep end.

There were mumbles, the phrase repeated, the audible raising of eyebrows. McNaghten quietly tapped his pipe on the desk until the amount of tobacco cascading into his tea obliged him to stop. The noise abated of its own accord and Lestrade went on.

'All of them perpetrated within the last six months, scattered almost the length and breadth of the country. All of them by person or persons unknown.'

'Come on, Lestrade, you must have more than that.' It was Abberline, newly promoted, from the corner.

Lestrade protested. 'I feel this ought to be classified, sir. Remember the Ripper case.'

'I do,' snapped McNaghten, squirming at the memory of it. 'That was an entirely different business. Please don't bring it up again.'

'You were saying, Lestrade.' Abberline was persistent. The Superintendent was crisp in his light-blue suit and sniffed his gardenia ostentatiously. Lestrade's look should have withered it and him on the spot. He contented himself with the realisation that promotion to the river police was no promotion at all. He must spend his time chasing foreign sailors and stinking dockers up and down the Ratcliff Highway.

'What I have, gentlemen, is this.' He ignored Gregson's snort and went on: 'The murders conform closely to a children's book of cautionary tales called *Struwwelpeter*. If I had time I would itemise them.'

'Spare us the quotations.' Jones had regained his smugness.

'Murder one. *Struwwelpeter*, or *Shock-headed Peter* himself. A middle-aged male found walled up, possibly alive, in Shanklin Chine, Isle of Wight. Still unidentified. Cause of death – asphyxia. Suspects . . .' He dried.

'Well?' McNaghten prompted.

'Alfred, Lord Tennyson.' Howls of derisive laughter.

'I thought he was dead, Lestrade,' said Abberline.

'He is certainly not sufficiently mobile for my purposes. But at the time he had access to the Chine out of season, when it was normally kept securely locked. Once I'd met him I was able to eliminate him from my inquiries. Subsequent inquiries produced no individuals. All I can say is that the murderer was someone who knew the Chine, had access to it and was probably a dab hand at cementing, by candlelight.'

More assorted snorts.

'The more I dwell on the Chine murder, sir,' addressing McNaghten, 'the more I believe the similarity to the *Struwwelpeter* stories was pure coincidence. It was widely reported in the papers. Anyone could have got hold of the idea.'

Abberline broke in. 'This . . . er . . . *Struwwelpeter*. Who wrote it?'

'A German doctor. Heinrich Hoffmann.'

'Well, he's your man. I've never trusted these krauts. Not since Sedan.'

Abberline had blundered nicely into that one. 'I checked him, Superintendent. He really is dead – seventeen years ago.'

Abberline suddenly found something of great interest

in the end of his pipe. Gregson was quietly sniggering.

'The second murder. Victim – Lord Hurstmonceaux.'

'I thought that was a hunting accident,' commented Jones.

'The press deferred to the aristocracy. Lord Rosebery was a witness. Family scandal and all that.'

'Are we in the business of hushing up murder?' It was Jones's question but the look on McNaghten's face told him and everyone else that it was not his day. Lestrade remembered the Ripper File and smiled to himself.

'I know the cause of death – and how the murder was committed. Other than that, I drew a blank.'

'As usual,' grunted Jones. McNaghten reprimanded him.

'Murder three,' Lestrade went on, his jaw flexing, 'a seventeen-year-old girl, Harriet Wemyss, burned to death at her father's home at Wildboarclough, Cheshire. She burnt her clothes and person with a cigarette end. Her murderer knew that she had a secret smoking habit.'

'Tut,' broke in Gregson, 'the youth of today.'

'I believe her murderer encouraged the habit for several weeks, having planned this all along. And for the first time we have an eye-witness description. That of a travelling salesman who came to the house on the day of the murder. The same travelling salesman who, I have reason to believe, was Harriet's lover. He was described as a big man with a dark hat and a muffler.'

'Hardly conclusive,' grunted Abberline.

'Murder four. Or should I say, four, five and six. Three upper-middle-class layabouts – Edward Coke-Hythe, William Spender and Arthur Fitz. You may have come across them in the *Gazette*; they were bound over by the magistrate for baiting the visiting celebrity Atlanta Washington. I came across them in Battersea Park, painted with black enamel from head to foot.'

'You questioned Washington, of course,' said Abberline.

'I did, sir, and decided he was in the clear.'

'Other suspects?'

Lestrade hesitated. 'I traced the paint to the studio of Mr Lawrence Alma-Tadema' (he'd got it right again) 'the artist.'

'Lawrie?' McNaghten broke in. 'You didn't tell me that.'

'He's hardly a suspect in the conventional sense, sir. He told me the stuff had been stolen from him.'

'Well, of course,' agreed Jones.

'Certainly not,' snapped McNaghten. 'Lawrence Alma-Tadema is a very great friend of mine. Why, at one time or another, he has painted all my family. It is only modesty which forbids me hanging his portrait of myself and my lady wife over that mantelpiece.'

Jones shifted awkwardly in his seat. Today he was very definitely under the weather.

'It was at this point that I saw the connection between the letters. After each murder, or set of murders, I had been receiving, here at the Yard, unsigned mourning letters in the form of verse, each verse relating to the specific murder committed. All of them from *Struwwelpeter*.'

There was a silence. 'You mean' – Abberline was first to break it – 'some maniac is going round the country, finding victims to order just to fit in with a kiddies' rhyme? Fantastic! Stuff and nonsense!'

'The facts speak for themselves,' was Lestrade's levelling answer. 'The final murder occurred three weeks ago. A certain Albert Mauleverer, a resident of Warwickshire, found shot with a twelve-bore down a well near Guy's Cliffe in that county.'

'Who does all the murders in the book?' asked Gregson.

'Not all of them result in death. What they have in common is that they are moral or cautionary tales – not to play with matches, not to bait blacks or be cruel to animals and so on. In most of them, the perpetrator survives. In the Inky Boys story, the victims are turned black by a tall magician named Agrippa.'

'No, I'm sorry,' persisted Abberline, 'I just can't accept it.'

'You can't ignore it either,' said McNaghten. 'The fact is that so far the murders have fitted the book like a glove. It's uncanny. Funny,' he mused, 'to think that stories I used to read to my children should be taken so literally, used in such a sinister way.'

'What concerns me, sir, is the future. We are all of us, in this room, concerned with the prevention as well as the detection of crime. If the murderer runs true to form, there are five more to come. How are we to prevent it?'

McNaghten rested back in his chair. 'That's quite simple, Lestrade. Catch yourself a murderer.'

The season was nearly at an end. Lestrade should have taken a holiday late in August, but he could not. He had asked McNaghten for more men. At all costs he must keep the lid on things before the national press began to see the connection which was now all too apparent to the Yard. McNaghten could spare him two constables and a young, impressive detective-sergeant, John Forbes. Lestrade had to admit the man was smart, eager and resourceful – a sort of Bandicoot with a brain. But he could not bring himself to like him. He was too arrogant, to opinionated. Five years on the Force and rapid promotion under Gregson had given him airs and graces. Lestrade preferred well-tried police methods, documents filed in shoe boxes, the banal joviality of Bandicoot and the doe-like loyalty of Dew.

'I think we're dealing with terrorists, sir. Take my word for it. Anarchy is at the heart of this.'

'How long have you been under Gregson?'

'That's a malicious rumour, I . . . Oh, I see.' Forbes grinned rather painfully. 'I have served in the Special Irish Branch for three years.'

'And do you see terrorists under *every* bed?'

'That's not fair, sir. And if Inspector Gregson were here . . .'

'I would show him the door,' Lestrade finished the sentence for him. 'Tobias Gregson was never this much of a pain in the arse when he was with A division. He's become obsessive.'

'With respect, sir,' Bandicoot raised his curly head from a mountain of paper, 'the sergeant may have a point.'

Lestrade glared at his newest recruit through slitted eyes. 'All right, Forbes, and make it convincing. It'll need to be to persuade me we're looking for Irishmen and Russian sympathisers, bent double under the weight of their bombs.'

He slowly lit a cigar, pointing to the kettle as Dew entered the room under yet another pile of paper.

'Motive – anarchy,' Forbes began. 'To embarrass the British police. To cause such uproar in the peace-keeping forces of the nation that the people would rise up and overthrow existing order. It's happening in Europe, as we speak.'

'Looking around me,' Lestrade commented, drawing slowly on the cigar, 'I believe I was the only senior officer present at Bloody Sunday in 1887. I didn't see any Anarchists, Forbes. I saw starving women and children, people in rags and dirt. Dockers who worked one day a month. Girls who had been selling their bodies from the time they were eight. Women who hadn't seen a bed in weeks. I also saw the truncheons of the police, Forbes, and the bayonets of the Grenadier Guards. Don't talk to me about Anarchists.'

'They're scum . . . sir.'

Lestrade leaned on his desk, pointing his cigar like a finger.

'I don't like you, Forbes. I don't like ambitious policemen who get where they're going by climbing over people. I've listened to your theory and it smells. Until you can show me evidence and a suspect based on the facts of the case, keep your opinions to yourself.' He flicked his ash down Forbes's waistcoat. The younger man leapt to his feet, brushing himself down. He made for the door. 'And if you want to put in for a transfer back to Special Branch, remember to fill in the forms in triplicate.'

Lestrade caught the broad grins on the faces of Dew and Bandicoot as Forbes disappeared.

'Gentlemen, to work.'

It was the night of the Police Ball. A starry night, pink with the glow of the fires of the metropolis. It was the end of September, cool after a week of rain. Lestrade was late. Lestrade disliked unpunctuality, but he disliked the annual Police Ball even more. This year the Commissioner had excelled himself. The venue was the elite Metropole, shimmering with its polished glass and candelabra, the four ballrooms heavy with opulence and dazzling with chandeliers. He had also excelled himself, in Lestrade's opinion, in stupidity, by insisting that this be a fancy dress occasion. Lestrade, therefore, felt particularly ridiculous in his Harlequin outfit, but nonetheless hurt when he counted three others in the foyer alone. He hoped that the mask would conceal his embarrassment and hopefully his identity as well, but in the latter, alas, he was mistaken.

'Good evening, sir.' It was Bandicoot, burnt cork from head to foot, with a grass skirt and assegae.

'Bit tasteless after the Inky Boys, isn't it?' Lestrade snatched a passing glass of champagne.

'Sorry, sir, I hadn't thought of that.'

'No matter, with the exception of McNaghten, you and I will be the only ones to grasp the significance. Who's here?'

'Well, sir, I've just met an old school chum of mine, Ferdy Rothschild.'

'I didn't ask for a Burke's Peerage,' Lestrade snapped. Oh dear, he thought to himself, he was taking this evening worse than he thought he would. 'From the Force, man.'

'Ah, well, Inspector Gregson of course – over there – I

think he's supposed to be Charles the Second, but he really hasn't the presence for it.'

'No,' murmured Lestrade, 'more like Nell Gwynne.'

'But I do like Inspector Jones's Julius Caesar. He's already tripped over his toga twice tonight.'

'After a few more of those he'll fall over his shadow.'

'Evening, Lestrade. Good God, who's this?' Superintendent Abberline breathed champagne over the native gentleman.

'Good evening. This is Constable Bandicoot, my assistant.'

'Constable?' Abberline shepherded Lestrade away. 'Look here, old man, one doesn't want to pull rank at all, but a constable at the Ball. It isn't done. Have him wait with your horses.'

'I don't have any horses,' Lestrade replied. 'And, anyway, he is an Old Etonian.'

Abberline paused. His artfully painted clown's eyebrow disappeared under his orange hair. 'Ah well, I suppose . . . Well, keep him out of the way. I hear we're expecting a Very Important Guest tonight.'

'Mrs Abberline?' Lestrade suggested archly, glancing in the direction of the ravishing young creature now in flirtatious conversation with Bandicoot. Abberline spluttered on his champagne. 'Where? Oh, I see, er . . . This is my . . . er . . . niece, Miss Hartlepool.'

'Ma'am.' Lestrade gave a stiff unHarlequin-like bow and Abberline whisked the girl away. 'Ha, ha, keep your wits about you, Bandicoot. Tonight could be more fun than I thought.'

Lestrade and Bandicoot began to work their way through the vast buffet supper, the inspector tending to follow the lead of the younger man in the hope that Bandicoot's breeding would enable him to make sense of the obscure French terms and to identify the multifarious delights on the table. Lestrade was happy enough with the cooked meats and roasts and even vaguely recognised escargots, but there were things there in aspic he'd only seen on mortuary slabs. Surprisingly, it was all beautifully edible.

He was just moving out of earshot of the Cannon Row and District Band when he noticed the McNaghten entourage enter by the far door. The redoubtable Miss McNaghten, eldest of his boss's crew, was with them and Lestrade felt the usual impulse to bolt for the terrace. But he had fled from her in Bandicoot's presence before – time to stand his ground. And, as a trombone slide whizzed past his ear, to face the music.

'Inspector Lestrade, isn't it?'

Lestrade recognised the public voice and the apparent distance.

'Ah, Miss McNaghten. I'm surprised you knew me in the mask.'

By now the daughter of the Head of the Criminal Investigation Department was close to him. 'Sholto, my dear, I'd know you anywhere. Oh, you poor darling, what happened to your face?'

'Oh, I walked into a plate-glass window in Cambridge.'

'Tut, tut. And what were you doing there, chasing the blue-stockings?'

'You know there is no one in my life but you, Arabella.'

For a moment, a hint of sadness flickered across Miss McNaghten's face, then the public face was visible again. 'You cad, Sholto. I don't believe a word of it.' She flipped him roundly with her fan. It would have broken the jaw of a weaker man. 'Shall we dance? I love the gallop.'

'Has no one ever told you, gentlemen are supposed to ask ladies to dance?'

'I haven't all night, Sholto dearest. It's nearly half past nine. Besides, I'm nearly twenty-eight. Mama tells all her friends I'm on the shelf. Time I rectified that. How do you like my Marie Antoinette?'

'Where am I supposed to be looking?'

'Oh, you naughty man. Keep your mind on the job. Which reminds me, what are you working on?'

'Arabella, you know I can't –' he was whisked away by a gawky girl he vaguely recognised as old Inspector Beck's youngest. She was having great difficulty galloping in her mermaid's tail and also in keeping her long wig plaits stuck to her breasts, covered in pink body-stocking though they were. . . ' – divulge anything of that nature,' he called as Arabella swept past him in a glitter of sequins and lace. Lestrade had to admit that the redoubtable Arabella McNaghten did look surprisingly ravishing. Perhaps it was the white powdered wig, the low-cut bodice, the incandescence of the light. Or perhaps it was merely the champagne.

'Oh, come, Sholto, don't disappoint me. You know Papa doesn't tell me a thing. Is it a murder?'

'Arabella, I am not at liberty to . . .'

'Oh, Sholto, that's what I love most about you, your sense of duty. Not to mention that fetching little moustache.'

It was Lestrade's turn to tap Miss McNaghten's hand away before new partners swept them apart. The dance at last came to an end and Lestrade seized the opportunity to palm his boss's daughter off on Bandicoot. After all, they had met and Bandicoot was rather more Arabella's size. The lozenged inspector deftly extricated himself and rather furtively slid around a marble pillar and out of sight.

'I still think we're looking for international terrorists, sir.' Sergeant Forbes tried to look casual in the orange hair of an orangutang. 'Mind you, if their game is to embarrass the police, they need only to turn up here tonight and take a few photographs.'

'That's the Commissioner for you,' commented Lestrade. 'And you're still wrong. I'm thinking of working on a new tack now.'

'May I know?'

Lestrade checked that the coast was clear as though he were about to burgle a house.

'If you wanted to murder someone, Forbes, how would you do it?'

'Well, I'd . . . I haven't been long in homicide, sir. I'd need time to think.'

'Come on, man, this isn't a board examination. Try a method.'

'Poison,' said Forbes.

'Too easily traced. Where would you buy it? How much? What type?'

Forbes looked flustered.

'No, Forbes. Poison is risky. Long range, I'll grant you. Ah, good evening Doctor Cream,' Lestrade raised his glass to a medical acquaintance who was waltzing nearby. 'Where did he find *her*?' he muttered to Forbes, 'a Hyde Park girl if ever I've seen one.'

'Riff-raff,' was Forbes's stereotypical comment.

'It gives you an alibi,' Lestrade went on. 'Administer some poison in Winchester, you could be in Dundee before it worked. But it's too hit and miss. Too risky by far.'

'Gun, then. A shot through the head.'

'At point blank range, yes. Any further away and you might miss. But at point blank range, chances are you'd be covered in your victim's blood. And what about the noise? If you killed your man in a house, there would be other occupants, neighbours, itinerant pedlars with your luck. Always assuming you owned or had access to firearms, of course.'

'Well, I don't know,' Forbes snapped. He had the distinct impression he was being baited.

'Keep your fur on, Forbes. There is no safe way to murder. But there is a pattern. A poisoner always poisons. Goodnight, Doctor Cream,' he called. 'Take William Palmer, the Rugeley poisoner in the '50s.'

'A little before my time,' said Forbes smugly.

'And mine, Forbes, and mine,' Lestrade was at pains to point out to him. 'But the *Struwwelpeter* murderer has killed several times and with the exception of three identical methods in the Inky Boys case, because the plot, as it were, called for it, we have death by asphyxia, walling up alive; death by burning; death by asphyxia, but by the totally different method of painting the skin; death by training a pack of hounds; and death by shotgun. Not necessarily in that order.'

'I am aware, sir. What is your point?'

'That chummy is damned clever, very versatile and . . . and this is where my thinking is really taking me – that our man is intent on killing *one* victim. Someone he wants dead, out of his way, for reasons or reason unknown. The others are red herrings, deliberately to put us off the scent.'

'Good God, Inspector.' Forbes swigged his drink. 'But if that is so, which is which?'

'That,' said Lestrade, exchanging his empty glass for a full one, 'is what we shall endeavour to find out. Tomorrow morning, you and I are going to start requestioning the next of kin of the victims. I shall start with Mrs Mauleverer.'

'Any reason?' asked Forbes archly.

Lestrade looked at him with disdain. 'She has better legs than Lawrence Alma-Tadema.' He'd got it right again. It must be the champagne.

In another corner of the ballroom, much later, Lestrade propped himself up against a handy rail. He had had just a little too much of the bubbly and Melville McNaghten's banal conversation was sending him gradually to sleep. Only the gold braid on the Commissioner's shoulder kept winking at him in the candlelight, keeping him awake.

'Arabella must be such a comfort to you, Lady

McNaghten,' some faceless boot-licker was saying.

'Indeed she is,' crowed Mama, 'but she's a dutiful niece too. She's always visiting her aunts and uncles. It's one of the duties – and blessings – of a large family. It's so nice to see you dancing together, you young things.'

A nudge in Lestrade's shoulder informed him that Lady McNaghten was talking to him.

'Enchanted, ma'am,' he said, raising his glass a little faintly, appalled to realise that Arabella's mother had seen them together, perhaps even, horror of horrors, 'linked their names romantically', as such mothers always do. Luckily for Lestrade, the band suddenly struck up the National Anthem.

'He's here,' the Commissioner was heard to cry, flinging his wife to a lackey and making a beeline for the main staircase. Those who were seated, rose and it dawned, with differing degrees of sobriety, on all of them who the surprise guest of honour was. In fact, there were eight of them, but the two at the head were the best known. The first was a balding, bearded man with poppy eyes, his immense girth somehow tucked into the elaborate mess dress of a colonel of the 10th Hussars. It was 'Bertie', the Prince of Wales. Behind him, younger, taller, slimmer, with a long neck and thin moustache, but the same uniform and poppy eyes, stood his son, Prince Albert Victor Christian Edward, the Duke of Clarence.

'Good God,' Lestrade hissed to himself, 'they've let him out.'

'No ceremony, no ceremony,' the Prince was saying. 'Sorry, gentlemen, to come unannounced. And indeed, out of costume. Another beastly regimental dinner. Couldn't turn up at the Mess in a Guy Fawkes suit, what?'

The assembly shook with laughter at the inane remark. Lestrade caught McNaghten's face as he watched the Duke of Clarence, every move registering itself. In that immense room, in that august gathering, only two men knew the significance. The name of Eddy, the heir presumptive to the throne, the Duke of Clarence, old 'Collars and Cuffs', was not just associated with homosexual brothels in Cleveland Street. His name should also have been on McNaghten's Ripper File. McNaghten knew it. Lestrade knew it. Eddy rarely appeared in public, but here he was in the middle of Scotland Yard's finest. There was a horrible irony.

Lestrade relaxed a little as Eddy was introduced to various dignitaries. He appeared to be normal, polite, suave, if a little stupid. Lestrade chuckled as Eddy was introduced to McNaghten himself and he watched the Head of the Criminal Investigation Department straighten out the cravat, which, by virtue of his suit of armour, he wasn't wearing. His gauntlets rattled ridiculously on his beaver and he escaped into the refuge of the Dashing White Sergeant with the nearest woman.

'Remember, Eddy,' Lestrade heard the Prince say as he joined in the revels, alcohol having lightened his lead feet, 'the Tenth don't dance.'

'Quite so, Father.' Eddy sulked in a corner for the rest of the evening.

The storm arose when Lestrade had been out on the terrace for some minutes. The night air was cool and there was no rain at first. He puffed gratefully at his cigar and rubbed his nose where the mask had been chafing. Now and then, a flash of lightning lit the terrace and the shrubbery beyond. He caught the wandering forms of patrolling constables. All was well, all was calm. But he had a murderer on his hands. And so far, all efforts to catch him had failed.

'Oh, ho, Harlequin.' Lestrade spun round. A large bearded officer of the Hussars emerged into the lightning flash.

'Your Royal Highness.' Lestrade bowed.

'Glorious night,' said the Prince. 'Rain soon, I

shouldn't wonder.'

'Quite so, sir.'

'Who are you?'

'Inspector Sholto Lestrade, Your Highness, Scotland Yard.'

'Ah, one of McNaghten's detectives, eh?'

'Yes, sir.'

'Good. Good. Got a light?'

'One thing Hussar uniforms and Harlequin costumes have in common, sir, is that they have no pockets. I got my cigar from a subordinate.'

'Quite right,' roared the Prince, 'that's where I got mine from too.'

'Would it be too presumptuous of me, sir?' Lestrade offered his cigar.

'No. Damned civil. I've been longing for a smoke for hours.' The Prince of Wales puffed heartily on his own cigar, pressed end to end with Lestrade's. He blew rings into the air with undying gratitude. 'Mama – that's the Queen you know – doesn't really approve of my smoking. Silly, isn't it, Inspector? I'm fifty years old and I still care what my mother thinks. Do you have a mother?'

'It happens to us all, sir.'

'Yes, yes, quite. Now tell me, I have a taste for the lurid. What case are you working on at the moment?'

'I'm sorry, sir, I cannot divulge, even to the heir to the throne . . .'

'Oh, balderdash, Lestrade. I know about Freddie Hurstmonceux, and a little bird tells me there were others in the series, as it were. It's not generally known that I am something of a sleuth myself. Perhaps I can help.'

Lestrade began to feel uneasy. The bushes below him were illuminated with lightning. 'May I ask the source of your information, sir?'

'Freddie Hurstmonceux from Rosebery. The business

rattled him a great deal. He's sweating on Mama giving him a Garter, you know. He's prepared to do a lot of talking at the moment – in the right quarter, you understand.'

'And the others?'

'So there are others?'

Lestrade realised he had been caught out.

'Very clever, Your Royal Highness.'

The Prince chuckled. 'Yes, I thought so. No, actually, I wasn't, what's the phrase . . . fishing. You're not telling me anything new, merely confirming it. I'm afraid I can't tell you any more. It would be betraying a confidence.'

'Then you understand, sir, that I must be equally discreet.'

'Oh, you disappoint me, Inspector. A man without a mother must be a totally free agent.'

Before Lestrade could answer, they were joined on the terrace by a bevy of officers from the Tenth.

'I hope you are not checking up on me, gentlemen,' grumbled the Prince. The company dutifully chuckled. 'Onslaught.' He summoned a young lieutenant to his side, 'Inspector Lestrade, this is Henry Onslow, my son's A.D.C. He has allowed my boy to escape him. The least he can do is to get you a drink. I have detained you long enough.'

Lestrade was grateful for the escape clause and returned with the lieutenant to the main ballroom. It seemed of little moment to the Prince that Eddy had given his watchdog the slip, but to Lestrade, it meant more. It meant more still when he saw his quarry in earnest conversation with a shapely raven-haired beauty at the far corner of the room. His arm was resting firmly against a pillar as if blocking her line of escape into the room. Two other things quickened Lestrade's step as he snatched a passing champagne glass and made for the couple. One was that the young lady was Constance

Mauleverer, the other was that McNaghten had good
reason to believe the man was Jack the Ripper. It was
irrational, perhaps, of Lestrade to behave as he did,
chivalrous to the point of folly. First he shoulder-barged
the Duke of Clarence with something more than
necessary force and then he poured champagne over his
jacket with a scarcely concealed tip.

'Dolt!' The Duke was not pleased.

'My apologies, sir. Your gold lace blinded me.'

'Liar!' The volume was such that guests in their finery
stopped waltzing to stare at the ugly scene developing.

'Mrs Mauleverer, isn't it?' Lestrade was attempting to
change the subject. She smiled as the inspector kissed her
hand. He was jerked upright by a strong right hand. For a
split-second Lestrade glanced at the gloved fingers on his
sleeve. If McNaghten were right, either of those hands
had the power of life and death. The large eyes bulged
and flashed. 'You have insulted me, Harlequin. Choose
your weapons.'

'My dear Duke,' Mrs Mauleverer intervened, 'I'm sure
that Inspector Lestrade meant no harm.'

Clarence checked himself a little. 'Inspector. So you're
a policeman.'

'Most of us are, sir. This is a police ball.'

'And my father and I are guests of honour.'

'Well, your father is.'

'Damn you, Lestrade. You've insulted me again.'

By now three or four officers of the Tenth had joined
them. 'I will have satisfaction.' This was delivered at such
a pitch that the band began to waver. When Clarence's
left hand snaked out and caught Lestrade across the face,
it stopped altogether. 'My second will call on you.'

Lestrade recovered his composure although Mrs
Mauleverer pressed his arm in a silent plea for restraint.
'If you are challenging me to a duel, sir, you are some
decades too late. Duelling has been illegal in this country
since Thornton and Ashford.'

Simultaneously, the silence was broken by two shouts, both harsh and guttural, both acutely embarrassed. One, from the Prince of Wales, 'Eddy!' The other, from McNaghten, 'Lestrade!' Both men reached the quarrelsome pair simultaneously. 'Lestrade, you will apologise to His Highness immediately.'

'I already have,' said Lestrade, unperturbed.

'Eddy, it is time we were away.' The Prince and his entourage bustled Clarence towards the door, Eddy scowling and muttering the while. The band struck up the National Anthem discordantly. McNaghten whisked Lestrade into an ante-chamber and proceeded to lecture him on the need for protocol and not upsetting Royalty.

One of many witnesses to the scene, Sergeant Forbes, was chuckling helplessly in a corner. Bandicoot was straight-faced and sober.

'Come on, Constable. Your inspector's had it. He's cooked his goose good and proper.'

'I don't care for your homespun smugness, Sergeant. The inspector always has his reasons.'

'Oh, good God, Bandicoot. I didn't think they made sycophantic policemen any more. If you want a *real* boss, go to Gregson, transfer to Special Branch.'

'I'm happy with Lestrade.'

'You'll never learn, will you. Waiter . . .' Forbes snapped his fingers and helped himself. As the ballroom returned to normal, Forbes spotted another target for his razor wit.

'Isn't that Sherlock Holmes?'

'I believe it is the Great Detective.'

Forbes looked heavenward.

'God, Bandicoot, there you go again. Toadying.'

'Steady, Sergeant. That's a little harsh.'

'Look at them. Holmes and Watson, like a bloody music-hall double act.'

'Excuse me, Sergeant Forbes, I think I'd prefer the conversation of the double act.' Bandicoot crossed the floor to Holmes, decked out like an Egyptian Pharoah. Watson had discarded the gorilla mask by this time as it was too difficult to get the champagne past the rubber lips.

'Hello, Banders, old boy. Didn't think you'd be here,' said Watson. 'Holmes, have you met Harry Bandicoot? Old Etonian, friend of my nephew, Edward.'

'Ah, yes.' Holmes suddenly came alive. 'The Atlanta Washington case. I read in what Fleet Street laughingly calls the newspapers that your Lord and Master, Lestrade, let him go.'

'I believe that was because he was innocent, Mr Holmes.'

Holmes shook his black wig tragically. 'What a pity. There seems to be no improvement in these Scotland Yard fellows. But then,' archly to Watson, 'he is a friend of *your* family.'

'I wanted to ask you, sir, if I may, about the . . .'

'Watson will answer any questions. I don't discuss my cases in public. God, Watson, why ever did I allow you to talk me into coming to this charade? I feel ridiculous.'

'Oh, I don't know, Holmes. It's difficult to tell you from Rameses himself.'

Holmes flicked up his flowing robes and swept majestically towards the ante-rooms. 'Bring your bag, Watson.'

The doctor's normally jovial moustaches drooped somewhat. He patted Bandicoot on the arm and followed the Great Detective. The constable saw Lestrade cross the hall in the opposite direction.

'You'll need a second, Inspector,' he said, intercepting him.

Lestrade looked at him hard. 'You don't imagine I'm going to fight that royal buffoon, do you?'

'If you were an Etonian, sir, you'd have no choice.'

'Where's Mrs Mauleverer?' asked Lestrade.

'I haven't seen her, sir. But Sergeant Forbes seems to

be . . . er . . . looking after Miss McNaghten for you.'

Forbes was standing embarrassingly near the daughter of the Head of the Criminal Investigation Department. She seemed not to be displeased by it. 'Are you going to barge into him too?'

Lestrade flashed anger at Bandicoot. It had not been his night. 'Miss McNaghten can take care of herself.' And he moved to the door. A gloved hand caught his arm. 'Sholto.' It was Constance Mauleverer. Lestrade glanced behind him. Both Forbes and Arabella McNaghten had noticed. Bandicoot tactfully faded into the background.

'Sholto, what's happening? You can't fight the heir to the throne, especially over me. Why did you insult him?'

'I can't tell you, Constance.'

'You won't go through with it?'

'Of course not. Constance . . . I didn't think I'd see you again. Especially here.'

'I came with my uncle, John Watson.'

'Watson? Doctor Watson?'

'Yes, do you know him?'

Lestrade laughed. 'Indeed. Don't you read the rubbish that he and Conan Doyle cook up between them? One day I'll sue them both.'

'*You* are in Uncle John's short stories?'

'Some of them. Dear lady, I am cut to the quick. Not that my "appearances" are very flattering. Mr McNaghten is far from pleased that Scotland Yard detectives are held to ridicule and scorn.'

'Sholto.' Constance was suddenly serious. 'I hate to bring this up, but are you any nearer to finding my husband's murderer?'

Lestrade looked hard into the dark eyes of this woman who had captivated him. 'I didn't know John Watson was your uncle.'

'I don't understand.'

'You didn't know his nephew was murdered recently?'

'Edward Coke-Hythe. Of course, he was my cousin.'

'Why didn't you tell me?'

'I didn't think it necessary . . . You mean the two are connected?'

'I don't know, Constance. But I do know that most people have no connection with murder at all. You have a connection with two. You are a dangerous woman to know.'

'Am I accused, then?'

'Ma'am, I never arrest ladies at police balls.' Lestrade kissed her hand. He led her on to the steps of the hotel amid leaving guests. Suddenly, a deputation of Hussars stood before them. Onslow stepped forward.

'Inspector Lestrade, I am instructed by His Royal Highness the Duke of Clarence to offer you choice of time and place to settle this affair of honour.'

'Affair of . . . oh yes, of course.'

'Sholto.'

'No, Constance. This won't take long. Dawn, gentlemen. That gives us three hours or so. Time enough to get to the Headless Chicken at Highgate.'

Onslow saluted briskly. 'Very well, sir. His Highness chooses sabres.'

Lestrade thought of the débâcle of his constable days struggling through cutlass drill.

'Naturally,' he smiled.

Onslow and his party departed.

'Sholto.' Constance took the Harlequin's hand. 'He'll kill you.'

'Over my dead body, Constance,' smiled Lestrade.

Duels

True to the spirit of melodrama and Gothic novels, a chill mist swirled around the gravestones of Highgate cemetery. Two parties emerged through the wet greyness of the dawn, walking in parallel down the overhung greenness of Swain's Lane. To the left walked His Royal Highness, the Duke of Clarence, in the patrol jacket and forage cap of the 10th Hussars. Behind him, draped with cloaks and rattling with spurs and accoutrements, four of his brother-officers, grim-faced and moustachioed. To the right, arm in arm against the chill of the morning, Inspector Lestrade, wrapped in his Donegal, and Mrs Mauleverer in a velvet walking-out dress. Behind them, crisp in morning coat and non-regulation bowler, Harry Bandicoot, and, in his one and only suit, Walter Dew, constables of Scotland Yard. It made a faintly ludicrous and extremely unlikely picture. It was the morning of September 16th, 1891. It was the modern world. But one man was not going to walk away.

The officers of the law took their positions at the gates of the Egyptian Avenue. The Hussars tramped to the top. There was an awkward pause and then two of them came down to the centre.

'Sholto, do you read Sir Walter Scott?'

'Alas, no, Constance.'

'If you did, you would know that knights in the Courtly Age carried a lady's favour when they fought.

Please, wear this for me now.' She tied her silk scarf around his neck. He held her hand briefly.

'I think they're waiting for us, sir,' said Bandicoot.

Lestrade turned to him. 'Bandicoot. Dew. Neither of you should be here. You are officers of the law. You should both know better. Bad enough if I'm caught in this nonsense, but you two . . .'

'You need a second, sir,' Bandicoot broke in. 'Who will hold your coat?'

Lestrade allowed himself a smile for an instant. 'Very well, but Mrs Mauleverer should not be here. Dew, escort the lady back to the Headless Chicken. Inside the carriage, please.'

'I've come this far, Sholto. I'll stay with you a while longer. And besides' – in a stronger voice – 'you wouldn't order Constable Dew away at a time like this.'

'So be it.' Lestrade grinned. He threw his Donegal to Bandicoot and stripped to his shirtsleeves. The two men walked uphill to where Clarence and Onslow waited. To their surprise, it was Onslow who took off his cloak and jacket, rolling up his sleeves.

'Etiquette demands that I cannot fight you, Lestrade,' Clarence delivered haughtily. 'I am after all the heir to the throne. Besides' – he produced a handkerchief – 'I have a cold coming. I trust Lieutenant Onslow will do as my substitute?'

Lestrade bowed.

'Rather a sacrilegious choice, this place of yours, I must say,' the Duke remarked.

'It'll save the cost of burial,' quipped Lestrade, 'for one of us.'

Clarence drew a cloak from two cavalry sabres lying across his arm. Bandicoot, with his Etonian grasp of these matters, inspected both carefully and nodded. Lestrade took one and turned to take up his position. The sabre was a good foot longer than the cutlass he remembered and he had forgotten how damned heavy the thing was. He took his cue from Onslow, who bent his knees and assumed the 'en garde' position, having saluted Lestrade with his sword. On one side, Clarence drew his sabre and on the other Bandicoot held the points of all three blades together.

'What now?' Lestrade broke the silence, unable to take the while thing seriously. 'Do we all pirouette to the right?'

Clarence scythed his blade upward and Bandicoot sprang back. For a second which seemed to Constance an eternity, nobody moved, then Onslow swept forward, his blade licking in over Lestrade's guard to find his arm. The white sleeve darkened red and Constance started forward, checking herself before Dew had a chance to restrain her. Onslow straightened up, saluting.

'Sir,' he said to Clarence. Lestrade felt dizzy and not a little sick. There was a numbness in his left elbow.

'Again,' Clarence sneered.

Bandicoot cut in. 'By all the rules of duelling, sir, even among the less salubrious schlagers of German universities, first blood is sufficient.'

'I will decide what is sufficient. Onslow, again.'

Onslow saluted again and came to the ready. Yards away, Dew gripped Constance's arm. Silently her heart went out to Lestrade, left arm hanging useless, facing a professional swordsman again. Onslow's attack was slower this time and Lestrade banged it aside.

'You're not trying, Onslow. I want him taught a lesson.'

Onslow's pace increased. His feet slid forward, faster, faster, his blade circling Lestrade's, inches from the inspector's body. Lestrade was retreating, trying to keep in step as best he could. He could hear words of encouragement from Bandicoot on his right. Further away the shouts of the Hussars and the angry yells of Clarence. The family vaults in their granite silence swept by him, but all he could see was that flashing, probing blade and Onslow's sweating face behind it. Desperately he parried and cut, using two hands once when he felt his back against an Egyptian column. Onslow's sword crunched inches from Lestrade's face. He ducked under his arm and caught him high in the ribs, purpling the white shirt. He dropped to his knees, fighting for breath. Onslow staggered back against a vault.

'That's it,' Lestrade rasped to Clarence, 'no more. No more.'

'Damn you, Lestrade. You're not cutting up one of my officers and getting away with it. Onslow, can you stand?'

The lieutenant somehow came to attention.

'Then get on with it.'

Lestrade flinched as the sabre flashed past his face, slicing off the very tip of his nose. He lunged from the ground and grazed Onslow's thigh.

'You boys, stop that!' All eyes turned to the distant voice. At the top of the slope, beyond the knot of officers, silhouetted against the dawn sky stood a lone figure. The outline presented an immediate problem. It wore a Hussar busby and presented a generally military outline, but apparently wore a skirt as well, and was leaning against a bicycle.

'God, it's the Colonel,' whispered one of the officers.

For a fleeting second Clarence toyed with the notion of its being his formidable Grandmama in one of her unused Colonel-in-Chief's uniforms. But the preposterousness of the idea banished it from his mind. With astonishing presence of mind, Bandicoot threw Lestrade's Donegal over both sabre blades and the combatants, sweating and bloody, tried to look as nonchalant as possible, as though it were the most natural thing in the world for two men to be in Highgate Cemetery this early in the morning, bleeding from sabre wounds.

The intruder leapt on to the saddle of the bicycle and scattered the Hussar officers, who sprang back in amazement. The figure screeched to a halt in the centre of the duelling ground. All parties present stared in astonishment. Before them stood an elderly lady, with grotesque theatrical make-up, in the heavily braided fur-edged pelisse and tall busby, complete with lines and plume, of the 11th Prince Albert's Own Hussars.

'Ah, I know you, my boy.' She pointed an imperious finger at Clarence, 'You're Eddy aren't you? Oh, I haven't been allowed at court for years. Your grandmother never forgave James for marrying me. But I keep abreast of court gossip, you know. "Collars and Cuffs", eh? Yes, I see it. Besides, you've got your father's poppy eyes.'

'Madam, I don't know from which asylum you have escaped, but I strongly suggest . . .'

'Come, sir,' one of the Hussars intervened, 'shouldn't we be away?'

Reluctantly Clarence was led towards the main gates and the hill where the carriages awaited. As he left, Onslow shook hands with Lestrade.

'If you ever tire of the Force, sir, we'd be proud to have you in the Tenth Hussars.'

Constance wrapped the Donegal around Lestrade's shoulders, dabbing the blood from his mouth and chin. Her eyes were wet and hot. 'Your colour, my lady.' Lestrade managed an uncharacteristic flamboyant flourish, removing the scarf.

'Come on, you need help,' announced the old Hussar lady. 'You, young man' – this to Bandicoot – 'take my bicycle and go on ahead. I've a private retreat nearby at the top of the hill. It's called Quorn. Tell them to prepare a room –' she glanced at Constance '– for two.'

There were silent protests all round, but between them the ladies helped Lestrade, dizzy from loss of blood, to the gate. Dew walked paces behind, anxiously peering through the lightening day for signs of coppers on their beat. To meet a constable in the pursuit of his duty would have been singularly unfortunate.

Lestrade fell into a fitful sleep. His head throbbed, his arm hurt, his nose was indescribable. But he had survived a duel and fell asleep holding the hand of a woman who had certainly become very important to him. It was not until he awoke that he began to take stock of the situation. The room in which he lay was pleasant enough, typically upper-middle-class, hung with mementoes of an earlier age. From somewhere he heard a clock strike – four. The blinds were drawn but it was daylight outside. Four in the afternoon. God, he was on duty in an hour. Time he roused himself.

'Sholto.' Constance swept noiselessly into the room. 'You shouldn't be getting up yet, dearest.' Lestrade realised the wisdom of her remark when he sat upright. His left arm was very stiff and his nose felt as if it reached the far wall.

'What time is it?' he asked.

'Just gone four. Shall I ring for tea? Lady Cardigan's staff are most obliging.'

'Cardigan? Oh, I see. That accounts for the uniform.'

'Yes, my dear. I've talked a great deal with her in the last two days. Ever since her husband, the seventh Earl, died, she has worn his uniform when in public. It somehow eases the pain of his going. Oh, he had a full life and she knew only too well that he was not exactly faithful, but they were fond in their own way. She took up bicycling a few years ago. She bicycles everywhere.' Constance chuckled. 'Even, it seems, around the colonnade in Highgate Cemetery.'

'Two days?' Lestrade stood up suddenly and immediately wished he hadn't. 'Good God, woman, have I been here for two days?'

'Calm yourself, Sholto. I am not used to being referred to as "woman", especially by a man I hardly know.' She was smiling tauntingly at him.

'I'm sorry, Constance. Good God, woman, here I am in my combinations at four o'clock in the afternoon and here you are, a recently widowed lady, in the house of a mad, old eccentric who . . .'

'That's less than kind, Sholto. Lady Cardigan is certainly eccentric, but she has placed her London home and its staff completely at our disposal. She has returned to Deene, her country home. She finds London a frightful bore now the season has ended. Anyway, I didn't know you were such a prude. This is 1891, you know. I have heard the new decade will be known as the "naughty nineties". Wouldn't you like to be just a little bit naughty with me?'

'Madam, you miss the point. I fought the duel on the morning of Saturday the sixteenth. What day is it today?'

'Tuesday the nineteenth.'

'Exactly. I have missed one turn of duty and am about to miss a second.'

'Bandicoot has reported you down with influenza, dearest. There's a lot of it about. No one will query your absence. Aren't you allowed to be ill in the Metropolitan Police?'

'In H Division, no.' Lestrade sat back heavily on the bed. He was beaten, he realised that. The thought of a cab or train ride to his lodgings and then to a pile of paperwork at the Yard did not appeal. Still less did applying his mind to the *Struwwelpeter* case. And before him, in the semi-darkness of the room sat the most beautiful woman he had ever seen. He looked at her smiling face, warm and soft. He reached out his good arm and ran his fingers round the smooth curve of her cheek. She pressed her head into the palm of his hand and kissed the fingers. Lestrade took her head with both hands and kissed her forehead lightly.

'I'm not going to break, Sholto,' she said, and their lips found each others in the darkness. It was not the most romantic love-making on record. Sholto Lestrade had never been a lady's man, until now. He was no novice, of course, but certainly a little rusty and most of his muscles had been put to the test too recently for this to be easy for him. Constance was of course no virgin, but despite her outward forwardness, she was still a woman of her times and the new decade was still too new to sweep away the time-honoured traditions of a lifetime.

The second time was better, however: both of them relaxed. It was nearly midnight before Constance lay curled up in Lestrade's arms, nuzzling her raven hair against his chest.

'Tell me about "Shock-headed Peter",' she whispered.

Lestrade shifted uneasily. 'At a time like this?' he asked.

'Sholto, you could have been killed two days ago. My husband and my cousin are dead already. This may not be the time. But it may be the only time. You will return to your beloved Yard tomorrow or the next day. I must go home to Warwickshire.'

He turned her head to him. 'What if I want you to stay?' he asked her.

She took his hand, squeezing it hard. 'You are a policeman, an Inspector of Detectives. I am a widowed lady with modest means and no future. We don't suit, Sholto. We wouldn't fit.'

'You once told me you didn't give a damn about convention,' Lestrade reminded her.

'I didn't think I did,' she answered. 'With another man, another time, I might not. But tell me, what would happen if your superiors found out that you were here and that I was here with you?'

Lestrade chuckled. 'I'd have another drubbing down from Sir Melville, then there would be a brief inquiry and I'd be kicked out of the Force. Your name would probably be dragged through the mud, though they wouldn't get it from me and they'd probably board this place up as a bawdy house and arrest Lady Cardigan as a brothel-keeper. The Commissioner's a stickler for the morals of his men.'

'Exactly. That's not a bright future for either of us, is it?'

He began to say something, but she stopped him with a kiss.

'How did you know about *Shock-headed Peter*?' he asked her afterwards.

'It was just something I overheard at the Ball. An orangutang was talking very confidentially to Marie Antoinette, I believe.'

'Oh, God, Arabella McNaghten wheedled it out of Forbes. I'll kill him.'

'Oh, Sholto, is it that secret? Isn't she the daughter of the Head of your . . . what do you call it, S.I.D.?'

'C.I.D. That doesn't matter. Regulations are very clear. All cases are classified information. They must not be divulged to any member of the public. Forbes knew that. I'll have that bastard . . . begging your pardon, my dear . . . I'll have that bastard back on the street for this.'

'Sholto,' she turned in the bed, pressing her naked thigh against his. 'You mean you aren't going to tell me anything about the case?'

She caressed Lestrade between the legs, her fingers sliding lightly at first, then harder as he rose to the occasion. 'Stop it, Constance,' he shouted hysterically, 'I'm too ticklish.'

For a while, as he travelled back to the Yard, Lestrade let his mind wander over the leave-taking. She said she was going. Back to Warwickshire. To sell the house. To move away. To begin again, without memories, without heartache. Change her name, perhaps. Go somewhere where no one knew about Albert Mauleverer, where Struwwelpeter with his sad cheeks was simply a child's fairy tale, not some sinister, ghastly reality. Lestrade had shaken his head as he held her hands. He had felt an iron lump in his throat. He was not a man of words. He was not a troubadour from one of Walter Scott's novels. He was not as silver-tongued as he wanted to be for Constance. 'I'll find you,' was all he had said. 'When this case is over, I'll find you.' Then it was her turn to shake her head. She did not cry. Her voice remained strong, her smile as dark and deep as ever. Lestrade had cried, inside, alone, but he was a hard-bitten copper and he betrayed no emotion at all. At least he hoped he hadn't.

Despite all this whirling in his brain, the atmosphere at the Yard was tangible. He noticed that in his brief absence, the scaffolding had been removed and that the new quarters gleamed in the afternoon sun that flashed on the river. But the place was like a morgue. A grim, silent desk-sergeant saluted him. He entered the lift with two ashen-faced detectives from Gregson's division.

'Sir Melville would like to see you, sir,' said Constable Dew as Lestrade reached his office. There was no cheery greeting, no cup of tea, no inquiry into the inspector's health. Lestrade knocked on the veneered door. A growl told him to go in.

McNaghten looked ten years older. Lestrade suddenly saw his whole career flash before him. Someone, Lady Cardigan perhaps, regretting her kindness, or Clarence, in a fit of pique, had shopped him. He even felt himself reaching into his pocket to hand over handcuffs and whistle.

'Forbes is dead,' McNaghten told him.

'Forbes?' Lestrade repeated.

'Dead. Gangland slaying. His body was found in an alley off The Minories this morning. I sent constables. Where the hell were you?'

'Er . . . recuperating.' No point in giving the game away now. There was nothing to be gained by it.

'I don't like it, Lestrade.' McNaghten was rubbing his moustaches repeatedly, smoothing the cravat every third or fourth rub. 'When a policeman is killed in the execution of his duty. I don't like it at all.'

'But what was he doing in The Minories, sir? He was supposed to be on the *Struwwelpeter* case. All my men are.'

'According to Bandicoot he'd had a tip-off. A nark, I suppose, told him to go to The Minories at midnight last night.'

'And he went alone?'

'Good God, Lestrade, you and I have done it dozens of times.' Lestrade laughed inwardly. He knew he had, but doubted it of his rather more feather-bed leader. He knew McNaghten had never walked a beat in his life. 'You don't take half the force with you for fear of scaring your tipster off. Come alone, the man says, and if you want what he's selling, you go alone.' The advice and the reasoning were sound enough.

'He must have been robbed. His watch had gone. We don't know if he was carrying money. Presumably, going to see a nark, he would have been. I want the man that did this, Lestrade. You are to drop the *Struwwelpeter* business and use all your available men on this. You can have dogs, back-up from Jones's division, anything you like. But these scum have got to learn.' He thumped the desk for effect. 'On my patch, no one kills a copper and gets away with it.'

Lestrade clattered down the corridor towards the mortuary. McNaghten must have been upset for he had not asked him to account for the bandage across his nose. He had worked out elaborate plans to explain an accident with the door of a hansom. He had also wrenched his arm, just for the record, should anyone ask, which would account for it hanging stiffly at his side. In the event he needn't have bothered. McNaghten's mind was elsewhere. It was largely in fact on the body of the man who now lay before Lestrade on the slab in the gleaming new white-tiled mortuary at Cannon Row. Forbes lay contorted, twisted slightly to one side, his body still stiff with *rigor mortis*, his face still wearing a slight look of surprise.

'Stabbed through the heart,' said the mortician cheerfully. 'Slim-bladed weapon. Might have been a hat pin.'

'A hat-pin?' Lestrade was incredulous. 'They're breeding a new type of East End rough, aren't they?'

'I thought that. Mind you, I had a subject in the other day. Now where was it? Yes, that was it, washed up near Shadwell Stair, stark naked. Exactly similar stab wounds, but through the back.'

'I should have thought a common or garden chiv would have suited a sailor or a doxy.'

'You'll pardon me for saying this, Inspector. I mean, it's not strictly my job, I know, but I'm something of a student of the criminal classes. I've noticed that murders go in waves. A certain type of weapon catches on and hey presto, they're all at it.'

Lestrade looked at the cadaverous features of the mortician and the centre-parted, lank hair. All in all, he looked a lot worse than Forbes. Sensing that the inspector did not care particularly for his amateur sleuthing, the mortician shifted his ground.

'Of course, it could be a *lady's* hat pin.'

If anything, that suited Lestrade less.

'Stabbing is not a female technique,' he said. 'Too physical, too messy. In twelve years of murder enquiries, I have never known a female knifer.' But at the back of his mind, and not entirely for reasons of pleasure, lurked the face and form of Constance Mauleverer. He dismissed the notion immediately. She had been with him at the time Forbes had been killed. All the same, he felt vaguely uncomfortable. Something about Forbes's death did not sit well.

'Of course, this is odd as well,' the mortician was saying and he pulled back the green sheet to expose the pale corpse. Lestrade visibly rocked backwards. Forbes's hands lay across his private parts. The mortician had forced them into that grotesque position as *rigor* was beginning to lessen, minutes before. Lestrade could not believe it. Both the thumbs had gone.

'Hacked off with a pair of scissors, I shouldn't wonder. Tough work, mind. The bone is very clean.'

But Lestrade had gone, nursing his arm as he leapt up the three flights of stairs to his office.

'No stomach for it, these brass hats,' muttered the mortician.

Feverishly Lestrade opened the book. There it was –

> . . . *The great tall tailor always comes*
> *To little boys who suck their thumbs,*
> *And ere they dream what he's about,*
> *He takes his great sharp scissors out*
> *And cuts their thumbs clean off – and then*
> *You know, they never grow again.*

'Dew, where's Bandicoot?'

'The Minories, sir. He said he ought to follow the trail while it was still warm.'

'You mean he's alone?'

'Yes.'

'Good God, man, you should have gone with him. What's an Old Etonian going to do in the East End? They'll have him for breakfast. Get a Maria and hurry.'

It was dusk before Lestrade and Dew found their quarry. Bandicoot was sitting in a corner in the dimly lit cellar bar of the White Elephant in Portsoken Street.

'I've been all over Aldgate and Houndsditch, sir. Nothing.'

Lestrade pointed at Bandicoot's beer. 'I hope that's not on expenses. Dew, your round.'

Dew disappeared into the jostling and the smoke.

'Who have you spoken to here?'

'No one, sir . . . yet. But I'm told an eye-witness comes in here every night about eight.'

'Who?'

Bandicoot reached for his notepad. 'A man named "Skins", sir.'

'Skins?' Lestrade leaned back in his chair, chuckling silently.

'Sir? Do you know this man?'

'The only one I know called Skins is one Albert Evans, a down-and-out. He'd tell you he'd stolen the Crown Jewels if you promised him a pint. Ah, thank you, Constable.' Dew arrived with the drinks.

'But what if he did see something?'

'All right, I'm prepared to wait. What else have you got?'

'Not a lot, I'm afraid. Sergeant Forbes received a note from a street urchin just before the end of his shift yesterday.'

'Did you see the boy?'

'No. The desk sergeant did. But that was the first place I asked. They hadn't seen the boy before and probably wouldn't know him if they saw him again.'

'That's what I like,' mused Lestrade, 'efficient, observant police work. What else?'

'I then thought to check the note – handwriting or something.'

'You're improving, Banders. And?'

'Sorry, sir. Sergeant Forbes must have taken it with him, but it wasn't on him when they found him.'

'Have you been to the scene of the crime?'

'Yes, sir. Two hundred yards from here in Gravel Lane. The constable who found the body was on a routine beat. He heard nothing, although he had passed the spot minutes before. Sergeant Forbes was due to meet his informer at midnight. His body was found round about half past two – the constable's watch was not accurate.'

'This constable, did he find any clues?'

'Nothing, sir. Which is odd. Sergeant Forbes was an experienced policeman and a well-built man. I would have expected him to put up something of a fight against the gang.'

'Gang?'

'The men who killed him, sir.'

Lestrade leaned forward again. 'Have either of you gentlemen seen the body?'

'No, sir,' the constables chorused.

'His thumbs are missing. We are not looking into a beating-up that went too far. We are looking for Agrippa.'

Dew and Bandicoot were astounded.

'So that's why Forbes didn't fight!'

'Whoever the murderer is, he took Forbes sufficiently by surprise.'

Bandicoot was thinking. Lestrade saw the strain showing on his face.

'If I recall rightly, sir, the next victim ought to have been little suck-a-thumb, named Conrad. Did Sergeant Forbes have that habit?'

'We needn't be too literal, Bandicoot. But you've got a point. I think Forbes was on to something. The murderer knew that and had to get rid of him. This is the first time we've rattled him. He's broken his pattern. Oh, the method is correct – the thumbs removed with scissors, but he's been so close to the text so far, I can't believe he wouldn't have had a Conrad in mind had he been given a little more leisure.'

'Wouldn't he have found it rather difficult to find a Conrad, sir?' asked Dew. 'There can't be many of them.'

'I'll grant you that,' Lestrade replied.

'Why not stay with the text, though?' asked Bandicoot. 'And bump off Sergeant Forbes anyway. Make it look like a gangland slaying, as we thought it was.'

'I don't understand Agrippa's motives, Bandicoot. If I did, we'd have him in custody, wouldn't we?'

'Excuse me, sir, isn't that Skins?'

Dew pointed to the door through which an ageing wreck of a man, toothless and grey, had shambled.

'Bandicoot, your round. Three beers and two gins. Dew, bring him over.'

The constables departed to their various tasks. For almost the first time Lestrade took in his surroundings. The cellar was filling up with people, beer fumes and smoke. Here and there carousers rolled drunkenly around a piano-accordion. A harlot was singing tipsily in a far corner. Three men had their hands up her skirt, but she appeared not to have noticed. The East End was crowded again after the recent return of the hop-pickers from the Kentish countryside. All human life lay before Lestrade as he watched Dew drag the struggling Skins across the sawdusted floor. Prostitutes, thieves, murderers, even the odd curate in silk top hat flashed before his gaze.

''Ere, wa's your game?' Skins was still squawking at the pressure of Dew's hand on his none-too-savoury collar. 'Oh, it's you, Mr Lestrade, sir.' Skins seemed to have gone even paler under the lurid lights when he saw Lestrade.

'Hello, Skins, how's the dead-lurking business? Set them down, Bandicoot. The gin is for Mr Evans, here.' Skins leapt for the glass, but Lestrade's hand slammed down over the top of it. He placed his bandaged nose an inch from the grey whiskery face of Skins. 'When he's told us what we want to know.'

'Look, guv'nor, you know me. I been in and out o' the Bridewell all me life, but there's some 'ard men around these parts now. 'onest, if I gets seed by one of them talking to the likes of you, why, then you'll find me floatin' and that's the Gospel truth.'

'"The likes of me," Albert. That's not very charitable.'

''Ave an 'eart, guv'nor.' Skins's eyes flashed round the room. The man was obviously terrified.

'Last night. Midnight. Gravel Lane. What did you see?'

'Nothin', guv.'

Lestrade sat up, staring long and hard at the other man. 'Albert Evans, dead-lurker, noisy racket man, snoozer, sawney-hunter, skinner . . .'

'Oh, no, sir.' Skins was indignant. 'Don't you know that's why they call me Skins? 'Cos I wouldn't do it. It's not natural.'

'You're missing my point, Albert. Do you know there are 20,883 men and women in prisons in this country? How would you like it to be 20,884? And I'm not talking about theft, Evans. Failure to report a murder will mean the crank and the treadmill.'

Skins fell back against his chair. He was steadied by Dew on one side and Bandicoot on the other. 'Think of it, Skins. Six hours a day, fifteen minutes on, two minutes off. You'll climb 8,640 feet a day. And of course for you we'll apply the brake to make it even more difficult.'

'Oh, no, sir. Not at my time of life. I couldn't take it, not again.'

'There again, murder carries the drop.' Lestrade quaffed his pint, artlessly. 'I was talking to James Berry the other day . . .'

'The public hangman?' Skins was pure white.

'That's him. He was telling me how he miscalculated the drop at Preston last week. Pulled the lever and the villain goes down, wham!' Lestrade brought his good fist down on the table. 'Unfortunately the rope was too short and his head came off. Blood all over the place . . .'

'All right, guv,' Skins sobbed. 'I get your meanin'. I'll tell you. Only I got to 'ave police protection.'

'We'll walk you to the door,' said Lestrade.

'Well, I was mindin' me own business . . .'

'Dead-lurking.'

'Shut up, Dew,' said Lestrade.

'An' I seen two men talking in Gravel Lane. It was a dark night last night so I couldn't see 'em clear, but they was both toffs. One of 'em had a topper and cloak. I thought, it's the bloody Ripper come back, I thought.'

'And?' Lestrade couldn't wait for asides.

'I couldn't hear what they was sayin'. They both whispered like. Then, and I was just about to turn into Gaydon Square, the gent in the topper ups and stabs the other one, thumps him in the chest, like.'

'Did you see the knife?'

'No, guvnor. I ran. Last thing I seed was the toff kneelin' down over the other 'un. And I said to meself, that's it, 'e's done for 'im.'

'Why didn't you report the incident?' asked Bandicoot. All three men around the table looked at him with utter scorn.

'The murderer,' Lestrade said, 'is there anything about him you can remember?'

'Like I said, guvnor. It was real dark. 'e was a big bloke. A bit taller than you.'

'As big as Bandicoot, here?' The constable obligingly stood up.

'No, I wouldn' say so. 'E walked funny.'

'Walked funny? What do you mean, man? Out with it.'

'Well, sort of . . . I don't know, sir, as if 'is feet was 'urting 'im. Can I have a drink now, guv'nor?'

Lestrade gestured to the glasses. Skins downed one gin, then the other, as if they were life savers.

'Hello, Skins.' An alien voice made them all look up. Four big men filled the space in front of the raised table. Their spokesman was a sailor by his coat and tattooes. Bandicoot was particularly aware of the smell. 'Talking to coppers again?'

As if at a signal, the music and drunken revelry died down. Beyond the four men, Lestrade saw all faces in the cellar turned towards them.

'We're not looking for trouble,' Lestrade told the sailor.

'Well, you've found it all the same.'

Bandicoot stood up, massive and immaculate. 'I should warn you that we are officers from Scotland Yard,' he said.

One of the men behind the sailor spat on the floor.

'Haven't you read the sign?' said Lestrade, pointing to the far wall, 'No hawkers. No spitters.'

''E's a big boy, ain't 'e?' said another man to his mate, eyeing Bandicoot.

Lestrade turned to his constable, 'Why don't you tell them you won a cap at Eton for boxing? That'll really frighten them.'

'Don't you think that's a little arrogant, sir?'

'Skins, you're a dead man,' the sailor snarled and aimed a burly right arm at him. Bandicoot caught it in mid-air and, spinning the man round, kicked him into the crowd. A roar went up as the fight started and tables and chairs were scattered as the crowd took up the best vantage points. The sailor got up, his pride more hurt than the rest of him. Skins had vanished in the smoke. Two other roughs in caps and monkey jackets sidled up to the raised table. Lestrade and Dew were now on their feet and the inspector began to walk steadily towards the centre of the room. A hundred miles away, or so it seemed, the staircase was bathed in a lurid green light. He saw the blow coming from his left but his left arm was too stiff and painful to deflect it. He spun round and his brass knuckles crunched head on with the wildly swung fist. The rough fell back, his hand broken. Lestrade staggered, too, his wrist aching. Only the knuckleduster had saved him from a similar fate. Two of them rushed at

Dew and that valiant policeman was last seen by Lestrade
disappearing under a tangle of arms and legs. Bandicoot
was parrying blows with his shoulders and Lestrade saw
him pick up one of the smaller roughs and throw him the
length of the bar. More and more bystanders were
knocked about as the mêlée spread.

When it became apparent that all three policemen were
still essentially on their feet, and that three roughs lay
unconscious on the floor, the mood turned nasty. There
was an eerie pause, during which the cheering died down
and then four knives flicked out, almost simultaneously,
flashing in the sulphur light. Each of the policemen
prepared for it in their own way. Lestrade flicked his own
catchblade out, which certainly surprised Bandicoot and
Dew, if not the clientele of the White Elephant.
Bandicoot picked up a chair, like a rather unconvincing
lion-tamer. Dew grabbed the nearest pewter mugs, two
in each hand, and waited.

'Prepare ye for the Lord!' a harsh voice bellowed,
shattering the stillness.

All eyes turned at once to the stairs. Half way down
them, silhouetted against the gaslight green stood a
white-haired, wild-bearded man in a military frock-coat.
The light seemed to play around his head as if it were a
halo. Around him, a number of burly, uniformed young
men were gathering. He descended the stairs, his
footsteps the only sound in the entire cellar.

'Repent, sinner,' he snarled at the nearest rough and
brought his heavy Bible crashing down on the man's
head. The rough collapsed among the overturned chairs.

'You likewise, brother,' and he smashed the brass
clasps of the Bible into the teeth of a second. Before he
reached the third, the area had cleared and some of the
troublemakers had sloped towards the steps.

'No one leaves!' The terrible old man pointed towards
the stairs and his henchmen formed a solid wall of blue.
'Time for a prayer meeting.'

To the constables' astonishment, the assembly — harlot, sneak-thief and drunk alike, all bowed their heads, as though they were in a church. Lestrade crossed the floor quietly.

'Something for your collection, General?' he produced a sovereign from his coat.

'And something for yours, Inspector.' The old man produced a book from his and pressed it into Lestrade's hand.

'Take your hat off, Dew,' Lestrade growled, 'you are in the presence of a great man.'

The assembly at the head of the stairs parted to let the policemen through.

In the alley above, it was Dew who first broke the silence. 'Was that . . . ?'

'General William Booth of the Salvation Army, laddie. And thank his God he turned up when he did.'

From the cellar tap-room of the White Elephant, the strains of 'Abide With Me' and the incongruous rattle of a tambourine. Bandicoot glanced over Lestrade's shoulder at his book. *In Darkest England.*

'And is there a "way out", Inspector?'

'That's too clever for me, Bandicoot. Let's go.'

'One thing, sir. What did Skins mean when he said skinning was unnatural? What is skinning, sir? I'm afraid I didn't understand any of that conversation.'

'Skinning, Bandicoot, as any novice bobby will tell you, is the crime of enticing children into alleyways and stealing their clothes.'

'No wonder he thought it unnatural,' said Bandicoot, distastefully. 'He obviously has a moral streak.'

Lestrade chuckled. 'No, no, Bandicoot. Skins thinks it unnatural because skinning is women's work. It would be a blow to his manhood. Dew, call me a cab in The Minories. We've got some bruises to look after.'

And Dew's voice echoed back as he disappeared into the darkness, 'You're a cab in The Minories.'

This time there were two mourning letters for Lestrade. They both came two days after the murder of Forbes. McNaghten had intensified the search for 'Agrippa', Agrippa the Elusive. Twenty-six constables and three sergeants had been found from somewhere, but house-to-house searches had revealed nothing.

The first letter Lestrade had been waiting for –

> *The door flew open, in he ran,*
> *The great, long, red-legg'd scissor-man.*
> *Oh! children, see! the tailor's come*
> *And caught out little suck-a-thumb.*
> *Snip! Snap! Snip! They go so fast,*
> *That both his thumbs are off at last.*

'Agrippa' had become the 'great, long, red-legg'd scissor man.' It was the same man, unruffled. So Forbes had found something, but what? He was on to someone, but who?

It was the second letter that took Lestrade by surprise. The scissors man had struck again, even before there was a body, even before the crime was reported. Somewhere, Augustus lay dead –

> *Augustus was a chubby lad;*
> *Fat ruddy cheeks Augustus had;*
> *And everybody saw with joy*
> *The plump and hearty healthy boy . . .*

Across the twilight river, the trees of October were dark and gaunt. A curlew called from the heathland. A knot of men wound their way up from the moored boat. Their lanterns swung as they walked, flinging shafts of light across the walls of the mill. Inspector Hovey of the Kent Constabulary looked at the huge, black building ahead of him. To one side the mill stream rushed and gushed, the overshot wheel groaning in the green darkness. A solitary light flickered in an upstairs room, high on the right.

'Somebody's in,' a constable muttered.

'Inspector.' Hovey held out his arm to the front door, by way of invitation to his guest. Lestrade took the bell pull. Far away, down an echoing hall, a distant answering ring.

'Old Prendergast's too mean to pay servants. And, as he's deaf, you'll wait for ever,' Hovey observed.

'This is your county, Hovey. It should be your boot in the door.'

'Vowles. You're the one with the shoulders. Open that door.'

Constable Vowles passed his lantern to a colleague and tried the door. It opened easily. 'It was nothing, sir,' he beamed. Hovey and Lestrade ignored the levity and in a confusion of courtesy, the inspectors collided abreast in the doorway.

It was Lestrade who finally led the way through the darkened house. There was no gas, not even any oil lamps that he could see. The lanterns threw long shadows across the faded wallpaper, peeling in the passageway. There was dust everywhere and cobwebs thick and white in the torchlight.

'Oh Jesus!' Vowles cried out. The others turned, constables' hands poised over their truncheons. 'Mice,' said Vowles, a little sheepishly.

'For God's sake get off that chair, man. You're a policeman.'

The party continued on its way, room by room. Empty, silent, dark.

'The light was at the top of the house. Furthest away from the wheel,' Lestrade observed.

'That would be through here.' Hovey now led the way, elbowing aside cobwebs as he reached the first landing. 'God, it's cold.'

The door at the end of the corridor was firmly locked. It took Vowles and the two other constables several attempts to force it open. The stench in the total darkness forced them back.

'Christ, what is it?' a constable asked.

'That's the smell of death,' Lestrade told him.

'I'm sure this was the room with the candle,' said Hovey.

Lestrade took a lantern. 'Opening the door probably blew it out,' he said. His feet crunched on broken glass. He glanced about him. A bed, a chair, a sideboard near the window. His feet hit something else. It rattled, clanked. It was a chain, heavy, long. He picked up the cold links and pulled them taut. There was something at the end of it. Holding the lantern up, he saw what it was. An old man, greyish-green, in tattered nightgown lay face up on the floor. Near his body the chain divided, one length attached to a bracelet on his wrist, the other on his ankle. Lestrade saw that the skin around these bracelets was cut and chafed. The man was skeletal, the eyes sunken, staring blindly at the ceiling. Lestrade looked up. Silhouetted against the dark blue of the night sky was a bowl of fruit. He could see by the lantern light that it was mouldy and shrivelled. He understood completely.

'Augustus,' he said.

'No. Isaac Prendergast,' Hovey corrected him, peering over his shoulder. 'God, the smell.'

Lestrade saw effluent all over the dead man's clothes and the floor. There was no sound now but Vowles quietly vomiting on the landing.

'Have your constables stand guard at the front door, Inspector,' Lestrade said. 'We can't do much until daylight.'

Daylight brought an unkind drizzle from the west. Lestrade had spent a cramped night sitting bolt upright in the settle of the snug of the Folded Arms. He was wakened by a tweeny raking out the fire with myriad apologies for disturbing 'the gennelman from Lunnon'. Breakfast was a cup of very mediocre tea and the journey, by trap and rowing boat back to the old mill, was equally wet and nasty. Vowles huddled against the doorframe, dripping wet and nearly as blue as his helmet. Lestrade threw off his Donegal and hung the soaking thing on another constable in the hall. Isaac Prendergast was even deader by daylight than he had appeared in the dark. The room was vile, floor and bed covered in excrement and the old man's body at the full stretch of the chains as though he had been reaching with his dying breath for the window.

'This is unbelievable,' Hovey was muttering. 'It looks as if some bastard chained him up so that he couldn't reach the fruit, leaving it there just out of reach. I've never seen anything like it in twenty years in the Force.'

'Nor will you again, Inspector,' said Lestrade. 'Are your men reliable?'

'They may not be the Yard, Inspector, but they are Kentish men. They know what they are about.'

'Good. Then have them go over this house with a fine toothcomb, especially this room.'

Hovey looked at the state of it. 'You're asking a lot . . .'

'Look, Hovey'—Lestrade's patience, after such a night, was wearing a little thin – 'why do you think I'm here, man?'

'I was wondering that?'

'Well, call it sixth sense. Let's say it fitted a certain

pattern. Isaac Prendergast is not an isolated case. He is the
ninth victim of the man I'm after. And I'll hang up my
cuffs if he claims a tenth. So if you or any of your yokels
are going to get squeamish on me, God help me, I'll see
you drummed out of the Force.'

The silent response told him he had struck a chord.
Hovey spun round and barked orders to his men.
Lestrade went to find some fresh air. He watched the
raindrops make ripples on the river, and the dark lines of
the mill broke and shivered.

'He was a spiritualist, you know.' Hovey had joined
him. 'I wonder if he'll come back.'

Lestrade turned to him with a rising feeling in his heart
– the first he had had since the case began.

'Perhaps he will if we call him,' he said.

McNaghten's telegram was more encouraging than
Lestrade had expected. *Go ahead*, it had read. *Have great
faith in spiritualism. More Things in Heaven and Earth. Get
some results. McNaghten*. Lestrade was wondering how he
could implement this decidedly odd piece of extra-
curricular police work when the solution fell right into
his lap. He was visited by a deputation of sinister-looking
ladies and gentlemen from the Dymchurch Spiritualist
Circle. It had been some time, they said, since Isaac
Prendergast had joined them, but each member of the
Circle had once promised to do his or her utmost to reach
the others when he or she crossed to the Other Side and,
by a fortuitous coincidence, the great Madame Slopesski
had expressed a wish to attend a seance for this very
purpose as part of her European and American tour. The
time was Thursday at seven in the evening. The place
was Carlton Hall, the old manor house beyond Dymchurch Level. The Circle had heard from Inspector
Hovey of Lestrade's interest in the case (Lestrade hoped
that his colleague had not given too much away) and
invited both inspectors to the meeting.

In the event, Hovey had pleaded a previous engage-
ment and Lestrade went alone. He crossed Dymchurch
Level a little before seven. Far away he heard the rush of
the sea, haunting, lonely. It was a clear night, starlit,
cold. The turf was springy beneath his feet. He didn't
quite know what to expect. He had played with table-
rapping as a boy, when such things were more in vogue
than they were now. But he had never attended a seance
in his life. Those held by Mr Lees, the medium employed
in the Ripper case, had been observed by a very small,
select gathering, headed by McNaghten and Abberline.
Lestrade had not been present. His directions for tonight
had been very clear and by a quarter past seven his feet
crunched on the gravel drive leading to Carlton Hall, an
imposing mid-century house, turreted and bastioned.
Very Gothic, Lestrade mused to himself. As a boy his
favourite paper had been *Varney the Vampire*. He could
almost hear the leathery wings flapping through the
crypt.

A tall elegant Lascar took his hat and Donegal in the
porchway. He was shown into the drawing room, heavy
with velvet curtains, latticed screens and studded
doorways. A huge fire roared and crackled in the grate.

'Not a night for smuggling.' A cheery voice welcomed
Lestrade from an ante-room.

'If you say not,' he answered.

'No, too cold. Too clear. Hasdruble Carlton. Welcome to my home.' The squire extended a hand.

'Sholto Lestrade. Thank you.'

'Ah, yes, from Scotland Yard no less? Not much
chance you being a smuggler, eh?' Carlton chuckled.

'I don't look too good in scarecrow's rags.'

'Ah, so you know our local legend – Dr Syn, the
redoubtable Vicar of Dymchurch?'

'I get the impression that before the death of Isaac
Prendergast, people in this part of the world talked of
little else.'

'You may be right, Mr Lestrade, but please if I may be so bold, we of the spiritualist persuasion do not use the word "death", we don't acknowledge such a thing. We prefer "going over". Brandy?'

Lestrade accepted a glass gratefully and turned his backside to the welcoming fire. It looked as though they were in for another winter like the last, beginning in October and ending in May. Carlton was called away by the arrival of other guests. One or two of them Lestrade recognised as having been in the deputation who had called on him at the Folded Arms. Introductions over, the group was taken through into the ante-room from which Carlton had first emerged. The entire room was hung with black velvet and, under a single oil lamp in the centre, was a large oval table surrounded by nine chairs. Solemnly the guests took what seemed to be accustomed places. The Lascar showed Lestrade to a seat between two elderly ladies of the parish, lit a number of incense sticks and then retired, closing the double doors behind him.

'We have two surprises tonight, ladies and gentlemen,' Carlton said in a soft whisper. 'Apart, that is, from the welcome presence of Inspector Lestrade.'

Nods and beams all round in the direction of the inspector.

'One is that Madame Slopesski can be with us after all.' A ripple of applause. 'As some of you will know we thought yesterday she would be unable to be with us because of the pressure of her tour. I am delighted to report that I received a telegram but an hour ago and she will join us presently. The second surprise is that we have yet another guest, someone who is revered by you all and known I think to one or two of you, a founder member of the Society for Psychical Research, Mr Frank Podmore.'

Rapturous applause, somewhat at odds with the hushed tones which preceded and followed it, heralded the newcomer's arrival. Lestrade had heard of Podmore too, but in a rather different context. Gregson had mentioned him because the man was a Fabian Socialist and to Gregson, of course not terribly conversant with the finer points of politics, that smacked of anarchy. Athelney Jones was after him too, strongly suspecting that Mr Podmore was a secret cottage loaf who had other designs on a long string of paper boys and telegraph lads than merely cataloguing their supposedly paranormal experiences.

Podmore was tall, distinguished, with greying hair and side-whiskers, perhaps forty. His eyes were calm and kind and he showed a huge sense of occasion as he quietly took his seat. He made it clear that tonight's 'show', if such was the right term, belonged not to him but to Madame Slopesski.

It was some minutes before that Great Lady arrived. Carlton was the soul of courtesy and hostmanship, ushering the living legend to her place. Lestrade took her in at a glance. The light of the oil lamp shone mercilessly on her dull grey hair, wild and unruly by English standards. She was a woman of about sixty, he would judge, large, matronly with a chronic stoop and a pronounced limp. She bore a passing resemblance to the Queen, who also of course dabbled in such things, though hardly for a living. Her hands were strangely young with long, tapering fingers and when she spoke, it was in a deep, resonant middle-European boom. Gregson would no doubt have assumed her to be another anarchist, had he been here, Lestrade mused to himself.

For what seemed an hour, the Sensitive and her Circle sat in silence. The phonograph rasped out some anonymous music, somewhere behind Lestrade's head. Madame Slopesski spent most of this time with her eyes shut, breathing deeply ever sixth or seventh breath. The others sat with bowed heads, except Lestrade, who watched them all.

Then the Great Lady stretched out her arms. It was the

signal to commence. Carlton leapt to his feet with noiseless experience and turned off the phonograph. As he returned he dimmed the oil lamp and it went out. In the flickering firelight, Lestrade felt the hairs on his neck stand a little shamefacedly on end. He hoped he hadn't visibly jumped when he felt the two old ladies, one on each side of him, grab his hands, their bony fingers sliding into position until fingertips touched.'

'Is anybody there?' Madame Slopesski intoned.

Nothing.

Lestrade watched every face in the flickering light. They all had their eyes shut, except himself and Podmore, who was carefully watching the medium.

'Aaaggh,' Madame Slopesski cried out in a harsh guttural scream. Lestrade felt fingers tighten on his own. Madame Slopesski recovered her composure. 'Is it you, Isaac? Are you among us?'

Nothing.

A long silence followed. No one moved. Madame Slopesski occasionally murmured, sighed, arched her neck. Podmore gave nothing away. Lestrade was watching the others. Was it one of them? Was it Isaac Prendergast who was the real target? And had all the others been mere blinds? That was the theory he had put to Forbes the night of the Police Ball. The last time he had seen Forbes alive. Had Forbes followed up that line of inquiry? Had he been lucky where Lestrade had not? And was it that luck that had killed him?

'Isaac.'

A thump. Then another. The table shook and rattled. There were gasps from those present except Podmore and the medium.

'Knock once for yes, Isaac.' Madame Slopesski was swaying slowly from side to side. 'Twice for no. Are you near?'

A single thump. Lestrade tried to tune his ears to catch the direction of the sound. His detective's training had taught him to be suspicious of all this. It was trickery all right, but how was it done? He could not free his hands or break the circle and he could not see beyond the heads and shoulders of the members hunched around the table.

'Are you happy?'

A double thump and then several more, agitated, malevolent. The chandelier tinkled and rang, sending sparks of reflected light shooting over ceiling and walls.

'Have you a message?'

Yes, said the thump.

'Speak through me,' wailed Madame Slopesski, swaying now more violently.

Another long silence.

'Hypocrites!' It was Madame Slopesski's lips that were moving but it was not her voice. 'Isaac', whispered the old lady on Lestrade's left, 'that's Isaac's voice.'

'All of you, hypocrites. You left me. Deserted me. Where were you when I needed you?'

'Oh, Isaac,' sobbed another lady, 'we didn't like to disturb you. We know how you hated to be called upon.'

'Quiet, Esmerelda,' snapped Carlton, 'we'll lose him.'

Silence again.

'Mr Podmore.' Carlton turned to the *éminence grise* for advice. Madame Slopesski remained motionless, rigid in her chair. Podmore leaned forward without breaking the circle.

'Isaac,' he whispered. 'Is it warm, where you are?'

Nothing.

'Is it dry?'

Nothing.

'Are you cold?'

A thump.

'We've lost him,' hissed Carlton.

'Not yet,' Podmore answered. 'Isaac.'

Another silence.

'Is your murderer here?'

A single thump, followed by violent shaking of the

table. The fire spat and crackled.

'Who is it?' It was Lestrade's voice, to his surprise as much as to everyone else's.

A deep guttural roar came from somewhere within Madame Slopesski. She stood up, hands outstretched. 'Beware,' she growled in Isaac's voice, pointing to Lestrade, 'beware, you will join us before long. Beware.'

She slumped back in her chair. Lestrade's eyes flashed from side to side. Everyone was looking at him. Except Podmore, who was smiling to himself and looking at Madame Slopesski.

Hasdrubal Carlton re-lit the oil lamp and the Circle broke up.

'I believe this is all we shall have tonight,' he said.

Podmore took the limp wrist of the medium and checked the pulse. 'I think it would be unwise to ask Madame Slopesski for more,' was his verdict.

The Circle generally agreed that voice manifestation was enough for one evening. Madame Slopesski's speciality was ectoplasm, but all present, except Lestrade, knew that such physical manifestation was rare and that conditions had to be just so. The ladies in the Circle fussed around Madame Slopesski who began to revive. Some of the others began to make leaving noises. It was Lestrade who stopped them.

'May I remind you, ladies and gentlemen, that Madame Slopesski – or was it Isaac Prendergast? – told us that a murderer was present. I am afraid I must detain you for a while.'

'But you can't believe that one of us . . .' Carlton began.

'It is not a matter of what I believe,' Lestrade interrupted him. 'It is not my belief that is at stake here, but yours. If Madame Slopesski is wrong, then either she is a fake – or your whole spiritualist movement is.'

There were cries of indignation at this, but Lestrade had his suspects in a cleft stick. 'Mr Carlton, may I use your drawing room for the purpose of my interrogations?'

Grudgingly, mine host agreed. Lestrade began with Carlton himself, to give Madame Slopesski a chance to recover. He was aware of the danger of leaving the other members of the Circle together in an adjacent room, with a perfect opportunity to concoct and perfect a story. But without constables and without a telephone, he really had no choice.

'How long have you known the deceased?'

'We of the spiritualist persuasion . . .'

'. . . do not use the word "deceased". Yes, I know,' Lestrade chimed in. 'All the same, Mr Carlton, I am conducting a murder investigation and would be grateful for an answer.'

'About five years. I am not a Kentishman myself, Inspector. I was until lately in Her Britannic Majesty's Civil Service in India.'

'Hence the servant – the Lascar?'

'Jat, actually. Jemadar Karim Khan. Late of the Viceroy's Bodyguard. A capital fellow, Lestrade.'

'These fellows have some interesting ways of dispatching their victims, I've been told.'

Carlton laughed. 'I see your reasoning, Inspector. I am supposed to have sent Karim Khan to do the evil deed, thereby giving myself a suitable alibi.'

'The thought had crossed my mind.'

'May I remind you, sir, that you are a guest in my house? The audacity of it!'

'Murder is an audacious enterprise, Mr Carlton. Although this particular murder wasn't. It can't have been difficult to overpower a weak old man.'

'Weak? Inspector, I don't know who you have been talking to, but Prendergast was far from that. I'll grant you, he must have been seventy, but he must also have weighed over twenty stone.'

Lestrade found it genuinely difficult to conceal his

surprise. He had assumed that the emaciated corpse he had stumbled over at the mill was not appreciably lighter than the former living frame. Then *Struwwelpeter* came back ominously to his mind –

> *Augustus was a chubby lad;*
> *Fat ruddy cheeks Augustus had;*
> *And everybody saw with joy*
> *The plump and hearty healthy boy . . .*

'Yes, Inspector, your deceased was obese – and powerful with it. He would not have gone easily.'

'Did you like him?'

'God, no. No one did. I think it's probably true to say that the whole Circle hated him. He was an almost total recluse, especially of late. The only time he ventured out was to attend our meetings, and then grudgingly.'

'So why did he come?' probed Lestrade.

'He believed, Inspector.' To Carlton that was reason enough.

'When did you last see him?'

'It must have been three, no four, months ago.'

'And then he stopped coming.'

Carlton nodded.

'Why didn't you – one of you – check on him? After all, he was seventy.'

'I'm sixty-three myself, Inspector. Anyway, you don't bother a testy old gentleman like Isaac Prendergast. He hated callers. I've heard he put buckshot into the Vicar's breeches once. Vicar never admitted it, of course, but his progress to the pulpit each Sunday is painfully slow.'

'You attend church, Mr Carlton?'

'Why certainly, Inspector. And I am not, as you are probably thinking – what is the phrase – "Hedging my bets". I am simply a Christian spiritualist. There is no dichotomy here.'

Lestrade thought he had better change tack before the

dialogue got beyond him.

'When Madame Slopesski – Isaac – whoever that was in there,' he said, 'told us that the murderer was present, whom did you have in mind?'

'Inspector, I have known all these good people for five years. I would stake my life on the fact that not one of them is capable of such a deed. When you share the shadows of the night with a fellow human being you get to know these things.'

Lestrade interrogated all of them and he had to admit that Hasdrubal Carlton was probably right. He spoke to six anxious people, deep believers all in what they were doing. He saw gullibility, sincerity, hope, but he didn't see a murderer. But he still had two to go, to his mind the most likely of all – Podmore and the medium. It was by now well past midnight. As the genial host, Carlton, had asked if those who had been questioned might be allowed to go home. Lestrade saw no reason why not. He asked the dark, silent Karim Khan, who understood but spoke no English, to show Madame Slopesski into the ante-room. In the event, it was Podmore who appeared and seeing Lestrade's annoyance at having his instructions misunderstood, said, 'I'm afraid she's gone, Inspector.'

'Gone?' Lestrade was furious.

'Yes, I didn't think you'd be pleased, but, I beg you, don't be hard on poor old Carlton. She is a very eminent lady in our field. If she pleaded tiredness due to her tour and the strain of tonight, how could he do other than to let her go?'

'Go where, exactly?'

'To her hotel. I believe she told me it was the Postgate, here in Dymchurch.'

Lestrade's eyes narrowed, 'I have been in this town for four days.' The clock struck one. 'Correction – five days', he went on, 'and I have not seen an hotel called the Postgate here. In fact I have not seen an hotel at all. Which is why I am staying at the pub. Did any of the Circle overhear this conversation?'

Podmore stretched out on the sofa in front of the dying fire, chuckling to himself. 'No, Inspector, they did not. And suddenly, it's all fallen into place.'

'What has?' Lestrade sensed that Podmore was playing games with him. He didn't like it.

'Have you attended a seance before, Inspector?'

'I have not.'

'Watch.'

Podmore sat bolt upright. 'Put your hands on the table between us,' he said. Lestrade did. Podmore turned out the oil lamps and resumed his seat opposite Lestrade. 'I'm going to place my fingertips against yours. Can you feel them?'

'Yes.'

'Right. Now be still. Absolutely still.'

Silence.

Podmore broke it first. 'Is anyone there?'

Silence.

Again, the repeated question.

Then, a thump, muffled, far off.

'Isaac, is that you?'

A louder thump.

Lestrade's heart was racing.

'Is your murderer here?'

A series of thumps, rocking the table.

'You did that with your knee,' Lestrade shouted.

'Yes, that wasn't very good, was it? Madame Slopesski was better.'

'She was a fake?'

'Please relight the lamps, Inspector. I haven't finished my exposé yet.' Lestrade did so and returned to his position. 'You noticed how the thumps were soft, then loud?'

Lestrade nodded. 'The soft thumps are done like this.' Podmore produced them again. 'I am merely pressing my toes against the soles of my boots. The harder knocks, as you guessed, are done with the knee. It is easier through skirts, of course' – Lestrade wondered in passing if Podmore ever wore them – 'and with the atmosphere so carefully created in the other room.'

'So Carlton was in on it?'

Podmore chuckled. 'What a marvellously quaint way you policemen have of putting things, Inspector. No, I don't think he was. Like all the other members of the Circle, he is a true adherent. Just like hundreds I have met all over the country. It's just part of the ritual which mediums insist on. The darkened room, the soft music. Oh yes, and the spitting fire.' Podmore threw a handful of something into the dying flames. They crackled into life. 'Salt,' he said to Lestrade's surprised look. 'Common table salt. Most mediums carry it in a purse attached to their wrists.'

'But the circle of fingers was unbroken,' said Lestrade.

'Indeed so.' Podmore smiled. 'As you see.'

Lestrade could not believe it. Podmore appeared to have three hands.

'This one is wax,' said the ghost-hunter. 'Most mediums are essentially conjurors. They cheat people as surely as your – what's the phrase – confidence tricksters do. Most of them in fact are just that – frauds who dupe innocents for money or the limelight. I am looking for the one who is not. For the one who is genuine.'

Lestrade was examining the wax hand.

'There is ample room in a lady's nether garments to hide one of these. I always carry a spare. It's sometimes fun to confuse the medium by slipping it in. Henry Sidgwick and I both did that once and the medium was exposed with five hands – two of her own and three wax ones.' Podmore laughed at the memory. 'In the darkness a dexterous medium can usually switch one of these for her own fingers. In the charged atmosphere of a seance, no one will notice when the light is turned off.'

'Why didn't you turn the light on?' Lestrade asked. 'I thought you ghost-hunters made your living by exposing frauds.'

'I don't know about a living, Inspector. Curious choice of words, really. But certainly I would normally have done that.'

'And tonight things were not normal?'

'No. To begin with, whoever that medium was tonight, she was not Madame Slopesski.'

Lestrade found his jaw behaving as it was frequently supposed to in the dubious literary concoctions of Doctors Watson and Conan Doyle, while Holmes suavely unmasked a villain. 'Not?' he repeated stupidly.

'Not.'

'How do you know?'

'My dear Inspector. I know Madame Slopesski. Oh, not well, I grant you. But I have been introduced to her on three or four occasions. Our impostor must have known that. She was visibly rattled when we met in the forecourt and blamed her surprise on the chill night air. Mind you, the disguise was good, very good. The stoop, the make-up, the hair, all excellent. Three things however gave the game away.'

'Oh?' Lestrade was beginning to wonder why Podmore had not followed a career on the Force.

'First, the tricks were not quite so slick. Madame Slopesski – the real one that is – is a genuine adept and, although she plays to the gallery, she does it better than our guest this evening. You must remember of course that she did not expect to find me here.'

'Second?'

'Second, her eyes. Madame Slopesski's are a dull grey. Our impostor's were a clear blue.'

'How observant of you.' Lestrade was exhibiting a tinge of pique.

'You policemen do not have a priority in these things, Inspector.'

'Thirdly?'

'Thirdly, the voice. It was a shade too deep. So much so in fact that . . .'

'Yes?'

'Inspector, I can't explain this, but I think our Madame Slopesski was a man.'

Silence as the two men looked at each other. Lestrade sank back in his chair.

'Could I be right?' asked Podmore. 'It's a sense I have –and it is what made me let her . . . him go. It was not a conventional fraud. Does that make sense to you?'

'Oh, yes, Mr Podmore,' said Lestrade. 'The murderer *was* in that room. He was Agrippa, the long, red-legged scissor-man. He was Madame Slopesski . . . and I missed him again.'

It was nothing that Lestrade hadn't said to himself a thousand times as he rode in the train back to London. Even so, it came hard from McNaghten.

'It's out of my hands,' said the Head of the Criminal Investigation Department, folding down the cravat and sweeping up the ends of his neatly waxed moustaches. 'The Commissioner has asked that you be given a week's leave, Lestrade. Take it and be done.'

Lestrade looked at him sullenly. McNaghten felt even more acutely uncomfortable than usual. 'Look, Sholto,' the approach was softer, the tone more wheedling, 'you've had your share of bad luck in this case, I know. But God knows, man, you've made no headway.'

'And who will?' Lestrade asked. 'Who has my case when I'm thrown off it? Abberline? Gregson? Not Jones, surely to God?'

'No one, Lestrade.' Lestrade was pacing his office. 'I'm not taking this case off you, man. I'm merely saying, have a rest, come fresh to it in a few days' time.'

'By that time another three men may be dead. Remember the book – I've got Philip, Johnny and Robert to go. And I don't know where and when Agrippa will strike next.'

'That's exactly my point,' McNaghten railed on. 'With rest, you'll see things more clearly – connections, clues. This Agrippa – he isn't superhuman. He's made mistakes. Look, Sholto,' again the avuncular tone, 'you're tired, you're on edge. What do you do in your spare time? Fish?'

Lestrade grimaced.

'Well, whatever you do,' McNaghten blustered, annoyed at revealing his lack of knowledge of his subordinates' lives, 'for the next seven days you are to do it. That is an order.'

In his own office, Lestrade packed a few things into a Gladstone bag. He saw little point in looking at the mourning letter lying on his desk, but Bandicoot and Dew hovered, waiting to see what he would do, how he would play it. No surprises, no clues. Typewritten, London postmark, the final verse –

> *Look at him, now the fourth day's come!*
> *He scarcely weighs a sugar-plum;*
> *He's like a little bit of thread,*
> *And on the fifth day, he was – dead.*

'Gentlemen, I am ordered to take a week's leave. During my absence you will do nothing, talk to no one. And if any senior officer asks, you know nothing. Understand?'

They understood. Lestrade had summed it all up perfectly. They did know nothing.

'What will you do, sir?' asked Bandicoot cheerfully. 'Go fishing?'

Lestrade looked at him. He smelt conspiracy for a moment, but dismissed it. Bandicoot wasn't good enough.

'I have friends to visit, Bandicoot. I think a turn by the sea will do me good.'

It didn't do Lestrade good. On the contrary, he staggered against the squalls and gusts which threw spray over the promenade at Southsea. Somewhere beyond the mist

and the endless grey that was the Solent and the sky lay
the Wight, where all this had begun, an eternity ago. He
pulled up the collar of his Donegal and sank his hands
gratefully into its pockets. Urchins ran by, shrieking and
squealing in the fierce rush of the elements. It was
Sunday, wet and dismal. Behind the white respectability
of the houses he heard a church bell. Surely, he couldn't
be much longer. He had been waiting half an hour
already. A carriage hurtled from nowhere, smashing
through the puddles and spraying Lestrade from the
landward side. At least now he was wet all round. There
was a sort of resigned comfort in that.

Then he was there. Respectable, prim, proper. Neat
bowler, upturned collar. He wrestled manfully with his
umbrella. Agrippa? The long-legged scissor man? Or a
doctor-turned-author going to church of a Sunday
morning? Lestrade followed him with the effortless
casualness of fifteen years of such surveillance. He sat
four rows behind him in church. His quarry seemed
popular. People greeted him, laughed, joked. He was
on his home ground, careless, off his guard perhaps.
But this wasn't the time or the place. Lestrade had
watched him for two days. It was time to make his
move.

The afternoon brought the opportunity. Lestrade had
followed his quarry to the Sally Lunn Tea Rooms. Odd
that it should be open on a Sunday, out of season. But
Lestrade was grateful enough for the roaring fire and the
pot of tea that cheered. Apart from the waitress, a sour
spinster with a head of hair the colour of barbed wire,
they were alone.

'Lister,' said Lestrade extending his hand and
approaching the other man.

'I beg your pardon?'

'My name is Lister. Er . . . may I join you? So hate to
partake of tea alone.' Lestrade wasn't sure whether he
could keep this plumminess up. Still, there were enough

frauds and snobs in the world; a slip would betray his background, but not his occupation.

'Yes, do. Conan Doyle.'

Lestrade shook the offered hand. 'Not the writer chappie?'

'Why yes,' the doctor beamed, basking in the warmth of recognition. 'Have you read my work?'

'My dear chap, I am your most ardent reader. I never miss a copy of the *Strand* when I am up in town.'

Conan Doyle's face fell a little, 'Oh, I thought perhaps you meant *The Micah Clarke* – or *The White Company*?'

Lestrade looked confused, '. . . Er . . . oh, yes, yes of course, very good. Very good. But better than the . . . er . . . *White Micah*, I like your stories of detection – that fellow, what's his name, Burdock Holmes.'

'Sherlock,' said Conan Doyle, a little irritated. 'Sherlock Holmes. If you are in London regularly you must have heard of the man.'

'Oh, yes, in fact I'm only a visitor here, but I assume that your admirable works are not a statement of fact?'

Conan Doyle chuckled. 'No indeed. Mr Holmes is a celebrated amateur detective, but I fear he falls rather short of my hero. After all, my Holmes is superhuman.'

'I've often wondered, Mr Conan Doyle, this Doctor Watson, Holmes's friend and confidante – is he real?'

'Why, yes. He and I were at medical school together. At least, that's not quite true. He was attending a refresher course on comparative anatomy while I was a student. It was on his suggestion that I met Mr Holmes.' Conan Doyle sank his teeth into a Chelsea bun. Lestrade was glad to see that he was getting into his stride. 'It was Watson's idea to write a biography of Holmes, to do for him what Boswell did for Johnson.' Lestrade didn't know what that was, but he doubted whether it was legal. 'The snag was that poor old Watson isn't the world's best writer. So we agreed that I should write the thing – the old flair, you know, and he would feed me the information. Well, somewhere along the line, the serious biography went out of the window and the fiction started. Between you and me, Mr Lister, it has worked out very well. It appeals to Holmes's monstrous vanity, to Doctor Watson's need to idolise the man – and it pays my bills now that I've given up medicine, at least on a full-time basis – I too am visiting here as a change from town.'

'I've always thought,' said Lestrade, sipping his tea with a certain elegance, 'you and Watson are a little hard on the police force.'

Conan Doyle chuckled. 'Oh, Mr Lister, they do what they can, but you must realise, they are hampered by bureaucracy.'

Lestrade had realised this many, many times.

'And then of course, they are not among the brightest people in the world. Take Inspector Lestrade, for instance.' The inspector buried his slightly stiffening moustache in his tea cup. 'According to Watson, the man's a buffoon.'

Lestrade coughed, spraying the table with his tea.

'My dear chap,' consoled Conan Doyle, 'have a care.'

Lestrade was profuse in his apologies.

'Another cup?' the doctor asked.

They talked casually of this and that. Of the likelihood of Mr Gladstone's re-election now that Home Rule was the burning issue. Of the weather, threatening a repetition of last year's winter, of the return of the Ice Age. And as dusk threw long gloom across the silvered clutter of the tea-table, Lestrade edged the conversation around to spiritualism.

'I read somewhere,' he said, 'that you were convinced of the existence of another world hovering a little above our own?'

'A quaint way of putting it, Mr Lister, but yes, I am a spiritualist.'

'I attended a seance recently.' Lestrade was watching

the good doctor's every reaction. 'The Sensitive was Madame Slopesski.'

'Good God!' Conan Doyle slammed the cup down. Guilt, thought Lestrade. He was visibly rattled, agitated, 'How marvellous! I've only read her *Mistress of Two Worlds* – magnificent. Do you know it, Lister?'

Lestrade did not. 'I would have thought that such an ardent follower would have at least seen his idol.'

'Alas, no. But great as Slopesski is, "my idol" as you put it is Daniel Dunglas Home – the levitationist.'

'I thought he was dead.'

'Please, Mr Lister, we of the persuasion do not use such a phrase.' Lestrade had been here before too.

'Do you know Albert Mauleverer?' he asked.

'Mauleverer. Mauleverer. No, I don't believe so. Is he a spiritualist? I don't recall the name in the SPR lists.'

'No, he isn't a spiritualist. What about Edward Coke-Hythe? Harriet Wemyss? Isaac Prendergast?'

A shake of the head to all these. Lestrade was fishing, but in very shallow waters. Either Dr Conan Doyle was as innocent as the day was long or he was an accomplished liar. But then, Agrippa was an accomplished everything. The red, long-legged scissor man was a master of the ancient art of murder. It was to murder that Lestrade now turned, introducing it via the vehicle of detective fiction.

'How would you kill a man, Mr Conan Doyle?'

The doctor was a little taken aback by the question, but answered anyway. 'Suffocation,' he said after a moment's deliberation.

'Why?'

'Oh, I don't know. It seems quiet, particularly while the victim is asleep. I'll let you into a little secret Mr Lister. I don't like blood. A poor admission from a doctor, eh? But it's a fact. No, I couldn't kill anyone if it meant a lot of blood.'

'Not a shotgun then,' prompted Lestrade, remembering Mauleverer's blasted head.

Conan Doyle shuddered.

'Nor a hat pin, followed by removal of the thumbs?'

Conan Doyle grimaced.

'Nor a hound pack to tear and rip the corpse?'

Conan Doyle fainted.

Lestrade had meant to wait until the all-too-good doctor recovered, to offer his apologies for offending him. It must have been the conversation on top of those rather sickly pastries. But somehow he couldn't face it. Conan Doyle would have wanted to know why he had been asking those bizarre questions. And at the back of his mind, Lestrade wanted to preserve his anonymity, at least for the moment. He had not broken Conan Doyle down and yet his reaction, if he were not guilty, was surely an odd one. A squeamish doctor? Who wrote murder stories for a living? It strained credulity. And his chosen method of murder when pressed by Lestrade – suffocation. The Man in the Chine, the Inky Boys – four of Agrippa's victims had died by a form of suffocation.

Lestrade left instructions with the waitresses of the Sally Lunn and then, collecting his baggage, caught the last and only evening train to town.

'Devil of a time to call,' snapped Watson, looking ludicrous in nightcap and shirt.

'I have no time for niceties, Doctor,' Lestrade answered him. He was tired, wet, dispirited. In the reflection of the carriage lights, rattling north on the brave curve below Arundel Castle he had seen the face of Constance Mauleverer. Distant. Smiling. Then it had vanished, and he saw only his own face, darkened by the darkness of murder. In that carriage, he had faced Death itself. He imagined as he stared beyond his own shadowed face, scarred by plate glass and sabre, Agrippa, sitting opposite him and a little behind. A big man, one moment in broad hat and muffler, as he had been when furtively meeting Harriet Wemyss months before in Macclesfield. The next, hunched, ancient, gnarled – Madame Slopesski with her bright blue eyes – the wrong colour – and the curse in her throat and the pointing finger. Again, the apparition became a series of night- marish scenes from *Struwwelpeter* – tall Agrippa, the long scissor-man, the hare with a shotgun and over all there danced that face with its sad cheeks – 'anything to me is sweeter, than to see Shock-headed Peter.'

No, Lestrade had no time for niceties. He had roused the sleeping cabbie at Waterloo and the hansom had creaked and clattered its way through the dark Sunday night, through the shining wet streets. There had been no lights burning at 221B Baker Street, though a ragged urchin was nodding off on the steps. Watson glanced down at him and tapped him with his foot. 'Go home, boy. Nothing for you tonight.' He showed Lestrade in. 'One of our Irregulars,' he said, gesturing in the lad's direction. 'They are all so loyal, you know.'

Lestrade followed the flickering oil lamp up to the parlour. 'Mrs Hudson sleeps so soundly. Sleep of the just I suppose.'

'Where is Mr Holmes?'

Watson stared at him. 'But isn't that why you've come?'

'I'm sorry, I don't follow.'

Watson straightened himself. 'Sherlock Holmes is dead.'

Lestrade felt his jaw drop. He recovered himself. 'Cocaine?'

Watson flashed him an angry stare. 'No, by God, Professor Moriarty.'

'Who?'

'The Napoleon of Crime, Holmes used to call him.'

'Perhaps I'd better come in again, Watson. I don't know what you are talking about.'

'Have a seat, man. And a drink. God knows I need one.'

Watson poured them both a voluminous brandy and sat by the fire's embers. 'Holmes had been aware of Moriarty's activities for some time. One of three appalling brothers, the man is a monster – a villain of international reputation. I wonder you haven't heard of him, Lestrade.'

'That's Gregson's department, Doctor – the Special Branch.'

'Anyway, Holmes was determined to face the man. He traced him to Switzerland. Master of disguise though he is, he daren't show his face here in England, not with Holmes after him.' Watson swigged heartily at his drink. 'I received this letter from Holmes and two telegrams. They all speak of optimism. He was to meet Moriarty at the Reichenbach Falls – a well-known tourist spot near Interlaken.'

'And?'

Watson produced a voluminous handkerchief and blew his nose loudly.

'I received another letter only this morning, by special messenger. Holmes did meet Moriarty apparently. They fought. Moriarty had a pistol. Holmes grappled with him and . . . they both fell over the edge.'

A chill silence descended. Watson hung his head, visibly sobbing. Lestrade felt uncomfortable. He had never liked Holmes, but the man had gone bravely. In the way he would have liked. He poured another drink for himself and Watson. He nudged Watson's shoulder with the glass and grunted to him.

'They found their bodies. Locked together on a ledge one hundred and fifty feet below. Their necks were broken.' Watson drained the glass.

Lestrade sat down heavily. He sat up almost immediately, pulling a fiddling-stick from beneath him, with a grimace.

'Oh, sorry, Lestrade,' mumbled Watson, 'his last bow.'

'Quite.' Lestrade allowed a certain interval. 'Is there nothing else you want to tell me, Doctor Watson?'

Watson looked up at the ferret-like features. They weren't ferret-like really. That was unkind. And the man was no buffoon either. He must write to Conan Doyle about that. But then, there was no point now, was there? The Great Detective was dead. There would be no more Sherlock Holmes stories.

'How did you know?' he asked.

Lestrade stood up. He thought his heart had stopped. 'I didn't at first.' He was wondering which of them, Watson or Conan Doyle, had played Madame Slopesski so convincingly and he was on the point of realising that neither of them had blue eyes, when Watson handed him a letter.

'You'd better read this,' he said. 'It's from the Minister Plenipotentiary in Geneva. Came this morning by special messenger.'

'Sir,' Lestrade read silently, 'I regret to inform you of the death yesterday of Mr Sherlock Holmes, late of 221B, Baker Street. As you know, Mr Holmes had been staying at the Travellers' Rest Hotel in Interlaken for the past three weeks. During that time he became increasingly unwell and took to wandering in the town and on the hills. He was warned about the dangerous slopes and precipices, but he persisted. At approximately ten o'clock on the morning of the fourteenth inst., Mr Holmes was seen to be walking near the Reichenbach Falls when he became extremely agitated, eye-witnesses testified. He began screaming loudly, "Damn you, Watson, will you never leave me alone," and leapt at a gentleman who happened to be standing nearby – a Professor Moriarty of Heidelberg University, who was on holiday with friends studying the rock strata in that part of Switzerland. The Professor and Mr Holmes were seen to disappear over the water's edge and their bodies were later found on a parapet one hundred and fifty feet below. Their necks had been broken. It grieves me, sir, to be the one to break this news to you. The hotel authorities took the liberty of searching through Mr Holmes's papers and your name came to light. In the absence of any other information, I would beg you to inform his next of kin and make arrangements for burial. Yours . . .'

Lestrade dropped the letter to his side.

'How did you know,' Watson's voice was barely audible, 'about the cocaine, I mean? Did you know he'd always planned to kill me?'

'I guessed,' Lestrade lied. He wanted to stay on the offensive. Watson was vulnerable now and he might yet get a confession.

'Look.' Watson wearily dragged himself over to the wall. 'Had you asked about these bullet holes, Holmes would have told you they were target practice – neat in the Queen's cypher, eh? What he would not have told you was that every one of those shots was fired when I was only inches away. Yes, I know it defies belief. But eleven times Holmes pretended the gun went off "by accident". He never had the nerve, you see, to kill me. Until . . . five weeks ago we had a row. A blazing one. He accused me of treachery, deception, hiding his cocaine, pouring glue over his violin. Mrs Hudson left the room in sheer panic. I'd never seen him so incensed before, although, I suppose, I knew it was always coming. He packed his bags and left. He refused to say where he was going.'

'The letters? Telegrams?'

'I made them up. The only letter I have received is the one in your hand, telling me of his death. What hurts most is that in his deranged mind, he thought that poor old geologist was me. I suppose there may have been a passing resemblance.'

'And the Napoleon of Crime?'

'I made that up, too.'

Another long chill silence.

'Why did you come, Lestrade? At this hour of the night? If you didn't know about Holmes . . .'

'It will keep,' smiled Lestrade. He was getting soft. Or old. Or both. As he made for the door, he told himself it was because Watson was Constance's uncle.

'Lestrade.' Watson's voice was stronger now. He faced the inspector across the shadowed room. 'I'm not going to let Holmes die for nothing. I shall write to Conan Doyle tonight. Holmes will live again. He shall not die at the Reichenbach Falls – and a Professor of Geology at Heidelberg University shall achieve undying fame.' Watson was smiling. 'And you will never catch him, Lestrade, only Holmes will.'

As Lestrade reached the stairs, he heard the scratch of bow on violin. Rosin on catgut. He never went back.

On the day the papers carried the story of the return of Holmes's body to London for burial, the body of Philip Faye was being examined in the white-tiled laboratory at Scotland Yard. Around the corpse stood Melville McNaghten, moustached and cravated, Dr Forecastle, the pathologist, Inspector Lestrade, back on duty, and Constable Bandicoot, attending his first autopsy.

'I'm not one to carp, Lestrade,' whispered McNaghten, 'but if you're right in the supposition that the name fits, then this is the ninth victim in this case of yours.'

'Tenth,' Lestrade corrected him calmly.

'It can't go on, Lestrade. We're being made to look fools. All of us. Have you seen the morning papers?'

'Burial of Sherlock Holmes?' asked Lestrade.

'Damn you, Lestrade. Burial of us all unless this man is caught. It's not just your career at stake now. The Commissioner is most alarmed. The public won't remain patient for ever, you know.'

'Cause of death?' Lestrade ignored McNaghten's blustering, addressing himself to Forecastle and the matter in hand.

'Suffocation.'

Lestrade swept from the room without further ado. He was Waterloo bound, for the Southsea train. Bandicoot hesitated in mid-corridor. McNaghten stopped him. 'Lestrade!'

'It's Conan Doyle,' the inspector answered. 'I wasn't sure at first. I thought it was a double act – he and John Watson of Baker Street.' Lestrade was thrusting a few essentials into a Gladstone bag. He always kept a spare shirt and collars at the Yard for just such a sudden departure.

'Conan Doyle?' echoed McNaghten. 'What on earth made you suspect him?'

Lestrade paused, searching the middle distance for an answer. 'Call it intuition,' was all he could muster. Then he had gone, Donegal flapping, into the chill, morning sun.

Bandicoot looked at McNaghten. 'Should I go with him, sir?'

'No need, Constable,' was the reply. 'Had the inspector bothered to wait for one moment, he would have discovered that I was to have lunch within the hour with Doctor Conan Doyle. He is in London for the funeral of Sherlock Holmes. I wonder Lestrade was not there himself.' McNaghten turned to go. 'On second thoughts, Bandicoot, you'd better get after him. Lestrade would never forgive me if I let him go all the way to wherever Conan Doyle lives on a fool's errand. Besides, he'll charge expenses to the Yard, and that would never do.'

And so it was nearly two before Lestrade and Bandicoot walked the Embankment. Leaves, crimson and yellow, were curling at their feet, gusting now and then across their faces. Lestrade was silent, nonplussed for the moment.

'Would it help to talk about it, sir?' Bandicoot was first to break the silence. 'I mean, I hope to be a senior officer one day and I'd like to understand something of the thought processes involved.'

Thought processes? Lestrade mused to himself. What the hell were they?

'It's funny, Bandicoot.' Lestrade reached a bench and sat down, tilting the bowler back on his head. 'I felt so sure this morning, but now . . . Listen to this. John Watson is related to two of Agrippa's victims – your school chum, Edward Coke-Hythe and Const . . . the wife of Albert Mauleverer. What if Agrippa intended, for reasons we don't yet know, to kill a certain victim – or indeed two certain victims? What if those victims are Coke-Hythe and Mauleverer?'

'Then why go on?' asked Bandicoot. 'Why is Philip Faye lying in the Yard mortuary?'

'Because Agrippa is a methodical murderer. Because he has used the *Struwwelpeter* stories and intends to follow them to the letter. Who can explain the workings of a mind like his?'

'And Dr Watson is the common factor?'

'At first I suspected Mrs Mauleverer. Two reasons told me I was wrong. First, these murders are not the work of a woman. They are too physical, too violent. Second, she has a perfect alibi for the murder of Forbes.'

'Perfect?'

Lestrade shifted a little uncomfortably and muttered, 'She was with me.'

'Ah, quite.' Bandicoot tried not to let the smirk show on his face. Lestrade tried not to let him know he had seen it.

'The only other common factor is Watson.'

'But could not Mrs Mauleverer have killed her

husband and Edward Coke-Hythe?' Bandicoot persisted.

'Yes, she could, but that would mean that the murder of Forbes at least was the work of a copy-cat, someone who also knew the *Struwwelpeter* pattern. Remember, the press have not yet made that link. We are still the only ones who know the pattern. No, it strains credulity.'

'And Conan Doyle?'

'Co-author with Watson of *The Adventures of Sherlock Holmes* – you know, in the *Strand Magazine*.'

'I'm sorry, sir, I don't.'

'You're missing nothing,' Lestrade observed. 'In Kent I met Agrippa. Oh, I know, it's not in my report. I didn't tell McNaghten, you, anyone. But it was Agrippa all right; disguised yes, cleverly, very cleverly. But Agrippa nonetheless; I am sure of it. Through Watson I knew that Conan Doyle was an ardent spiritualist – and who better to play a leading medium than an ardent spiritualist?'

'So it was Watson and Conan Doyle?'

'Two murderers would be convenient,' Lestrade was talking to the middle distance again. 'Easier to accomplish the murders, provide alibis, leave a trail of red herrings, but . . .'

'But?'

'But, Bandicoot, it increases the risk enormously. Can one trust – *really* trust – the other? Remember his life depends on it. One slip, one wrong word – and the drop. No, that too strains credulity. Oh, I over-reacted this morning. Conan Doyle had chosen the method of suffocation when I asked him how he would kill a man. Suffocation, Bandicoot. The method of dispatch of one Philip Faye.'

'Then why don't you arrest Conan Doyle? Or at least interrogate him?'

Interrogate? thought Lestrade. Where did Bandicoot find these words? Had he perhaps swallowed a dictionary? Or perhaps his mother had been frightened by one?

'No, he's not our man. He's been in London for four days. And our revered Chief is lunching with him as we speak. Could we establish a link between the good doctor and our latest corpse, I wonder? I doubt it.'

Bandicoot looked confused.

'When you've been in this business as long as I have . . .' Lestrade checked himself; he'd always vowed he would never say that, but it was too late now, '. . . you learn to work on intuition – a feeling, vague, unsure, but there. Somewhere between your fob and your half hunter, Bandicoot. That something tells me Conan Doyle is not our man. We'll let him and Watson go on writing their detective rubbish. We can't hang them for that.'

Lestrade got to his feet. 'Come on, I'll buy you a Saveloy in the Coal Hole.'

Unsavoury was the word with which Bandicoot finally came up. The best word he could find in the circumstances to fit the late unlamented Philip Faye. Lestrade was cool, detached about the whole thing; he had after all seen it before, but it opened up a new world to Bandicoot. The radical press and the Evangelists called it White Slavery. Lestrade shrugged and called it a fact of life.

'Little girls,' Sergeant Dixon had repeated. 'Oh, yes, big market. Deflowering's the name of the game, Bandicoot. 'Course, it's not so common now as it was. When you've been in this business as long as I have . . .'

'So Philip Faye was a procurer of young girls?'

'So it says 'ere in records. 'Course it wasn't illegal until Mr Labutcher's Bill.'

'I think that's Labouchere,' corrected Bandicoot.

'Right. Well, anyway. There's still money to be made. Big money. There's many a gentleman will pay well for a virgin. Don't say much for London, do it, that you've got to find 'em about twelve years old for 'em to be . . .'

'Virgo intacta?' asked Bandicoot.

'I don't see their birth sign has much to do with it,' commented Dixon sagely. 'They say they're all the same length lying down. Mind you, I'm a family man, me. If any pimp laid hands on my girls, I'd break his neck.'

'Or suffocate him?' Bandicoot was proud of that quip. It was worthy of Lestrade.

'I don't think immoral earnings was Mr Faye's only vice,' said Lestrade, sweeping towards the lift. 'Come on, Bandicoot, we've got work.'

Faye had served a four-month sentence for procuring back in '86. Since then he appeared to have been clean – or lucky. But Lestrade had discovered, via his usual street sources, that the deceased had recently been moving in a rather different circle. He had gravitated, if that was the right word, from little girls to big boys.

'I always thought he had a hand in the Cleveland Street business in '87,' Jones grunted, picking his teeth with his gold pin. 'Mind you, there were too many big names involved in that. Half the Royal Horseguards, for a start.'

'For your benefit,' Lestrade turned to Bandicoot, 'a male brothel was uncovered in Cleveland Street. Some very prominent people, MPs, army officers and so on, were discovered to be using the place as a regular meeting point with errand boys.'

'Unfortunately most of them got off,' slurped Jones. 'Well, when you've been in the business as long as we have, Constable, you'll learn that the big fish usually get through the net.'

'And Philip Faye was a big fish?' asked Bandicoot.

'No,' said Lestrade levelly. 'And when you've been in the business as long as Inspector Jones has you'll learn that the little fish usually get through the net as well.'

The Cadogan Hotel was one of the most impressive in London. Like the Metropole it was one of the most fashionable among the Smart Set, in or out of season. It was mid-morning when Lestrade and Bandicoot arrived. They ordered coffee and brandy (Bandicoot was paying) and waited. Their targets were not long overdue. First, a large, scented man with a fur coat, thick, sensitive lips and a rather ridiculous Neronian haircut. With him, but always a little in his shadow, a slim, blond, young man with classical features.

'Mr Oscar Wilde?'

'I am he.'

'Inspector Lestrade, Scotland Yard. This is Constable Bandicoot.'

'Ah, how quaint. Part of the long arm of the law. You know who I am. May I present Lord Alfred Douglas?' The slim young man bowed. 'Bosie, be an angel and get us all a drink, will you? Unless of course you gentlemen are on duty and don't.'

'We are on duty and we do,' answered Lestrade.

'Now, gentlemen, pray be seated. To what do I owe the pleasure?'

'Pleasure, Mr Wilde?'

'Oh, Inspector,' Wilde tapped Lestrade's knee. 'You are a wag.'

'Philip Faye,' said Lestrade.

'Oh, dear me, yes. Poor Philip.' Wilde's face darkened and he rested his head in his hand in a flamboyant gesture. 'A tragedy. An absolute tragedy.'

'When did you last see him?' A waiter brought a tray of brandies to Lord Alfred Douglas.

'No, no,' he said, 'put them on Mr Wilde's bill.'

'Ah, let me see, Bosie, was it Monday last we saw poor Philip? At the Albemarle?'

'Possibly, Oscar. You know I always found him irritating.'

'Irritating, My Lord?' asked Lestrade.

'He had St Vitus's dance, Inspector.'

'Oh, come now, Bosie. He may have been a prey to nervous disorders. He always reminded me of a character in my *Canterville Ghost*. Have you read it, Inspector?'

'I only read the *Police Gazette*, Mr Wilde. Has it appeared there?'

'Oh, Inspector, I see I must watch out. You are within an ace of snatching my reputation.'

'Your reputation is quite safe with me, Mr Wilde.' Lestrade was emphatic. 'Have you any reason to wish Mr Faye dead?'

'Good heavens, Inspector, Philip was one of my dearest friends.'

'Did you know he had a criminal record?'

'You mean that phonograph thing old Tennyson did? Yes it was pretty awful, wasn't it?'

Lestrade brushed aside the attempt at levity. 'No, I mean procuring little girls and boys.'

Wilde licked his lips. 'He was just misunderstood.'

'Now he is dead,' Lestrade went on. 'Tell me, Mr Wilde, did you kill him?'

'Inspector, I have been patient.' Wilde's inane grin had vanished. 'But when you accuse me of the murder of a very dear friend . . .'

'I have accused you of nothing, Mr Wilde.'

'I must ask you to lower your voices, gentlemen,' snapped Douglas. 'Mr Wilde and I are regular patrons here.'

'So Faye's twitching annoyed you.' Lestrade now turned his attention to the young man.

'Eh?'

'You said he had St Vitus's dance. You said you found him irritating.'

'And that's not all I found him doing, eh Oscar?' Douglas smirked.

'You wicked boy,' scowled Wilde. 'Bosie, sometimes you can be so vulgar.'

'A lover's tiff?' Lestrade threw the challenge to the air.

Wilde and Douglas were both on their feet, protesting. Bandicoot thought he'd better get up too. He hadn't been

happy about the way Douglas had been looking at him.
Lestrade remained seated. 'He was a cottage loaf, My
Lord – a homosexual under the meaning of the Act.'

'Act?' Douglas was furious.

'Say nothing, Bosie. Remember your father.'

'Do you know who he is?' Lestrade asked.

Douglas aimed a punch which Bandicoot caught and
held easily in mid-air. Douglas scowled defiantly at
Bandicoot's collar stud, on a level with his eyes. 'Doesn't
say much for the Queensberry Rules, sir,' Bandicoot
couldn't resist saying to Lestrade.

'You obnoxious bastards,' Douglas screamed at the
policemen.

'Please, My Lord,' replied Lestrade, 'this *is* the
Cadogan Hotel.'

Wilde stopped in mid-fume. 'What a superlative
phrase, Inspector. I wish I had said that.'

And to a man, the clientele of the Cadogan Hotel
turned and with one voice chanted, 'You will, Oscar,
you will.'

The White Lady

McNaghten had reached the end of his tether. Complaints from the family of Queensberry had been flooding in all week. Complaints too from a story writer named Wilde. The latter McNaghten could ignore – he had never heard of the man. But the Marquis of Queensberry, objectionable little man though he was, was of the 'fancy', the coterie of the P.O.W. himself. And that could not be ignored. One more instance of innuendo without fact, threats without proof and Inspector Lestrade would become Constable Lestrade, directing traffic in Piccadilly.

In the meantime, the inevitable mourning letter had arrived –

> *Where is Philip, where is he?*
> *Fairly cover'd up, you see!*
> *Cloth and all are lying on him;*
> *He has pull'd down all upon him*

Lestrade checked his copy of *Struwwelpeter*. Bandicoot had not remembered this story. It was too trivial, too ridiculous. And even Agrippa, it seemed, was finding it difficult to match a homosexual pimp with the innocuous boy who fidgeted at his papa's dining table. Lestrade was wondering who Johnny Head-in-Air might be and what might befall him when Arabella McNaghten swept into his office.

'Sholto, you must come for Christmas. Papa is taking us all to Lynton. And I know you have three days' leave. Now, not a word. We shall expect you on the twenty-third.'

And she left.

Bandicoot buried his face in some suddenly absorbing papers. Dew was freezing quietly in the street some miles away, keeping a vigil near the house of Dr Conan Doyle, who had not yet gone south for the winter.

'Lynton,' Lestrade repeated mechanically.

'It's a rather quaint village, sir, situated above the mouth of the Lyn river, near Barnstaple.'

'Thank you, Bandicoot, we can dispense with the guide book. Is the woman mad?'

Was this another of Arabella's flights of fancy, he wondered to himself, continuing the rhetorical questions in the confines of his own mind. Or was it a clumsy attempt by McNaghten Senior to patch up the damage of a whole series of recent stormy exchanges in his office? Certainly Lestrade had not been invited before, although it was not unheard of for McNaghten to invite his staff, singly or in pairs, to his country house in the west country. But he had no more time to ponder it at the moment. A tall young man with waxed moustache and centre parting appeared at the door.

'Mr McGillicuddy, sir,' a constable announced him.

'Oswald McGillicuddy,' the young man extended a hand. 'I expect you know my father, the balloonist?'

'No,' said Lestrade. He was not at his best at this hour of the day, especially as it was Saturday and he had just been rattled by the unrattlable Miss McNaghten.

'I've come to report what I think may be a murder.'

Lestrade felt even worse.

'Bandicoot, some tea for Mr . . . er . . .?'

'McGillicuddy. Oswald.'

'Tea for Mr McGillicuddy.'

Exit Bandicoot.

'I reported it at Bow Street yesterday,' the young man went on. 'They wrote it all down and then told me to see you. Er . . . you are Inspector Lestrade?'

'At the moment. What is your news?'

'Well, perhaps I should explain, if you are not aware' – McGillicuddy looked a little hurt – 'that I come from an aeronautical family.'

Lestrade attempted to look sage. 'Do you mean you are a trapeze artist?'

'No, no, Inspector. We are balloonists. It is a little-known fact that my great-great-grandfather gave Etienne Montgolfier his first lesson. Anyway, more recently, we have become interested in other forms of flight. My cousin Albert, you may remember' – Lestrade did not – 'leapt from the Eiffel Tower the year before last in an attempt to prove da Vinci's theory.'

'Which was?'

'Wrong.'

'Ah.'

'Well, we are a family used to sudden bereavement, Inspector. And to injury in the cause of aeronautical science. You'd never guess, would you, that this arm is not my own?'

'Good God,' marvelled Lestrade, 'whose is it?'

McGillicuddy waved a marvellously wrought limb. 'It's made of painted gutta-percha, you know. I can do almost anything with it, but I must take care when toasting crumpets.'

'A wise precaution.'

'It might melt, you see.'

Lestrade was becoming convinced he was in the presence of a madman when Bandicoot arrived with the tea. McGillicuddy deliberately used his left hand, curling the fingers by means of a switch wired beneath his coat lapel.

'Another of my family's interests,' he beamed.

Lestrade left that stone unturned. 'Your murder?' he said.

'Ah, yes. My cousin, John Torquil. He died when his Maxim steam-powered Bisley hit a tree at thirty-eight miles an hour.'

'You mean he was driving a horseless carriage?'

'No, no, Inspector. The Maxim Bisley is an aeroplane. A featherless bird. The tragedy was that Hiram Maxim was there at the time. I do hope he doesn't lose hope. It was not his machine that was at fault, you see.'

'Do I understand,' persisted Lestrade, 'that your cousin, the deceased, was actually flying?' He and Bandicoot felt their chins hitting their respective desks.

'Ah, there's the rub, Inspector. For flight to be called flight, an aviator must take his craft off the ground for a reasonable period of time. It cannot in other words be a fluke – a spring bounce or a freak gust of wind. John was, in my opinion, as a somewhat partial observer I admit, about to manage sustained flight, when the machine dipped and his superstructure disintegrated. Without wings, of course, he ploughed through a hedge, hit an oak and ended up in the lake. There was a resounding crash. We all ran to him, but it was too late. Poor fellow had broken his neck.'

'Forgive me, Mr McGillicuddy, but isn't what you're describing merely a regrettable accident?'

'Ah, no, Inspector. I thought you would say that, so I took the liberty of bringing along proof.'

McGillicuddy stepped into the corridor, operated his artificial arm and lifted in a piece of steel about four feet long, from which hung wires and wooden struts, dangling with canvas.

'Observe the end,' he said. 'Sawn through, gentlemen. Sawn through. When one is a scientific aviator, one is aware of stresses in metals. If steel sheers off, it does not do it like that. This machine was tampered with before John Torquil took to the air – if took he did.'

'And who had access to the machine prior to the . . . er . . . flight?'

'The mechanics who built it. Hiram Maxim who designed it. Myself and John Torquil. Oh, and possibly Armytage Monk.'

For a brief moment, Lestrade toyed with a Catholic-inspired plot, then he rejected it.

'I have been in the Force long enough to know that I cannot exclude you, sir. Oh, please, do not take umbrage. I suspect that Bandicoot here is of the opinion that no sane murderer would walk voluntarily into two police stations and obligingly point a finger, albeit a false one, at himself.'

Bandicoot nodded. Lestrade felt a little pompous, rather like the late lamented Sherlock Holmes, but he was in his stride now and refused, mixed metaphor though it was, to back up.

'I, however, have known guilty parties do just that, in the mistaken belief that suspicion may be averted. Tell me, did the deceased leave a will?'

'I don't believe so. Both his parents are still living and he himself was unmarried. Presumably his worldly goods revert to his mater and pater.'

Lestrade faced the window. 'Where did this accident take place?'

'At Bisley, on the rifle ranges. Hence the machine's name. One needs the level ground, you see, for take-off.'

'Bandicoot, inform the desk sergeant. You and I are bound for Bisley.'

It was mid-afternoon when the three arrived. Raw. Cold. The sky promised snow, a return of the bitter weather of the previous winter. Lestrade inspected the mangled wreck of the Bisley, housed in an improvised shed McGillicuddy referred to as a hangar. Hiram Maxim, the inventor of the famous machine-gun whose carriage had once run over Lestrade's feet, was a large voluble American, though his accent broke through the interminable jargon of the scientifically obsessed only occasionally.

'The Bisley's wingspan is a hundred feet. The body is sixty-seven feet. The propellor is driven by a fifty-horse-power steam engine weighing three and a half tons. I think on my next attempt I'll use rails to help stabilise the thing.'

'You mean you're going to try this again?' said Lestrade.

'Of course,' Maxim and McGillicuddy chorused. 'The march of science,' Maxim went on alone.

'As I told you, Inspector,' McGillicuddy continued, 'the Bisley's prop was sawn through. This was no accident.'

There were only two mechanics who had worked on the Bisley on the days before the tragedy. Lestrade and Bandicoot interviewed them together and Lestrade was convinced at any rate they were honest as the day was long. Bandicoot was less certain; one of them, it came out in conversation, was a socialist.

Over brandy at the Commandant's house where the American inventor was a guest, Hiram Maxim that evening also convinced Lestrade of his innocence. Bore he may have been, murderer he was not. And as the snow flurries thickened across the silent ranges at Bisley, Lestrade became more convinced than ever that he had his eleventh victim. Agrippa had struck again. John Torquil was Johnny Head-In-Air.

'Tell me about Armytage Monk,' said Lestrade, rolling the brandy balloon between his hands.

'Not much to tell,' McGillicuddy answered. 'John brought him over to Bisley about a fortnight ago. I hadn't met the man before and I gathered John didn't know him well. It seems he was a keen aviator though and very anxious for John to fly the Bisley.'

'If he was such a keen aviator, why didn't he fly it himself?'

'Ah, he couldn't. He'd had an accident the year before

himself, and had permanently damaged his neck.'

'His neck?'

'Yes, he couldn't speak properly, poor chap. Had a guttural, sort of rasping voice – and he always kept his throat muffled, even indoors. There was one odd thing though.'

'Oh?'

'Well, this is going to sound ridiculous, but John and Armytage often seemed to be . . . well, giggling is about the size of it. Exchanging the odd glance as though they were enjoying some sort of private joke. Probably at our expense.'

'Is Monk a big man?'

'Yes, I'd say so. About six foot and broad.'

Lestrade leaned forward penetratingly. 'What was the colour of his eyes?'

'Good God, Inspector, I haven't the faintest idea.'

'They were blue, Inspector,' Maxim offered from the corner. 'Icy blue.'

'Why should you remember that, sir?' asked Lestrade.

'Why should you ask it?' Maxim countered.

'I have my reasons, sir.'

'I am a scientist, Inspector – a trained observer. I notice all sorts of things about all sorts of things – and people.'

'And what else did you notice about Armytage Monk?'

'I didn't like him, certainly. He had an air of falseness about him. And he didn't know a great deal about aeronautics for all that, as McGillicuddy says, he was so keen for Torquil to fly the Bisley.'

Lestrade tried to forget, at least for a while. It was Christmas, or nearly so. He caught the west-bound train to Swindon and cursed Mr Brunel anew for his wide gauge. One day they would change the damned thing and there would be no need to sojourn in Swindon again. By midday he was at Minehead and made the rest of his way by coach. This was a mistake and he regretted his momentary whim for the old-fashioned. Porlock Hill was still slippery with the morning frost where the sun had not penetrated through the thickly clumped trees. After a few horrendous slides and the whinnying terror of the horses, the driver gave up and demanded that the passengers get out and walk on up with their baggage. After an hour or so of whipping and yelling, the coach reached the top. Lestrade sat frozen on his Gladstone bag. The Christmas spirit, not surprisingly, had left him.

Consequently, it was nearly nightfall before the inspector arrived at The Tors. It was an immense house rather more like an hotel than anything, jutting out boldly from a dense covering of evergreens on the craggy outcrop below Countisbury Foreland. Lestrade looked out at the wintry sea curling under the ringed moon. What was he doing here? He looked at the opulent house and voiced silently his suspicion of a policeman with private means. Such things shouldn't exist. Then the house was alive with shouts, dogs barking and lights scurrying here and there in the driveway.

'Sholto!' It was Arabella, looming large and comfortable out of the dusk. She gave Lestrade a peck on his frozen cheek. 'You darling man, you're quite numb. Come in. Papa's expecting you.'

After hours in a draughty coach and on the road with silent or surly fellow travellers, Lestrade had about lost the use of his tongue, but a brandy and a crackling log fire soon revived him.

'I know it's Christmas, Lestrade,' McNaghten poured them both another drink, 'but I brought you here for a purpose. Tomorrow my other guests will be arriving. There'll be no time to talk to you then. Tonight, I want you to forget that I'm your superior. I want to talk to you man to man. The *Struwwelpeter* case. Do you have a suspect?'

'Several,' said Lestrade.

'Come on then, man. Let's have it.' Even in his dressing gown and smoking cap, McNaghten straightened the ever-present cravat.

'As you know, sir . . .' Lestrade began.

'Ah, no, Sholto. Man to man, remember. Sir *Melville* . . .'

Lestrade twitched his moustache at the unbridled generosity of that.

'At first I suspected Lawrence Alma-Tadema' – right again! – 'the artist.'

'Poppycock . . . Sholto.'

'As you implied . . . Sir Melville. You are of course quite right. I put some men on him.'

'Really, Lestrade, Lawrence is a family friend.'

'Even so, sir, I could not leave a stone unturned.'

'Very well.'

'He had a perfect alibi for the next two crimes. He is not Agrippa.'

'Quite.'

'But there is a connection. The black enamel that killed the Inky Boys did come from his studio, I'm sure of that.'

'How does it help?'

'I don't know . . . yet.'

'Go on.'

'Then it occurred to me that Agrippa might be killing red herrings. Multiple murders to disguise his *one* actual target.'

'Risky,' mused McNaghten, but both he and Lestrade knew it had been a prime suspicion in the Ripper case.

'But worth it. The question is, which is the real crime? My men and I have taken nearly two hundred depositions, Sir Melville. Perhaps somewhere in that two hundred is the man we are looking for.'

'Or perhaps not.'

'I then reasoned that Mrs Maulverer was the murderer. She was related both to Albert Mauleverer and one of the Inky Boys, but that I rejected.'

'Why?'

'It's not a woman's crime, Sir Melville. Physical strength was required in almost all the murders. Constance Mauleverer is a small woman. It would have been beyond her.'

'What of Conan Doyle?'

'Ah, yes. I suspected him and Doctor John Watson of a double act. Their motives I could not guess at, but the fact that there were two of them explained Agrippa's rapid and effortless disappearance. One killed while the other kept watch and covered tracks.'

Again, unknown to each other, both men thought of the Ripper case.

'Again, I had them both watched. Their alibis are sound. And I know John Watson. Bad writer he may be, mediocre doctor he may be, but he is no murderer.'

'So where does that leave us?'

'The Tors, Sir Melville, Christmas 1891.'

'What? Oh, yes, I see. No more suspects?'

'Agrippa is elusive but he is not superhuman. We know some things about him. First, he is a big man, about six foot tall, heavy and powerful. he is a master of disguise, able to play a passionate lover as in the case of Harriet Wemyss, an aeronautical enthusiast in the case of John Torquil.' And Madame Slopesski in the case of Isaac Prendergast, Lestrade added silently to himself. He could not bring himself still to admit to his superior, now suddenly his 'equal', that he had once been in the same room with Agrippa. 'We know he has a warped sense of humour, using the children's verse, *Shock-headed Peter*, as a pattern for his crimes. And one other thing – Agrippa is a snob.'

'A snob, Sholto?'

'Look at his victims. Where is the costermonger, fishwife, cordwainer, flower-girl? Every one of his victims was well-to-do, genteel, rich.'

'What about Peter himself?'

'Ah yes. I'm coming to the conclusion that Peter, whoever he was, was not one of Agrippa's victims.'

'Not?'

'No. The story of the finding of the body in Shanklin Chine was widely covered by most papers. Anybody could have read it, been reminded irresistibly of *Struwwelpeter* and gone to his grisly work.'

McNaghten sat down by the fire. 'What happens,' he asked Lestrade, 'when the murders end? Isn't there one to go?'

Lestrade nodded. 'Flying Robert,' he said.

'Will we see an end then, Lestrade? Will we see an end?'

The Valley of the Rocks lies on the edge of Exmoor. Blackmore's Exmoor, the Exmoor of the wild Doones of Badgeworthy, who had terrorised the moor in the seventeenth century. It was also the Exmoor of The Chains, near Brendon Two Gates, where a man might drown in the clawing, sucking mud if he took one wrong step. The Valley was hardly the spot for a walk in winter, but Lestrade had agreed to accompany Arabella: he felt a little out of place as the massive McNaghten clan and friends began to arrive the next morning and Arabella had promised to break his arm if he refused. Even Lestrade felt the atmosphere. The sea was chiselled into steel-coloured ridges below him and it was unnerving to be higher than the gulls on those narrow ledges. Here and there sheep and goats clustered close to the rock for shelter. Lestrade kept as far as he was able in the lee of Miss McNaghten.

'Stand here, Sholto,' she called above the wind.

Lestrade stood opposite her in a whistling gap in the rocks.

'Look around you,' she said. 'We are standing in the White Lady.'

'Oh?'

'If you look at these rocks from the Valley road, this

cleft is in the shape of a lady, outlined against the sky. Legend has it that if a girl stands with her lover in this spot, they shall be joined for ever.' Her hands reached out for his. He kept them firmly in his pockets. The silent pleading face turned to a smile as she turned out of the wind. 'Sholto, you've let me down. Again.'

'Arabella, there must be dozens of young men beating a path to your door. Why me? I can't rival all this – a house in the country, servants.'

'I don't want all this, Sholto.' She took his arm and pressed herself into his Donegal. 'Let's go home. Papa will be fretting.'

'Doesn't he trust me with his favourite daughter?'

'Oh, yes, Sholto. But he doesn't trust me with his favourite detective.'

Somehow Lestrade battled through the evening. Few people spoke to him. But in a way he was glad of that. He retired early and was in bed and asleep long before midnight. It must have been three or four and a raw, cold morning when he felt a body, a live one, sneak into his bed. He wasn't used to four-posters and completely misjudged the distance between it and the ground so that he fell heavily and hurt his shoulder.

'Sholto, don't be so ridiculous. You'll wake the whole house.'

'Arabella,' Lestrade hissed, 'what the devil are you doing here?'

'Get back into bed and I'll show you,' drooled the voice in the darkness.

'Good God, woman, have you no finer feelings? And in your mother's house.'

'Yes, and with my father's right-hand man.' She leaned over and tugged at his night shirt.

'It's nice of you to accord me that title, but I think you exaggerate. Anyway, you're missing my point.'

'Oh, I hope not.' And she heaved him into bed.

For once in his life, Sholto Lestrade laid his scruples aside. Arabella McNaghten was quite attractive in an odd sort of way. And it was dark. And it was Christmas. He put all thoughts of McNaghten Senior and of Constance Mauleverer out of his mind and rolled, a little coyly, into the arms of Arabella.

'Merry Christmas!' The noise boomed through the house. There were clashings and hurryings. Lestrade sat bolt upright as a scarlet- and white-clad Sir Melville swept into his bedroom. In a blind panic, Lestrade turned from right to left looking for Arabella. He thought in a split second of the feeblest of excuses – she had found the wrong room. The bed was so big he hadn't realised she was there. She had fainted, and he had taken . . . Oh, no, that sounded dreadful, but in the event, she wasn't there.

'Merry Christmas, Sholto.' Father McNaghten shoved a huge Havana into Lestrade's open mouth. 'Yes, I know it's a shock. And it's not something I'd care for you to relate at the Yard, but it's something of a family tradition here at The Tors.' And he scuttled off to distribute his other goodies to his other guests.

Lestrade somersaulted off the bed, landing on the same shoulder, of course, and peered beneath the gloom of the coverlet. An elegant chamber-pot, but no Arabella. Behind the curtains? No. The wardrobe? Only his one good suit.

There was a knock on the door to interrupt his search. It was the maid with his morning hot water and shaving tackle. In the corridor, Arabella swept past in a flurry of silk. 'Good morning, Inspector. Merry Christmas.'

It had been a long time since Lestrade had known a family Christmas. The glittering tree, the gaily wrapped presents, the chattering and squeals of children. Luncheon was splendid – goose, chicken, pheasant, dumplings, a light wine and seemingly endless claret. After the meal, during which Lestrade was bored to death by

Arabella's deaf grandmama, who persisted with her reminiscences of her holidays in Hastings, charades was the order of the day. Lestrade grinned icily throughout the lame performances, but he had to admit secretly that he quite enjoyed himself. Arabella was busy with the children for most of the day and that night Lestrade locked his door and slept more soundly.

The feast of St Stephen was celebrated with rough shooting. McNaghten enlisted the aid of local beaters and Lestrade was given a twelve-bore. As he crooked it in his arm, he thought of Albert Mauleverer. And he was still thinking of him when the explosion ripped through his cap and collar. He felt the sting in his cheek and ear, which spun him round. He lay floundering awkwardly in a ditch. At first he thought he was dead, but the frozen bracken sticking in his ear convinced him otherwise. Next he thought his own gun had gone off and how stupid he would feel trying to explain that. Before he could realise anything else, he was being peered at by blue, anxious faces wreathed in icy breath. Hands lifted him out and on to a blanket. There were shouts, dogs barking and he passed out.

He awoke to the chime of the great-grandfather clock downstairs. He heard eight chimes, but he suspected it was later. He moved his right arm. Still there, still intact. And felt the crisp, clean bandage round his throat. He hauled himself upright. The room. The Tors. He was alive.

'My dear chap . . .' McNaghten swept in, brushing his wife and daughter back out of the room. 'How do you feel?'

'Would it be too much of a cliché, sir, to ask what happened?' He'd already answered his own cliché – 'Where am I'.

'Damnedest thing,' flustered McNaghten, 'my gun went off. I'd just loaded the thing and was bringing it up when I stumbled on a tussock and it went off. I could have killed you, Sholto.'

Lestrade mumbled that it didn't matter. All in a day's shoot, etc. etc.

'Doctor says you've a clean wound. Your hat and coat stopped most of it and you'll make up the loss of blood in no time. Feel up to some broth, old chap?'

Lestrade felt more up to some broth than the old chap routine. He felt even more embarrassed at being in this situation now that he was confined to bed. He stood it, the fussing of the McNaghtens, for one more day and then, despite their protestations, he struggled into his bloody Donegal and hailed a cab for the station

> As he trudg'd along to school,
> It was always Johnny's rule,
> To be looking at the sky
> And the clouds that floated by;
> But just what before him lay,
> In his way,
> Johnny never thought about;
> So that everyone cried out –
> 'Look at little Johnny there,
> Little Johnny Head-In-Air!

Lestrade read it – the mourning letter. Posted on Christmas Eve. London postmark.

'In the book, of course,' Bandicoot was musing intelligently (Lestrade surmised that Santa must have brought him a brain for Christmas), 'Johnny is nearly drowned. Falls into a river carrying a writing case. Agrippa must be slipping.'

'Agrippa's done a pretty good job so far,' answered Lestrade, settling into his chair as gently as he could without moving his head. 'He's entitled to a little lapse now and again.'

'May I venture an observation, sir?'

Lestrade nodded.

'I think you have quite a soft spot for Agrippa. Oh, it's grudging all right, but a soft spot nevertheless.'

'I do admire his planning, I'll admit. But it'll give me great satisfaction to see his neck stretched.'

'Tell me, sir, what happens when Flying Robert is dead? Will that be the end of Agrippa?'

Lestrade looked at him levelly.

'You have my word,' he said, 'that Flying Robert will not die, not unless Agrippa goes with him.'

Bandicoot chuckled awkwardly. 'Forgive me, sir, but how do you intend to protect all the Roberts in Britain?'

'I don't have to, Bandicoot. I only have to protect one.'

It was the first day of the New Year. 1892. The old Queen entered the fifty-sixth year of her reign. The constable entered the front door of the Yard to collide sharply with a grubby-faced street urchin on his way out.

'Now then, now then,' growled Dew, looking enormous above the lad, 'you're in a hurry, sonny.'

'I don' wanna be seen round 'ere, do I?' squawked the boy, trying to struggle free, 'I'd never live it down.'

'Why are you here, then?' asked Dew.

'Hold him, Constable.' Sergeant Dixon, crimson and sweating came tumbling along the corridor. 'This little bleeder was hanging round the front desk. I've been chasin' him all over the building.'

'No need, mister, I was only deliverin' a note.'

'Note?' asked Dew.

'Iss on the desk. I was puttin' it there when 'e come chargin' up.' The urchin jabbed a revolting thumb in Dixon's direction.

'Bring him along, Constable.' The sergeant picked up the note, sure enough where the boy said he had put it, and perused the contents. His eyes widened as he did so.

'Inspector Lestrade about?' he whispered to Dew.

'I don't know, Sarge. I've just come on duty.'

'Bring him!' The policemen and their struggling

charge made for the lift.

Lestrade lolled back in his chair, feet crossed on the desk. He balanced his nose, tipless since the duel of last year, on his fingers. He suddenly found himself wondering what this street-Arab must think of his appearance. His face was seamed by myriad old cuts – the plate glass from the Albino Club in Cambridge; he had the crimson wrist from Bandicoot's careless tea-making on his first day and his neck still encased in bandages. He read the note again –

> Come to Hengler's Circus, January 1st 1892
>
> Agrippa.

It was typewritten, the paper and envelope edged in black. There was no stamp, no postmark.

'Who gave you this?'

'A bloke.'

'Bloke?' Bandicoot asked.

'Yer – a bloke. 'E's a bloody toff, ain' 'e?' observed the boy. Dixon cuffed him round the ear.

'What did this bloke look like?' asked Lestrade.

'I dunno.'

'Think!' Lestrade slammed his fist down on the desk. The boy jumped. ''E was tall, wiv a titfer and muffler.'

Bandicoot looked perplexed. 'I'll explain it to you later,' said Lestrade. 'What did he say?'

'Nuffin. 'Cept give this note to them at the Cop Shop.'

'Which Cop Shop?' asked Dixon.

'*This* one, o'course.'

'How do you know?' asked Lestrade.

'Stands to reason, don' it? 'E was only 'cross the road and 'e pointed in 'ere.'

Bandicoot and Dew raced to the window, but of Agrippa there was no sign.

'Look, guv'nor,' the boy went on, 'I was only doin' a job. I didn't mean no 'arm.'

'How much did the bloke tip you?' asked Lestrade.

'A tanner.'

He felt in his pocket. 'Dew' – the constable fished out some coins from his pockets and handed them to Lestrade – 'here's a bob. Go on, get out.' Lestrade flipped him the coin. 'And sonny,' the boy stopped, 'tell your grandchildren you once spoke to the long-legged scissor man.'

The boy looked puzzled, bit his shilling piece and disappeared.

'I'll reimburse you, Constable.' Lestrade quieted the anxiety forming on Dew's brow.

'You're not going, sir?' Bandicoot asked.

Lestrade looked up at him. 'With your background, Bandicoot, you're not very good at working-class slang are you? Cockney patter?'

'No, sir.'

'What do they call policemen, Bandicoot?'

'Sir?'

'The great British public – what do they call us?'

'Er . . . Peelers, sir.'

'Sometimes . . .' Lestrade waited for more.

'Er . . . Bobbies?'

'Better. Why, Bandicoot?'

'Why, because the Metropolitan Police was founded by Sir Robert Peel, sir, then Home Secretary.'

'Quite so,' nodded Lestrade. 'You asked me a couple of days ago how I intended to protect all the Roberts in Britain. There is only one Robert at risk, Bandicoot – only one Bobby – and that's me.'

Finale

Melville McNaghten could not believe his eyes. There it was, on the front page of the *Evening Standard* that he had bought on his way into the Yard. 'Shocking series of murders,' it said. 'Eleven Dead – Whole Affair Based on Children's Rhymes – Scotland Yard Have Known For Months'. The editorial railed on about police incompetence and Sir Melville's name loomed larger than life, in thick black print. So did Lestrade's. McNaghten was still reading the fine print, his job becoming less secure every second when he overheard two women talking on the tram next to him. He didn't normally go by public transport, but he had returned from his Christmas vacation earlier than planned, leaving his vehicle at The Tors for the convenience of his family and guests. One woman said to the other, 'Really, my dear, these policemen. I just don't know what the world is coming to. And Scotland Yard, the paper says, Has Known for Months. Isn't it criminal?'

'Indeed, ma'am,' McNaghten butted in. 'Criminal's the word.'

The ladies huddled closer together, the furthest clutching her infant to her bosom.

'I don't believe we were addressing you, sir.' The nearest woman was arch.

'Forgive me, madam, I am not normally so discourteous, but you see, I am a policeman. Sir Melville McNaghten, Head of the Criminal Investigation Department.' He tipped his hat with unusual malevolence. 'And you are?'

The ladies hesitated. 'I am Miss August and this is Mrs Miller,' came the frosty answer. 'Don't tell me you're going to arrest us.'

'No, ma'am. I just feel that one good name deserves another. For your information, one of these victims was a policeman. And I've the best brains at my disposal tirelessly working around the clock to catch this man.'

The ladies were on their mettle. 'Huh!' it was Mrs Miller's turn to sneer. 'For all the success you've had my little Agatha could solve crimes more quickly than you.'

McNaghten snapped shut his paper and stood up. The ladies gasped, Mrs Miller burying little Agatha's face in her shawl, but they were witnessing not a defeat exactly, more a tactical withdrawal. Anyway, it was McNaghten's stop.

In his office, the Head of the Criminal Investigation Department twirled his moustache and smoothed down his cravat.

'Tea,' he bawled at Dew, 'and Lestrade. Not necessarily in that order.'

'I'm afraid the inspector is out, sir.'

'Out?' McNaghten was pacing the room. 'His duty doesn't end for . . .' he checked his half-hunter '. . . another hour. Where's he gone?'

'I don't know, sir.' Dew had his fingers crossed behind his back.

McNaghten fretted and fumed. Then he rang the offices of the *Evening Standard*. The line was dreadful, crackling and erratic, the incessant click of the presses and his own stirring of the tea didn't help. He ascertained from the editor that the reporter who had written the article was T. A. 'Scoop' Liesinsdad. 'Foreigner is he?' grunted McNaghten. 'Welsh,' was the reply. 'Thought so,' rejoined McNaghten. Liesinsdad, or at least his voice, appeared on the other end of the telephone. Yes, he had been given the story personally, over the telephone, by a man. Yes. Yes. With a husky voice. But it could have been the line. There's a lot of noise here, you know. McNaghten knew. Yes, it was true. Liesinsdad had no reason to doubt it. Could McNaghten comment? No, he could not. How had one man deluded the Yard for so long? And was it possible he was Jack the Ripper? McNaghten had had enough. 'Stay there,' he bellowed. 'I'm sending constables round. If you've heard Agrippa's voice, I want to talk to you face to face.'

As he hung up the receiver a thought occurred. Why not go himself? It could only be a matter of minutes before someone told the Commissioner that the press had the whole story. Tomorrow it would be in *The Times* and the Home Secretary would read it. Then the Prime Minister, then the Queen. Heads would roll, and the first to bounce in the gutter would be McNaghten's. But, if he could move fast enough, pick this reporter's brains for some minute but vital clue. If he could follow up this clue. Today . . . now . . . then he might just save himself. Damn the constables. He'd go himself.

Lestrade did not, despite what he told Bandicoot, go alone. He carried in the pocket of his Donegal the Apache knife and knuckleduster which he always carried when danger lurked. Besides, there were hundreds of people thronging through Argyle Street that crisp January evening. Upon the chatter and the laughter, the bright expectant faces of the children and the smell of roasting chestnuts, the stars looked down.

'How much?' inquired Lestrade of the ticket man at the Corinthian Bazaar.

'Yer pays yer money, guv'ner, yer takes yer choice. Move along now, there's lots wants to get in.'

Lestrade produced the coins and found a seat. The ring was lit with sulphur and electricity. Everywhere was the smell of greasepaint and elephants. In the centre was an artificial lake, with a real tree in the middle of it and armfuls of imitation shrubbery round the edge. The band of the Grenadier Guards no less had been hired to play for the evening and all the tunes of glory were trotted out. Lestrade had not been to a circus for years. The glitter and the dazzle made him forget, temporarily, why he was there. The clowns rolled about, spraying water over each other and throwing buckets of confetti at the crowd. Elephants danced and pirouetted, bespangled young men and women swanned through the air on their flying trapeze. Over it all were the roars and gasps of the crowd – as the foot slipped momentarily on the high wire, as the lion snarled and would not back away, as the dwarfs and giants and armless men and pig-faced ladies ambled in grotesque postures. There was even a touch of the Music Hall, the house roared along with the lyrics of a popular song, but it was a sudden memory, the music perhaps, that reminded Lestrade once more of *Struwwelpeter*. He knew the whole book off by heart, the whole stinking thing. And the last verse, the one yet to be acted out, he felt sure, on him –

> *Now look at him, silly fellow,*
> *Up he flies*
> *To the skies.*
> *No one heard his screams and cries,*
> *Through the clouds the rude wind bore him,*
> *And his hat flew on before him . . .*

'Sir.'

Lestrade spun to his left, jarring his neck. It was Bandicoot bending over him.

'Siddown,' yelled a man behind. A lady hit Bandicoot with her umbrella. He squatted awkwardly at Lestrade's knee.

'What in blazes are you doing here?' Lestrade hissed

at him. 'I thought I gave instructions.'

'I'm sorry, sir, I couldn't stay away. If there's a chance to get Agrippa, I want to be there.'

'This is my collar, Bandicoot.' Lestrade didn't want this young man there. It was not something he'd dare admit, but he had a strange feeling that he would not come through tonight. He remembered the letter in his pocket. The one which served as a last will and testament. He had meant to post it outside the Corinthian, but the moment had gone.

'Now you're here, you can take this.'

'What is it, sir?'

'Even at Eton, Bandicoot, they must have told you what a letter looks like.'

'Yes, sir, of course. But it's addressed to the Commissioner.'

'Very good, Bandicoot. You're improving all the time.'

'Do you wish me to deliver it personally, sir?'

'Yes, but only in the event of my death.'

'That settles it!' Bandicoot stuffed the envelope into his pocket and forced himself down on to the floor. 'I'm staying.'

'Bandicoot,' Lestrade's voice had changed, 'do you think I'd let a social misfit like you interfere tonight? I've spent ten months chasing Agrippa and this is the nearest I've come to catching him. The last thing I want is your great feet getting in the way. Now go home. That is an order. Ignore it and I'll have you off the Force so fast you won't be able to say "Dry Bobs"!'

Although he was amazed that Lestrade should know Eton terminology, Bandicoot was genuinely stung by the rebuke of his superior. He was, as Lestrade knew, a sensitive lump of a man at heart.

'Very well, sir, but at least take this. It belonged to my father.'

'The *Evening Standard*?'

'No, sir, what is wrapped in it. I'm not a particularly Godly man, Inspector Lestrade, but I hope He's with you tonight.'

'You and me both, laddie. On your way.'

'Siddown,' yelled the man in the row behind again, but Bandicoot had gone into the shadows before the same umbrella could descend.

Lestrade looked down. Gleaming in the newspaper was a revolver. A beautifully chased pearl-handled Smith and Wesson, .44 calibre. He had seen drawings of guns like this at the Yard, but never in the flesh. On the barrel, in the half light, he read the inscription: *To H.B. May you always have the last shot*. How Lestrade echoed those sentiments tonight.

Then Lestrade saw the headlines for the first time. Like Melville McNaghten, he couldn't believe it. He dashed for the door and read the story with the aid of the bright lights in the foyer.

'Are you feeling good-natured, dearie?' An ageing hag with rouge and bad breath fondled his arm.

'Not now, I'm not,' mused Lestrade, half to himself.

'Perhaps I can interest you in something juicy, dearie. My niece has just come up from the country. Thirteen, she is.'

Lestrade came to. 'Is that so, madam?' he rounded on her. 'Then you'd better send her back to the country, or I might start to remember Mr Labouchere's Bill concerning the use of young virgins for illicit purposes.'

The prostitute gave up, flounced her feather boa and swung her backside into the night. 'Suit yourself, dearie, she's no virgin anyway.'

Lestrade's brain was whirling. What he had dreaded for months had happened. Now it would be common knowledge. There would be panics, hysterics, witch-hunts. It would be the Ripper case all over again. He could just imagine it. Anyone who knew the *Struwwelpeter* rhyme would be under suspicion. Any tall tailor with scissors in his hand, any painter with a pot of black paint, any smoker with a box of lucifers. He and McNaghten could kiss goodbye to their jobs, of course. But then, he reflected, after tonight that wouldn't matter, would it?

He heard the finale beginning. Clowns dressed as policemen, grossly fat and crimson-faced were chasing sea-lions around the lake. Inevitably, with the perfect timing of circus clowns, one by one they slipped and fell into the water, the sea-lions applauding with the crowd as they clambered out, only to slip back again. The band struck up and out of the centre of the lake a tableau arose, mermaids and sirens dressed in dazzling colours, topped by Britannia, resplendent in helmet and shield. Fireworks shot starward through an aperture in the skylight. The crowd roared and roared again. Then the band fell silent. Only a drum roll carried on. The crowd were hushed. To one side of the ring a tall young man, glittering in spangles, climbed into a huge cannon. It was a new variation for a Hengler Circus, never seen in London before. All the handbills had carried the word 'Human Cannonball' and as soon as Lestrade saw it, he knew – 'Flying Robert'. Wherever Agrippa was, he planned to put Lestrade in there, and the last tale of *Struwwelpeter* would be acted out. The drum roll heightened. The fuse was lit. The ringmaster was shouting the numbers 'One – two – three – fire!' and simultaneously an explosion ripped through the hushed circus. The tall young man hurtled out, curled tight into a ball and splashed into the lake, inches short of the precariously balanced sea-creatures. There was silence. Even the sea-lions sensed the tension of the moment and then an astonishing roar of relief and delight as the young man straightened up out of the water and took his place beside Britannia. Lestrade's heart was in his mouth, as was the heart of every spectator there, but for different reasons.

Amid tumultuous applause, the parade of the animals began and the crowd, tired and happy, scattered for the exit. Lestrade sat there motionless, hands on his knees, the devastating newspaper on his lap. No one moved him on, no one approached him. Even when circus staff arrived to sweep the droppings and sprinkle fresh sawdust, they ignored him. Then he heard the main doors lock with a click and he was alone in the darkened circus. The moon and the stars lit the scene and what was colour and noise and life before was now silver-black and silent and dead. Lestrade stood up. He left his end seat and stepped down towards the deserted ring. His footsteps echoed in the vast emptiness of the Corinthian. He thought of cocking the revolver, but he might blow his foot off. What bothered him most was that his neck was so stiff from the gunshot blast. He could not move suddenly and that put him at a disadvantage.

Then he heard it, that low, whispering guttural voice. 'Down here, Inspector, by the lake.' This was the voice that Harriet Wemyss had been wooed by, the voice that had coaxed old Isaac Prendergast, at least momentarily, out of his seclusion.

'Agrippa?' Lestrade faltered on the final step. He couldn't see anything. 'I presume the cannon is reserved for me?'

A chill, hollow laugh. 'Flying Robert,' the voice said.

Lestrade had pinpointed the voice. Its direction. Yes, there in the shadows. He was sure of it. A shaft of moonlight fell on to the buttons of a clown-policeman, grotesquely rotund in a hoop and braces. Lestrade stood in the open, with his legs apart, ready to roll either way if he had to. He levelled the Smith and Wesson and cocked it. Once . . . Twice. He saw the hand rise to twirl the moustaches and fall to straighten the non-existent cravat.

'Come into the open, Sir Melville, the game is over.'

'How did you know it was me?'

'I didn't. Not until The Tors. That morning you came

in as Father Christmas. You were wearing built-up shoes, weren't you?'

'Very observant, Inspector.'

'The eye-witnesses who saw Agrippa all mention the bulk of the man. You are too small. But that disguise convinced me that you might be capable of others more convincing.'

'And the voice?'

No one had moved yet.

'Come out of the shadows.' Lestrade's palm began to sweat.

'And the voice? What about the voice?'

'It's good. Madame Slopesski, the travelling salesman, all very professional.'

'But did you know I could throw my voice, Sholto?'

'What?'

'You see, I'm not really here at all.'

The figure in the shadows raised something. It looked like a stick and it threw it at Lestrade. Instinctively the inspector moved sideways, jerking his neck and firing simultaneously. There was a crash of splintering glass and a heavy object caught Lestrade round the ear. He lay stunned in the sawdust and by the time his consciousness had focused on the gun lying some feet away, somebody else had picked it up.

'Then, of course,' the clown policeman bent over him, 'then there are the eyes. Did none of your witnesses mention them? It is one of my failings, Sholto. I cannot bear to have my eyes covered or drops put in. My sight is not all that it should be. Have you spent these *three years* working with a man and you don't know his eyes are grey? But mine, Sholto, are blue.'

The voice had changed. It was softer, warmer. The clown policeman swept off his helmet and let the long dark hair cascade on to his shoulder. Lestrade blinked up in disbelief.

'Arabella?'

She straightened and walked away from the recumbent form of the inspector.

'What I suspect you never discovered, Sholto, with your appalling working-class background, is that the original Agrippa was a German magician of the sixteenth century. I fancy I have produced more magic in these four years than he ever could.'

'Why?' Lestrade had struggled to his knees.

'Clever little trick this, isn't it?' She indicated the broken glass, 'it's all done by mirrors, you know. By standing behind you and throwing my voice – well, Papa's voice – I was able to steal quite a march on you, wasn't I?'

Lestrade rose to one knee.

'Stay where you are!' Arabella's voice was harsh, her meaning unmistakable. 'In all my murders, Sholto, I never gave my victims an even chance. After all, like Queen Elizabeth, I have only the body of a weak and feeble woman . . .'

Lestrade would have found some humour in that, had he not been staring down the muzzle of Bandicoot's .44. 'Pretty little gun,' mused Arabella, following his gaze, 'you didn't draw this with Father's permission, I'll be bound.'

Lestrade's one hope was to keep her talking, to play for time. 'You know as well as I do he doesn't know I'm here. The gun belongs to Constable Bandicoot.'

'Ah yes, sweet boy.' Arabella smiled. 'I toyed with making him one of my victims, to show you all how unsafe you were, how easy it was to strike into the very heart of the Yard itself, but Bandicoot was too endearing. Forbes took his place in my scheme of things.'

'Tell me about your scheme of things,' said Lestrade. He had hoped that someone would have heard the shot and the breaking glass. But it was as though Arabella could read his mind.

'You're playing for time, Sholto, you crafty old cove.

Well, why not? You want a tedious run through all the *Struwwelpeter* victims?'

'It would be interesting.' Lestrade was collecting, as unobtrusively as he could, a handful of sawdust from behind him.

'Very well, but first, I think we'll tie your hands.'

Lestrade saw his chance, threw the sawdust in Arabella's face and deflected the gun. What he did not know, however, was that the iron bar she had lobbed at him minutes before was still in her other hand. She brought this cracking down on Lestrade's bandaged neck. He dropped as though poleaxed and was only barely conscious of her tying his wrists firmly behind his back. She hauled him with little effort into a sitting position, his back against the cannon.

'To begin with . . .' Arabella sat cross-legged in her enormous trousers opposite him. She produced a cigar from nowhere and lit it, passing it to Lestrade for one last smoke. She puffed rings into the air. 'The Man in the Chine had nothing to do with it. Had it not been for the description the local papers carried it would never have reminded me of *Struwwelpeter* in the first place. I don't know who killed your labourer, or fisherman or whatever he was, but the whole bizarre thing was perfect. The long hair, seemed an exact replica of Shock-headed Peter himself. And the name stitched into the smock – unbelievable.'

'And the regimental lace of the Thirteenth Hussars?'

Arabella laughed. 'God knows, but it was the first of many delightful red herrings. Papa, of course, kept me informed.'

'Of course. Which is why I thought he was our man.'

'Shame on you, Sholto Lestrade. To think such things of your superior.' Arabella clicked her tongue.

'Tell me about Freddie Hurstmonceux. How *did* you do it?'

'Ah yes, that was difficult. It's so useful, knowing so

many people in so many walks of life. Papa has many contacts. One of them is . . . well, his name doesn't matter, after all he is an accessory to murder. He is Master of the Pytchley Hunt and knows more about dogs than you do about flat feet. Well, I bet him, to cut a long story short, a hundred pounds that he couldn't train a dog to go berserk at the mention of one word.'

Lestrade smiled to himself that his assumptions had been correct. 'The word being harrow?'

'Exactly. The old school of the Master of the Pytchley. We both laughed at that, but I already had my target – Lord Freddie, a thoroughly detestable pig of a man – and my means. I met Freddie through this intermediary and used all my wiles to make him buy a new hunting pack – the one with the lead hound Tray, who'd been taught to kill at the mention of a word. The rest of the pack would follow suit if he led. The most difficult thing was getting the harrow into position. It was all rather hit and miss of course: four earlier hunts had gone the wrong way. Even I can't control foxes, Sholto.'

'You amaze me,' said Lestrade. 'What about Harriet?'

'Yes, I didn't like doing that one. She was a very stupid girl, but I felt a certain sympathy for her. It was also riskier than Hurstmonceux. I had to be seen in public, as a man. Luckily, poor Harriet didn't know one end of a man from another. I played her along with secret rendezvous, flowers etc. and, of course, I taught her to smoke.' Arabella blew more rings skyward.

'Of course,' said Lestrade.

'It was simple to get into the house and pour petroleum spirit into the lavatory. Oh, sorry, Sholto, Chapel of Ease – I didn't mean to offend your sensibilites.'

Lestrade found himself smiling.

'It was beginning to get embarrassing. The silly little dolt talked of marriage. It was all rather sick. After all, Her Majesty has said that such unnatural acts do not go on between women.'

'What about the Inky Boys?' asked Lestrade.

'Ah well, the visit of Atlanta Washington had been planned for months. It fitted well, but the actual method of murder was tricky. I wasn't sure it would work. I spent hours poring over Papa's chemistry books and the Yard library. In the end I took a chance. I selected my trio of racists and invited them to a secret rendezvous in upper rooms in James Street. I drugged them, tied them up, painted them in black enamel . . .'

'Which you stole from Lawrence Alma-Tadema's studio?'

'Yes. I thought Papa would give the game away there, when he told you he knew the artist. I was the sitter who cancelled my appointment at the last moment so that I would have a chance to go to St John's Wood anyway and steal the paint. But you didn't get the point, dear Sholto, did you?'

'How did you get the bodies to the Park?'

'The same way I just overpowered you, Sholto. A combination of cunning and brute force. It was risky, of course – but there are many drivers and hauliers carrying bundles in the early hours. No one asked questions. The hire of the van was simple enough.'

'And Tall Agrippa appeared for the first time in a mourning letter. Tell me, Papa's typewriter?'

'At the Yard actually. I typed most of them together, feet away from your own office, Sholto.'

'Albert Mauleverer?'

'He was a non-event. The most difficult thing in the provincial murders, especially Macclesfield and War-wick, was getting away from the family for long enough. Luckily, we have dozens of distant aunts who do not contact us much. I was supposedly visiting them. I invariably used a male disguise at hotels so that there should be no awkward questions about a woman travelling alone. Of course, I didn't bargain for you falling for Mrs Mauleverer.'

'Did I?'

Arabella's tone changed. 'Oh, Sholto, I loved you. If you had shown the slightest interest . . . well, none of this would have happened.'

'Why Forbes?'

Arabella had nearly finished her cigar and Lestrade was anxious to keep her going.

'Conrad is the name in the *Struwwelpeter* rhymes. I couldn't find one. Anyway, I disliked Forbes intensely. He had an arrogance above his station. I got him, shall we say, interested in me at the Commissioner's Ball. Then I sent him that farcical note, as I did you; it never fails.'

'Was it a hat pin?'

'It was. Cutting the thumbs off was more difficult than you'd imagine. Ruined my dressmaking scissors.'

'And Augustus?'

'Ah yes, old Prendergast. I was staying – or rather wasn't – with another fictional aunt in Kent. As with Conrad it proved impossible to find an Augustus, so I selected this tyrannical old codger. Reprehensible, wasn't it, to tie him up out of reach of food like that? Even I had qualms. But then, I didn't have to find the corpse.'

'Why did you risk Madame Slopesski?'

'I don't know. Vanity, I suppose. I suggested to Papa he encourage the seance idea. I wanted to confront you, to be as close as we are now and to watch your reaction. I must admit, when I realised Frank Podmore was there, and I guessed he would know the real Slopesski, my heart sank. I think that was probably the most awkward moment of my life.'

'What about fidgety Philip?'

'Ah, yes, the unsavoury Mr Faye. I didn't like him at all. I'd met him through the Queensberrys. Friends of friends of friends, actually. He was physically very weak. I pretended to be enamoured of the ass, then pinned him down with my ample bosom and suffocated him with a

sheet. John Torquil called for more ingenuity, but you
know, Sholto, how I rise to a challenge. I played myself
with him, risky but fun, but as he pointed out a woman
aviator would be absurd, so again, male garb. I joined the
aeronauts and awaited my chance. He would keep
giggling to himself about the subterfuge. Pity really, I
think Maxim's machine might actually have flown if it
hadn't been for my tinkering.'

'Why did your father invite me to The Tors?'

'My idea.' Arabella threw the cigar butt into the
sawdust. 'A woman is only a woman, Sholto, but a good
cigar is a smoke. Come on.' She hauled him upright. 'I
was determined to seduce you before . . . tonight.'

'What about the shotgun blast? I thought it was Sir
Melville's deliberate attempt to kill me.'

Arabella chuckled. 'One of life's little accidents,
Sholto. It would have been ironic, wouldn't it Sholto, if
Papa had robbed me of "Flying Robert"? I'm sure you
can manage the steps with your hands tied.'

'I'm not going in there, Arabella.'

She raised and cocked the revolver. 'Sholto, I have
packed enough explosives into that breech to blow it and
you apart. That way at least, death will be instantaneous.
But there are five shots left in this revolver. That way,
death can be very slow.'

Lestrade summed up his predicament in a second and
reluctantly climbed inside the cannon's mouth. He slid
down until his knees were against the circular wall.
Above him, all he could see was the stars, crisp and
twinkling through the glass night. The last verse of
Struwwelpeter whirled through his brain –

> Soon they got to such a height,
> They were nearly out of sight!
> And the hat went up so high
> That it nearly touched the sky.
> No one ever yet could tell

Where they stopped or where they fell;
Only this one thing was plain,
Bob was never seen again.

'How did you get the use of this place?' Lestrade's voice was echoing in its death chamber. Arabella was busy with the fuse.

'Charlie Hengler is a law-abiding soul,' she answered. 'And he doesn't know Papa. I came to see him yesterday claiming that I, Melville McNaghten, had an undercover job to do of the gravest importance. International espionage, no less. I needed to take part in the show as a clown and to have the theatre to myself at the end of the show. Oh, don't worry, Sholto, we shan't be disturbed.'

'One last thing.' Lestrade was still hopeful, the eternal optimist.

'What's that, Sholto?' Arabella struck her match.

'Why? Why?'

'Have you heard of Sigmund Freud, Sholto?'

'Is that a penny dreadful?'

'No, my dear.' She smiled acidly, looking up at the smooth-painted sides of the cannon. 'Mr Freud is a psychologist. His wife Martha and I were at school together. We keep in constant touch. His theory is that all little girls at some point want to be little boys. Penis envy, he calls it – oh there, I've shocked you again.' She clicked her tongue derisively. 'Willy envy, is that better? Well, I suppose I'm the classic case. Ever since I can remember I wanted to be a policeman, to join the Force, to be what Papa was. I couldn't do that, Sholto. Society wouldn't have it. But what I could do is to beat you all at your own game. All you men. With your cigars and your arrogance and your hypocrisy. I have killed ten people, Sholto, tonight will make it eleven. And you didn't have a clue. I left plenty, God knows, and the nearest you got was my father. And you're about the best of them, Sholto. Oh, by the way –' she applied her match, slow burning, to the fuse. It flashed and crackled. She stepped back. '– The Ripper File I stole for you, an eternity ago . . .'

'What about it?'

Lestrade could hear the fuse as well. His heart was thumping.

'There was one name missing from the last page, Sholto. The name of Arabella McNaghten.'

'You . . . you are Jack the Ripper?'

'An earlier, more amateur attempt, my dear boy. Rather ironic they should put Papa on the case at the end, wasn't it? Still, from tomorrow, Papa's job will be up for sale to the highest bidder. As will yours, but you won't be there to see it.' She lingered below the cannon for a few seconds. 'Goodbye, Sholto. I loved you once.'

Lestrade was still muttering in the echoing chamber. But Arabella was striding up the steps to the exit.

'Miss McNaghten.' A voice made her turn. A tall, square figure stood to her left in the next aisle. She drew the revolver and was levelling it when a shot rang out. Arabella McNaghten jerked back, eyes staring in disbelief, dark crimson spreading over the police tunic. She crashed heavily down the steps. The tall figure dashed from the pall of smoke his gun had left and scrabbled frantically for the fuse. It had an inch or a little less to go when he put it out.

'Bandicoot?' Lestrade's voice had a strange maniacal quality about it.

'Sir?'

'Bandicoot, Bandicoot, wherefore art thou, Bandicoot?'

'Are you all right, sir?' The blond, curly head appeared anxiously in the cannon's mouth.

'Yes, Bandicoot. It's just my appalling working-class background. Get me out of this.'

The constable helped the inspector out and untied his hands. 'Arabella?' asked Lestrade.

'I'm afraid I had to kill Miss McNaghten, sir.' Bandicoot looked decidedly shaken. 'I didn't tell you that my father had a brace of these things.' He brandished the other gold-chased revolver. He straightened. 'Sorry I disobeyed orders, sir . . . and came back.'

Lestrade looked at him. 'Tonight, Bandicoot, I looked death in the face. Thanks to you, I've got to do that all over again.'

They crossed to where the body lay, face down in the sawdust. Lestrade knelt and turned her over. He looked at the pale face, still streaked with make-up and looked at the blood on his fingers. 'You're wrong, Bandicoot.' He closed her eyes. 'You didn't kill her. Agrippa did.'

'Sir?'

'Give me a hand.'

Together they carried Arabella to the cannon and loaded her in. 'Now get back.' Bandicoot dashed for the tiers of seats as Lestrade relit the fuse. He had just time to reach the edge of the ring when the explosion ripped up and out, smashing the plate glass of the roof and sending debris in all directions, splashing into the lake and knocking over the tree.

Lestrade and Bandicoot were into the night air and away as the crackling flames behind them brought shouts and cries for water.

'I don't understand, sir,' said Bandicoot.

Lestrade stopped and faced him. 'You don't have to, Bandicoot. The world must know, Sir Melville must know, that Arabella McNaghten was the final victim of Agrippa, the long, red-legged scissor man. We never caught him, Bandicoot. He lives on, he walks the streets of London yet. Oh, people will panic for a while. There'll be demands for resignations.' They walked on. 'But you're safe, and perhaps I am too. In time people will forget. We'll make the right noises and pursue our inquiries, but you and I'll know it's all over.'

'Why, sir? Why did you put her in that thing?'

'Because . . . because I've got too much respect for a man to tell him his daughter is a monster. His favourite child an evil fiend without pity or remorse. Her death will finish him as it is, man. The least you and I can do is to leave him his memories.'

Lestrade was right. The story that Arabella had given the *Evening Standard* the day before appeared in *The Times* and all the other dailies the next morning. For a while, people panicked. There was a cry for heads and Sir Melville McNaghten, a broken man at the news of his favourite daughter's death, offered his. He retired in the summer to The Tors, where he lived on for several years with his other children and his memories. Walter Dew became an inspector eventually and achieved undying fame as the man who arrested Dr Crippen – by long-distance wireless. Harry Bandicoot left the Metropolitan Police the following year, married a rich widow and they lived happily ever after. Constance Mauleverer vanished. No one saw her again.

And Sholto Lestrade himself? Ah well, that is another story.